Crime Exploded

Crime Exploded

A Buck Taylor Novel

Chuck Morgan

CHARLES E MORGAN
LONE TREE

Contents

DEDICATION

Dedicated to law enforcement officers everywhere, who put their lives on the line everyday to preserve and protect.

Chapter One

He looked up at the uniformed guard as they stood waiting for the steel gate to roll back from its latching plate. He felt tiny next to the large black man with the bald head and dark-rimmed glasses. They weren't friends, but he felt a particular affection for the guard after all these years. Friendships were not encouraged, but this particular guard had been friendlier than some others, which made him feel a little more human.

The gate stopped, and the guard looked down at the frail man standing beside him. The clothes he wore were baggy, and he looked like he was wearing his father's old suit, a faded dark blue jacket with mismatched blue pants. The faded and yellowed white shirt was two sizes too big, and he had decided not to wear the tie they had given him because it hung funny around his neck. His brown shoes, one size too large, were scuffed, and the soles had seen a lot of walking over the years. He wondered who they had originally belonged to and why they were still in the storage unit.

He carried a small rectangular suitcase that was scuffed and had one latch that locked. It contained all his worldly possessions: a couple of books he had read over the years, three pairs of new underpants and undershirts he had bought at the commissary and two pairs of socks that had seen better days. The underwear had cost him a big chunk of his savings account, but someone had told him once that clean underwear could make a man feel wealthy no matter what he wore on the outside.

The guard tapped him on the shoulder. "It's time," he said, showing no emotion on his face. "Good luck."

He nodded at the guard, pulled his watch cap tighter onto his balding head, lifted the collar of the old wool coat and stepped out into the snow that was lightly falling. He checked the coat pocket once more and felt the bus ticket the assistant warden had given him. In his pants pocket were the hundred dollars he'd received as gate money, twenty-seven dollars and twelve cents that he had left from his savings account, and the bottle of oxycodone the prison doctor had given him.

The steel gate behind him rolled closed, and he took a deep breath of the cold morning air. He heard the gate clang shut, a sound that no longer bothered him after all these years, and he walked towards the steel gate in front of him. He stood and waited.

Time had become less important over the years, but he sensed that more than a few minutes had passed, yet the gate remained closed. He wondered if they were having second thoughts and had decided to keep him inside to finish his sentence. He started to feel panicky, but he dared not look behind himself for fear he would see the guards coming to take him back to his cell, so he stood motionless as the snow settled on his hat and shoulders. He looked down at the old King James Bible he held in his other hand and said a silent prayer that this was all for real and that the freedom he had started to experience a few minutes before wasn't going to be taken away as part of some sick joke.

He wasn't sure what to do next when the loud blaring horn sounded, and the red light over the gate started flashing. The steel gate started rolling open, and he breathed a sigh of relief. The gate stopped rolling, and a voice came over the loudspeaker.

"Move forward."

He straightened up his shoulders, pulled himself up as tall as his five-foot-nine-inch frame would allow and stepped through the gate into freedom. Freedom for the first time in forty-four years, six months, and twenty-two days. The gate clanged shut behind him, and he accepted, for the first time, that this was all real. He stepped over to the green metal trash can that stood next to the gate, looked at the King James Bible one more time and threw it in the trash can. He smiled and headed across the parking lot to the covered bus stop and the waiting bus that would take him to Denver and then on to his final destination.

Chapter Two

Connor O'Connor woke up from a restless night's sleep with terrible abdominal and back pains. The pain was so intense that he lay in a fetal position waiting for the oxycodone to take effect. The doctor at the prison had told him that the pain would increase, as would the nausea, and that there was nothing left to do but manage the pain. He had agreed with the doctor to stop taking the various chemo pills he had been offered, since they were no longer effective. He was also aware that he had only a couple of weeks to live.

The diagnosis of pancreatic cancer had come too late. By the time the doctors at the prison hospital, conferring with experts, had diagnosed it, the disease had metastasized into his lungs and his bones. Connor had always prepared for the fact that he would die in prison. He had been sentenced to two consecutive life sentences without parole, and he knew he was never getting out. He figured he would either die of old age or die of some kind of prison attack. He had many enemies in the real world, and any one of them could have reached into the prison population and found someone to kill him. His frail body bore the scars of several of those attempts, but he always came out on top.

Connor O'Connor was a survivor. He was also a predator of the highest order. After word got out to the prison population about Connor's victories in dealing with too many attacks to count, it became obvious that Connor O'Connor was not to be messed with. He'd spent the last ten years living in relative solitude. He was untouchable, and everyone knew it. They also knew that with two life sentences hanging over his head, he had nothing to lose.

Connor's life had been as peaceful as it could be, until a few months back, when he started having severe back pains and losing weight. When the doctors eventually diagnosed the cancer, he was relieved that his stay at the state penitentiary in Florence, Colorado, would end sooner than he had expected. Then came the surprise he never expected.

A national prisoner rights group called the Dignity Project had quietly petitioned the governor of Colorado to commute Connor's sentence to time served and allow him a compassionate release, so he could die peacefully on the outside instead of on the inside. After several weeks of lobbying and multiple lawsuits, finally, with the consent of the state prison board, the governor had reluctantly granted the release. Connor O'Connor was a free man—except as he thought about it, when he received the news of his impending release, he realized he was trading a life sentence for a death sentence, but at least he would die a free man.

The bus ride to Denver had taken over two hours, and Connor was in pain when he stepped off the bus with his meager belongings. He removed the slip of paper from his pocket that contained the name of a downtown hotel, where the Dignity Project had reserved a room for him. He found the hotel without issue and checked into the small but clean room. It was the first time he'd had a room, and a bathroom, all to himself in over forty years.

Connor had never realized how difficult it would be to fall asleep in a soft bed. He was exhausted from the trip, but in all that wonderful silence, sleep would not come. He tossed and turned all night until the pain in his abdomen hit and doubled him over.

The sun was peeking through the thin drapes when the pain finally subsided enough for him to take a long, hot shower and dress in his shabby prison hand-me-downs. He had several things to do while in Denver, one of which was getting some money and buying some newer clothes. The desk clerk had told him about a thrift store a block over that carried decent men's clothing, and that would be his first stop after eating a couple of slices of toast in the hotel breakfast bar.

It was a cold morning as Connor left the hotel

and walked to the thrift store. The snow had let up during the night, leaving an inch on the sidewalk, but walking in the cold snow with his prison shoes on chilled him to the bone. The man who ran the thrift store was a huge help to Connor, and by the time he came out of the changing room, he looked like a new man.

The jeans were a little loose, but the length was perfect, and they dropped just the way he liked it, over his new insulated hiking boots. He found a flannel shirt that fit his frail frame and an insulated jacket that was so thin, he never thought it would keep him warm, but he was surprised when he stepped out of the store. The only thing he kept was his prison watch cap, which was now pulled down over his ears. The insulated leather gloves helped keep his hands warm. When he looked in the mirror, he felt like a new person, and the whole thing only cost him twenty-five dollars, which made everything even better.

Connor stepped up to the bus stop and checked the schedule. He found the stop closest to his next destination, even though he had no idea if it was still there. He boarded the bus and settled in. Denver had changed a lot since the last time he had been there. But then, everything had changed since that day, forty-four years ago, when they put him in the back of the prison van and drove him to the place that would become his home for the rest of his natural life.

He fondly remembered fighting the two prison guards as they tried to put him inside the van and also remembered, not so fondly, getting smacked in the head with a wooden baton. He hoped that his so-called friends and people from the neighborhood had been watching. He wanted everyone to know he was still fighting. He wanted them to know that if he were ever released or managed to escape, that there would be hell to pay.

Chapter Three

1977

The trial had begun like every other trial Connor O'Connor had been forced to sit through. He was thirty-four years old and had been arrested more times than he could remember, but up till now, he had never seen the inside of a prison. Witness intimidation, juror intimidation and any other intimidation you could think of was his stock and trade, and he was always acquitted.

He had learned his trade from the best in the business, having spent several years learning how to build bombs for the Irish Republican Army. He always thought back to the first bomb he ever planted. That one had killed a local constable who had started working for the British Army, and two soldiers patrolling with him. Connor had watched from behind a fence as the bomb tore the men to shreds. He felt no pity for the poor men. As a matter of fact, he didn't feel a thing, and that surprised him. Over the years, the more he killed, the less it bothered him.

He had returned to Denver by way of New York City, where he had taken care of several loose ends for some friends in the Irish mob. His reputation was spreading, and no one wanted to mess with Connor O'Connor.

His life in Denver wasn't as exciting, but he managed to make good money working for his Irish friends and even did a couple of jobs for the Italians. He hated their guts, but they paid well, so he didn't mind.

What he did mind were people who reported on his Irish friends. One such person was a reporter for the old *Rocky Mountain News*. He had somehow gotten close to someone in the organization and was preparing to name names, as they called it. This would have been bad for a lot of people, including some influential politicians, so it was decided that the reporter needed to be taught a lesson. A lesson that would make other local reporters think twice before entering the dark world of the Irish mob.

Connor had sat outside the reporter's apartment on Pearl Street for several days to establish his routine. The reporter was so dumb, he thought. He followed the same routine every day, and Connor was quick to develop a plan. The reporter usually took the bus to the *Rocky Mountain News* building, but each Friday, he would slide into his car and head south to a nursing home in Lakewood. Connor found out that he was visiting his mom, and that would be perfect.

Connor had no qualms about killing up close. He

had killed using a gun, a knife and had even beaten one poor fuck to death using a lead pipe, but he still enjoyed the power of killing someone with a bomb. Not only was the power something to be enjoyed, but the pictures that would follow on the late-night news were a thing of beauty.

Connor had gathered all the materials he needed from several local hardware stores and a construction site that belonged to one of his friends. He had decided on a different kind of bomb for this job. One that wasn't connected to the car's starter, which was the usual way a car bomb worked. This bomb would use a timer that was set to go off at a specific time. He had used it in Ireland on several occasions, and it had worked well. It also messed with the FBI's heads because they weren't able to pin him down to one signature method, something he also learned working in Ireland.

That Thursday night was still warm as he waited in his car down the block from the reporter's apartment. Once he felt confident that there was no activity on the street, he grabbed his small duffel bag off the seat next to him and casually strolled up the street. He stopped across the street from the reporter's car and looked both ways.

Connor moved in the darkness like a cat. He crouched next to the car and pulled the bomb out of his backpack. He slid under the car and set the timer. A couple of wraps of black electrical tape secured the bomb to the car's frame, and he was back in his car less than a minute later. He was right on schedule. Now he just had to wait.

His internal clock woke him up just before eight, and he sat up in the seat and watched as the reporter came down the stairs from his apartment, but something was wrong. The reporter wasn't alone. He was standing next to the car talking to a woman, and next to them stood a young girl, maybe four or five years old. This wasn't the reporter's regular routine. So who were these other people, and what were they doing in his plan?

The reporter handed the woman something, kissed her full on the mouth and then kissed the little girl on the top of her head. He turned and walked down the street towards the bus stop he took every other day. The woman put the little girl in the back seat of the reporter's car, leaned in and belted her in. She stepped around the car and slid into the driver's seat.

Connor looked at his watch. "What the fuck?" he said out loud. He didn't know what to do. He had one rule: *No women or children.* He had to do something, but he felt like he was glued to the seat. He started to sweat as his eyes darted from the watch on his wrist to the car.

The woman had rolled down her window to adjust the mirror and had just pushed down the gearshift when the explosion went off, right on time.

Connor had used enough black powder to take out the car but not enough to cause a lot of collateral damage. However, the explosion still blew out the front-facing windows of several apartment buildings, and shrapnel tore through the cars parked to the front and rear of the reporter's car. He looked up in time to see the reporter running towards the burning car and watched as several neighbors held him back from the wreckage. He fell to the ground, and Connor could hear the bloodcurdling scream a block away.

Connor's hands were shaking as he pulled away from the curb and did a U-turn in the street. He drove two blocks, pulled into a gas station, parked and cried harder than he ever remembered crying in his life. He could hear the sirens in the distance as the fire engines raced to the scene, but they would be too late.

Calm enough to drive without killing himself or someone else, Connor pulled out of the gas station and headed up Lincoln Street towards Five Points. He drove the speed limit and stopped at every light. He looked around as he drove and imagined that all the people walking on the sidewalks were looking at him. For the first time in his life, he felt like a killer.

Connor pulled his car into the small lot next to Logan's Bar and Grill and walked inside. The minute he stepped through the door into the dark bar, he knew the word was out. Jacky Logan Sr. sat in his usual place in the back of the bar, counting the night's take from his various business ventures. The news was on the television at the end of the bar, and reporters were reporting live from the location of a horrific early morning bombing. Every eye in the bar was glued to the screen except for Jacky's. He waved Connor to the back and pointed towards the seat.

Connor was about to speak when Jacky held up his hand. Not a word was said as Jacky slid a piece of paper across the table. Connor looked at the address that was written on the paper and knew what it was. He looked down at the stacks of money sitting in front of Jacky. The job was supposed to pay five grand, but Connor knew that that was now out of the question. Jacky pulled a small pile of twenty-dollar bills off a stack, counted off twenty-five of them and slid them over to Connor.

Connor picked up the bills and the slip of paper and left the bar. He had fucked up badly, and the silence was Jacky's way of telling him that he was not happy. The silence also protected Jacky from any police surveillance that might be going on, the same way everyone sitting at the bar protected him since they never saw or heard a thing. Connor headed for the address on the paper.

Chapter Four

The cops hit the safe house at six a.m. the next morning using a battering ram that woke Connor from a restless sleep. All he could picture all night long was the face of that little girl. He had finally fallen asleep just before dawn when the door burst open, and a dozen cops ran into the apartment.

A bloody and battered Connor O'Connor, wearing his boxers, was dragged barefoot down the stairs and thrown into the back of a police van. What he heard, just before the van pulled away, were vile screams and curses from the crowd that had gathered outside the safe house. He was shocked and bewildered by everything that had happened, and he wondered how the cops had found him so quickly. He hadn't told anyone, not even his girlfriend, Carly, where he was heading.

Connor spent the better part of four months in the Denver County Jail as he awaited trial. He was finally placed in a protected cell after the fourth attempt on his life ended with a stab wound to his gut and another inmate lying beaten and bloody on the ground. He was never sure if the guards were protecting him from the general population or protecting the general population from him.

The trial lasted five days, and he was feeling good about what the jury was hearing. The case was entirely circumstantial, and he felt confident that Jacky Logan Sr. was making sure that the jury was playing ball. That was, until the last day of the prosecution's case.

The prosecutor called his next-to-last witness, and Connor almost shit himself when he heard the name.

"The court calls Jackson Logan to the stand," said the prosecutor.

Connor couldn't believe his ears, and he turned as the courtroom door opened and Jacky Logan walked down the aisle, but it wasn't Jacky Logan Sr. It was Jacky Logan Jr.

Connor and Jacky Jr. had grown up together, and Connor considered Jacky Jr. to be his best friend, so why was his best friend taking the stand for the prosecution? Connor was stunned silent. He also noticed that Jacky Jr. never looked at him as he was being sworn in.

The story Jacky Jr. told during the next two hours was unbelievable. And in reality, it shouldn't have been believed. Jacky Jr. had all the details needed to wrap up the case against Connor O'Connor, but Jacky Jr. had never been told the details. The only person Connor had told some of the details of the hit to was Jacky Sr. He never talked about a hit to anyone beforehand, so he couldn't figure out how Jacky Jr. knew those details.

The defense spent an hour trying to change Jacky Jr.'s story, but Connor could see the frustration in his eyes when his lawyer sat down. He also saw something else. He was going to lose the case.

As if the surprise of Jacky Jr. testifying against him wasn't enough, the last witness called was shocking.

"The court calls Carly Ryan to the stand."

Connor couldn't believe his eyes as his girlfriend walked down the aisle and stood in the witness box. Several times during her testimony, the judge had to reprimand his attorney to take control of his client, at one point threatening to duct-tape Connor to his chair.

Over the next hour, Carly corroborated everything that Jacky Jr. had told the jury, and under cross-examination, she never folded. She had put the final nails in Connor's casket even though she had never been told any of the details by Connor.

His lawyer presented little in the way of a defense, and by the end of the day, the jury was given the case. The jury deliberated for an hour and fifteen minutes before finding Connor O'Connor guilty of two counts of premeditated murder and two counts of murder for hire. Three weeks later, Connor was sentenced to two consecutive life sentences without the possibility of parole. Connor O'Connor would spend the rest of his life in prison.

Chapter Five

The bus screeched to a halt, and Connor stepped off and looked across the street. The old neighborhood had changed a lot during the last forty-four years, and the only thing Connor recognized was the bar. Logan's Bar and Grill had the same old entrance, but it was now huge.

The bar had taken over the next two spaces in the building and, according to the sign above the front door, now had live music five nights a week. Even Connor recognized the names on the marquee. He walked across the street and opened the door. The change on the inside was dramatic, and it was no longer the dark hole-in-the-wall he remembered growing up with. It was now bright and airy and reeked of sophistication.

Connor grabbed a seat at the bar and ordered a draft beer. At ten o'clock in the morning, the place was almost empty, and he looked towards the back to see if the booth was still there, where Jacky Sr. held court. The booth had been replaced with a freestanding table and two chairs.

He looked around to see if anyone recognized him or if he recognized anyone else. The bartender set the glass of beer in front of him and started to walk away.

"Excuse me, buddy," he said. "Does Jacky Logan still own this bar?"

The bartender looked him up and down. "Yes, sir. He does. Do you know Mr. Logan?"

"We were friends years ago, but I've been traveling and lost touch. What about his kid, Jacky Jr.?"

The bartender looked confused; then, recognition filled his eyes. "I'm sorry, sir. You must have been asking about Mr. Logan's father. He was the original owner of the bar. I'm sorry to tell you, he passed away a couple of years back. Mr. Logan is his son."

Connor smiled. "That's okay. I was friends with both of them. Went to school with your Mr. Logan."

He thought for a minute and decided to see if he was right. "Is he still married to Carly?" he asked.

"Yes, sir," said the bartender. "It's too bad you weren't here last Friday. Had a big retirement party for them both. Gonna be living the good life up in the mountains."

The bartender stepped away, and Connor finished his beer and left a dollar tip on the bar.

He put on his coat and hat and stepped out into the sunlight. The beer didn't sit well, and he felt the nausea coming on. He stepped around the corner of the building and puked up the beer and the toast from breakfast. He felt better.

"So, Jacky Jr. and Carly got married. How nice for them," he said to himself.

He rested for a few more minutes and then headed for Lawrence Street, coming to a stop in front of an old, dilapidated house. He stopped for a minute and rested against the rusted wrought iron fence that surrounded the property. He looked around. It was the last private house left on the street, which was now filled with small apartment buildings. It didn't look anything like it did when he grew up here.

The large sign on the fence noted that the property was being developed into lifestyle housing, whatever that was. It was slated to be torn down at the end of the month. He pushed open the gate and walked around to the back of the house. Looking around to make sure no one was watching, he broke out a windowpane in the back door and unlocked the door. He stepped inside.

The place was a mess inside—nothing like when his mom ran the house. The paint and wallpaper were peeling, and there were puddles on the floor where the roof had leaked. He thought about his mom and dad, and a tear fell from his eye. So much had changed since he was sent to prison. He wasn't allowed to attend either of their funerals or the funeral for his younger sister, who'd passed away a couple of years back. He was all that was left, and his time was drawing to a close. Prison had cost him so much. Jacky Logan Jr. had cost him so much.

He shook off the melancholy and opened the basement door. The lights didn't work, so he felt his way along the stairs until he could start to see shapes. The tiny basement windows helped once he reached the bottom of the stairs.

He looked around and was glad to see that nothing had changed since the last time he had been there. He stepped over to the old chimney from the original boiler and felt along the bricks until one of them shifted ever so slightly. Using his nails, he pried the brick out of the chimney and did the same with the six bricks surrounding it. He reached inside and felt the old oilcloth package, which he gripped and pulled out.

He took the package, headed up the stairs to the old kitchen and laid it on the counter. He undid the string and opened the package. Everything was just as he remembered it.

The package contained an old Colt 1911 pistol and a box of .45-caliber shells. There was also fifty thousand dollars, wrapped in plastic. Money he had been paid over the years and that he had been saving to marry Carly. He now had other plans for the money.

Connor loaded the pistol, put the remaining shells in his pocket, along with the money, and walked out the door. He never looked back.

***

Connor stepped off the Trailways bus and looked around the town of Montrose, Colorado. In his backpack was his gun, what was left of the fifty thousand cash and an envelope with a new driver's license and credit cards in the name of Sean O'Leary.

He'd known nothing about the town when he did an internet search in the prison library to find a room for rent. All he cared about was that it was a small town where he could live out his last days in peace and quiet; but first, he had some things to take care of.

He found the apartment above a small bookstore overlooking the main street in town, stepped into his new world and locked the door. He sat down on the old but still decent couch. The apartment came furnished, which was good because he couldn't see spending any money on furniture he would only use for a couple of weeks.

The eight-hour bus trip had taken a lot out of him, and he took another oxycodone and closed his eyes. When he woke up, it was dark, and he could see fat snowflakes coming down. He looked out the front window and could see all the Christmas decorations along Main Street. The falling snow made it look festive, something he hadn't seen in a long time. He closed the drapes and turned on the old television that sat on the small table in the corner of the room. He flipped channels until he found one of the Denver news channels and sat back down.

The top story was the explosion and fire that had destroyed Logan's Bar and Grill, one of Denver's oldest and most treasured eateries and nighttime entertainment venues. The fire chief told the reporter that they suspected the fire had broken out in the basement and that once it got going, it quickly rolled through the old wooden building. There were no injuries or fatalities, but the building was a total loss.

Another reporter had contacted the owner at his home in Vail, but the owner had refused to comment, other than to say they would build an even bigger and better venue to replace the old place.

Connor O'Connor sat back and smiled. He felt good for the first time in a long time, and he was ready to move on with the next phase of his plan.

Tomorrow he would start gathering the items he needed. If he lived long enough to complete it, everyone would know his name.

Chapter Six

The manifesto was finished. Of course, finished is a vague term. He had been writing the manifesto for ten years and had *finished* it numerous times, only to return to it and add more when something in his life pissed him off. This latest edition had seen the addition of rhetoric on diversity and inclusion and a questionable election. He had gone on for pages about the most recent presidential election and how the election had been stolen from the American people.

Diversity and inclusion were other issues for him. He'd had black friends and colleagues when he was a professor at the University of Colorado. He treated them with respect as long as they respected him, and he didn't see the need to have it thrown up in his face constantly. He liked who he wanted, and he didn't like people that made him mad, and lately, a lot of people had made him mad.

He scrolled through the internet and found a story about government spending to give illegal immigrants health care, and he opened the manifesto and started typing. Another fourteen pages later and he closed the *finished* manifesto. He sat back and looked at his laptop. It was time.

He closed the laptop, put on his cap and coat and headed for the workshop. The snow from the last storm had added another foot to the side yard, and he made a note to dig out the snow shovel and clear a path to the road. Jessie would be bringing by his groceries later today, or maybe it was tomorrow. Sometimes he forgot things. A terrible situation for a man who graduated first or second in every school he had ever graduated from, grade school through his second PhD. His IQ had always been off the charts, and sometimes he had trouble adapting to a new school or making friends, but no matter what, he always remembered.

He ran his gloved hand through his long gray beard and thought about the grocery delivery. That momentary lapse made him question whether he had left the grocery list in the mailbox for Jessie or if maybe he hadn't ordered the stuff after all. Oh, well. If she didn't show up today or tomorrow, he would leave her another note.

A hawk flew overhead and let out a screech, and he raised his hand above his eyes and scanned the sky. The hair on the back of his neck raised in alarm, and he scanned the area around the shed and the cabin, stopping every few feet to listen. He wondered if the hawk had spotted the FBI coming through the woods. He finished the scan and noted that none of his IEDs had gone off, so he assumed he was still safe.

He cleared his mind once again, walked past the snow shovel hanging on the side of the cabin and trudged through the foot-deep snow to his shed. The snow was piled up in front of the door, and as he started pushing it away with his hands, he wished he had a snow shovel. He found a flat piece of wood next to the door and used it to clear the way, finally able to pull open the wooden door.

The shed was dark and cold, maybe even colder than outside, if that was possible. He grabbed some tinder from the firebox, carried it over to the old iron wood-burning stove and loaded it. Then, using a match from the box on the workbench, he lit a fire and watched it burn, mesmerized by the flames. He added more wood to the pile of tinder and closed the door. He could feel the shed warming up, and he took off his gloves and coat.

He pulled back the old plastic tarp covering the one large window to let in some light over the workbench and looked at his assortment of supplies.

The small refrigerator would be the perfect container, so he removed the door and set it aside. He ran the wires through the hole where he had removed the drain and screwed the timer to the side of the container in the holes he had drilled the previous day. The timer was self-contained, and all he needed to do was add the three new triple-A batteries to it, and it would be ready.

He placed two blasting caps in the bottom of the refrigerator and screwed the straps to the bottom. Next, he set the first plastic milk jug of yellow liquid into the refrigerator and inserted a blasting cap through a hole in the cap. The second milk jug he placed next to the first and inserted the other blasting cap into it. He continued this process until there was no room left in the refrigerator. He checked the connections and liked what he saw.

He filled the rest of the refrigerator with old nails and screws he had accumulated since the last time he had built a similar device, a year or two back. It might have been more than a year or two, but who was counting.

The refrigerator was filled to the brim with the assortment, and he replaced the door and snapped the lock into place, sealing it. Everything was ready. The last couple of times, he had sent letter bombs to various government officials and corporate executives. But this time would be different. His target was bigger and more meaningful. The mosque had been in the news lately, and he had watched the stories with great interest. He had searched the internet and found several stories about how the mosque was harboring terrorists and that they were kidnapping babies and shipping them overseas to ISIS to be used as sex slaves once they grew up.

Of course, the stories he found on the internet

had nothing to do with reality, but that didn't matter. The night he first heard about the mosque, the story was about them opening their doors to a synagogue that had burned down, leaving its congregation nowhere to hold services. The local Imam had gotten together with the rabbi and offered him the use of the mosque's basement meeting room so the synagogue members would have a warm, safe place to worship.

It was a feel-good story for the reporter, but the internet made something else out of it. The stories on the internet twisted it into something unrecognizable, kind of like when little kids play telephone. He believed all the bizarre stories, and that mosque would be his target.

He put on his coat and gloves and carried the small refrigerator out of the shed. He walked to the lean-to structure next door and pulled the cover off his old pickup truck. He placed the refrigerator in the bed of the truck and covered it with an old blanket.

Locking up the shed and the house, he grabbed a jug of water and a couple of apples for the long drive. He climbed into the old truck and hit the starter. The engine balked, and he thought it might not start, but it had never let him down yet. He turned the key again, and the engine coughed and caught. A cloud of black smoke filled the shed as he revved the engine to keep it from dying.

He put the truck in gear, pulled out of the lean-to, circled past the house and turned onto a barely discernible trail that disappeared between two huge spruce trees. He was taking the back way off of his property. It would take longer, but he knew it was safer. He didn't think the FBI knew about the road, because he only used it when he needed to head someplace without being seen.

It would be dark when he got to Avon, and he wanted to be back safe in his cabin by first light. He would have to step on it once he reached the highway. He figured the traffic would be light, being that it was Christmas Eve, and he hoped to make good time in the old truck. He had planned his trip so he could place the bomb after everyone left the building.

He wanted to make a statement so people would read his manifesto. The fact that people were going to die, well, too bad. But he didn't care much if people died. The information he got off the internet said that the mosque was being used for a unity celebration service on Christmas morning. The Jews and the Muslims would be celebrating together, so he expected a lot of collateral damage.

Over the years, his bombs had claimed the lives of six people and injured many more. Besides, terrorists were hiding in the mosque. The government should give him a medal for what he was about to do.

Chapter Seven

Jacky Logan was pissed. "How the fuck did this happen?" he asked as he looked at the faces of the men gathered around the dining room table, his face becoming the same color as his fiery red hair. "That fire is going to cost me a couple of million bucks to replace the building and to cover the lost contracts for the entertainers. Plus, what it will do to my name."

He looked at Jimmy Sullivan, his oldest and most trusted friend. "What are you hearing from the fire investigators?"

Jimmy, who had his hands in all things government-related, flipped open the green folder in front of him. "The arson investigators couldn't find any signs of any kind of accelerant. Their findings indicated a short in one of the electrical panels. They're saying that the spark ignited all that dry old wood in the basement and then raced through the building."

Jimmy sat back. He knew this was not what Jacky wanted to hear, and he waited for the coming explosion.

Jacky stood up from his chair and looked out the

window at the mountain behind his house. Usually, the view from the window or the back patio was enough to calm him down. Today, that wasn't working.

Without turning around, he said, "So the fire guys are blaming me. Is that it? They think I run an unsafe building? What are they fucking kidding? We brought the electrical in the building up to code when we expanded into the rest of the building. Cost me a fucking fortune."

He turned and looked at Mike Raines. "Mikey, you get your dad down into that basement and have him look around. I want to know what he thinks."

Mike Raines and his dad were the electrical contractors who had done the rewiring of the entire building seven years ago. Tommy Raines, Mike's father, had been a colleague and friend of Jacky's dad for all their lives. He gave the eulogy when Jacky's father passed away.

Jacky next turned to Tommy O'Hara. "Who do we know who could do this without getting caught?"

Tommy O'Hara had been Jacky's enforcer for years. Part of his job was to keep track of anyone they'd pissed off or offended in some way. He ran a hand through his slicked-back hair.

"We haven't received any threats from anyone

recently. Things have even been quiet with the Italians. No one wants to go back to the way things were. Back in the day, everyone lost money; now we're all making money and as far as I know, everyone is happy."

Jacky slammed his fist down on the table, and glasses of wine and beer danced. "I want to know who burned down my place, and I want the son of a bitch dead! Now, put your heads together and let's figure this out!"

Jacky thought about who might want to hurt him until his son, Jacky III, looked at him. He had taken over running the business when Jacky announced his retirement a couple of weeks back. "What about someone from the old days. Someone with a grudge against you or Granddad?"

Jacky sat down and thought for a minute. Between himself and Jacky Sr. they'd made a lot of enemies during the early days, but they had made sure most of those guys were no longer around to cause any trouble. He was just about to blow the question off when his expression changed. He sat quietly for a minute.

"What?" said Jacky III.

"No. It's not possible. He's been in prison for over forty years, and he's going to die there. Must be someone else we pissed off," said Jacky.

"Jacky, who you talkin' about?" asked Jimmy.

"The one person from my past who would still have a grudge. He was also an expert in all things involving death and destruction. But like I said, he's in prison for the rest of his life, if he's even still alive."

A light bulb went off, and Jimmy looked at the group around the table. He looked back at Jacky. "You're talking about Connor O'Connor."

Most of the men gathered around the table were too young to remember Connor O'Connor, but not Jimmy. He had been right there, the day they raided the safe house and hauled Connor away. He'd sat through the entire trial, and he was there the day they read the verdict. He had been close to Connor O'Connor throughout his youth, and he was probably one of the few people who knew what Jacky and Carly did to Connor.

He had never told a soul about Jacky Sr. turning on Connor after the botched bombing and how Jacky Jr. and Carly had testified against him. He felt bad about how it all went down, but he knew it had to go that way for the sake of the business. Anything less would have brought too much unwanted scrutiny from law enforcement and from the Italians, who were slowly creeping into their turf. Jimmy broke off that thought and looked at Paul Kincaid.

"Paul, call your friend at the prison in Florence and see if Connor O'Connor is still safely locked away."

Paul stood up, pulled out his phone and stepped out of the dining room and into the kitchen.

Someone down the table asked, "Who is Connor O'Connor?"

Jacky looked around the table, took a sip from his wineglass and stared for a minute. Jimmy knew better than to say anything. Jacky composed himself.

"Connor O'Connor is a scumbag who killed a woman and a kid when he was supposed to kill the husband. He was a complete fuckup, and his incompetence led him to get pinched. He got like a hundred years in prison. He's nobody we need to worry about."

Paul stepped back into the room and whispered in Jimmy's ear. Jacky III looked over, and Jimmy held up his hand. Jacky glared at Jimmy. "You gonna share with the rest of us?"

Paul sat back down, and Jimmy looked at Jacky. "Connor O'Connor was released from prison two weeks ago. He got a compassionate release because he has stage four pancreatic cancer. He only has a few weeks to live."

Jacky turned white as the tablecloth. "Why the fuck weren't we told about this?"

"No one was told. It was something that happened suddenly, and our guys never got the word," said Jimmy.

Jacky looked ready to explode, and everyone at the table knew it. They had all seen it happen before, and when it did, it wasn't pretty. And somebody usually died.

Carly walked in just at that moment and placed her hand on Jacky's back. She looked at Jimmy and her son and mouthed, "Deal with it." She then took Jacky by the hand, helped him stand and walked him out of the room.

Everyone, including Jacky III, looked at Jimmy. He stood and walked around the table.

"Connor O'Connor was a bomber. He was trained back in Ireland during the Troubles and gained a reputation as someone you didn't want to mess with. The Brits considered him a terrorist. What he was, was a ghost. Jacky was correct when he said he killed a woman and her kid. His intel failed, and he missed his target. He got multiple life sentences. If anyone could have done this, it was Connor O'Connor, and now he's out."

Jacky III stood up. "I want this motherfucker found, and I don't want my father involved. Get out on the streets and talk to all your earners and snitches. Find this fuck before he causes my family any more pain. There's a hundred grand in it for whoever brings me his head in a bag."

Jacky III left to check on his dad, and everyone at the table stood up and gathered around Jimmy. They were all hungry for more information. Jimmy wasn't about to tell them how things had ended between Jacky and Connor, but he was willing to give them a warning.

"Connor O'Connor may be old and sick, but you can bet he is still deadly. Now, he may have had nothing to do with the bar burning down, but he's a threat to the boss if he is out there and still alive. You heard Jacky III. Find this fuck before something bad happens."

Everyone left and headed back to Denver. Jimmy sat and finished his wine. He had a bad feeling about this.

Chapter Eight

The snow on Christmas Eve had dumped another foot of snow on Gunnison, Colorado, and the decorations on the houses reflecting off the snow cast a warm glow over the town.

Buck Taylor didn't mind the snow. He had lived all his life in Gunnison, and weather was just something that happened, and you dealt with it when it was over. It was early in the snow season, and including this storm, Gunnison had already seen twenty-seven inches of snow, and the temperature the other night had dropped to fifteen below zero. So, Buck just figured it would be a bad winter as he pulled the snow thrower out of the garage and fired it up.

After finishing his driveway, he ran the snow thrower over to his neighbor's house and started on her driveway. After he had cleared all of her snow, he noticed Mrs. Graves standing in the doorway wrapped in a thick blanket. She held up a bottle of Coke, and Buck, kicking the snow off his boots, stepped up to the door as she opened it and stepped inside.

Ruth Graves and Buck had been neighbors for as long as he could remember. At eighty-four and a widow for five years, she was still spry, and her mind worked like a steel trap. Nothing that went on in Gunnison County got past Mrs. Graves.

"Merry Christmas, Buck," she said as he stepped through the door and into the warm, cozy living room. "Can we still say Merry Christmas, or is that not allowed anymore?"

Buck laughed and took a long drink of the Coke. "It's still okay, Ruth. Merry Christmas has always worked for me."

"You seeing the kids today?"

"Yeah, Cassie came in last night and is staying with David, as are Jason and his crew." He looked at his watch.

"I better get going. I'm cooking breakfast this morning."

He thanked her for the Coke, and she thanked him for clearing her driveway. He hugged her and headed back out into the early morning cold. He didn't want to be late getting to his son David's house and miss seeing his grandkids open their presents.

Cassie, his daughter, had flown in from Montana, and Jason and his family had driven in early the day before to beat the storm. This would be their first family Christmas with everyone together since Lucy had died five years ago. Cassie had even brought matching pajamas for the whole crew, including the dogs. Buck was looking forward to family time.

He loaded up the gifts and groceries and backed out of his garage. He could have walked to David's house quicker than driving down the unplowed street. David and his wife, Judy, lived around the corner from Buck, and they kept an eye on the house while he was away.

Buck pulled his state-issued Jeep Grand Cherokee into David's driveway and parked behind the Gunnison Police Department SUV sitting in front of the garage door. David was a sergeant with the Gunnison Police Department and was the night shift supervisor, a shift he had spent many years on as a patrol officer.

David was a shade over six foot and a few pounds heavier than his father, but he looked exactly like Buck had when he was David's age. It was almost scary how much they resembled each other. He also moved with the ease of a young man, which made Buck jealous at times.

Buck opened the back hatch, grabbed the bags of Christmas gifts and groceries and headed for the back door. He stopped inside the door to give Scruff the Siberian Husky a quick pat on the head, reached into his pocket and gave the dog a large dog biscuit.

Scruff headed for his favorite pillow in the corner by the fireplace, and Buck started putting the gifts under the tree.

With all the yelling and hollering, he could barely hear himself think, but after he finished with the gifts, he headed into the kitchen and started unpacking the groceries for breakfast.

Cassie walked in and hugged him. "About time, Dad. The kids are waiting," she said. She took the grocery bag from his hands and placed it on the counter and gave him a push towards the tree.

Cassie was Buck's middle child, and she was every bit a middle child. In high school, she'd played soccer, ran track and played volleyball. She lettered in all three sports. She was also the one who got in trouble for violating curfew, drinking and getting into whatever other mischief she could find. So Buck was surprised when she was accepted to the University of Arizona with a full volleyball scholarship. He was even more surprised when she was accepted into law school. Cassie had never been one for regimented education.

Several years ago, she'd suddenly dropped out of law school, and her career path took a different track. She joined the Forest Service and was now working as a wildland firefighter with the Helena Hotshots, one of the country's elite firefighting teams, based out of Helena, Montana.

Buck had not been surprised by any of this. He never saw her sitting behind a desk as a lawyer. She loved the outdoors, and she was as tough as they come. Lucy hadn't been pleased that she quit school without any discussion, and she always worried whenever Cassie was called out on a fire, but she also knew her daughter, and if this was where she was happy, then so was her mom.

Ever since Lucy died, Cassie had been Buck's sounding board, the way Lucy used to be. Another voice and another viewpoint to help him see a case more clearly.

The festivities started as soon as he sat down in the recliner, and all hell broke loose as wrapping paper and boxes flew through the air and landed everywhere. Buck thought about how much Lucy would have loved the scene unfolding before him. He wiped a tear from his eye and opened a gift from Jason and his family.

Once all the gifts were unwrapped and the kids started playing with that one special gift, Buck headed for the kitchen. He set all the ingredients for his world-famous huevos rancheros on the counter and started cooking. Judy and Kate, Jason's wife, walked in and started working on the side dishes while David and Jason set the dining room table.

Jason was Buck's youngest son and was a partner at an architectural firm in Boulder,

Colorado. He was a devout Catholic, which he got from his mom. He was also the one member of the family that took everything to heart, and he worried about Buck and his job.

During the past year and a half, Jason had worked as both Architect and Project Manager on the Lucy Taylor Memorial Riverwalk. The project was the brainchild of Hardy and Rachel Braxton, Lucy's sister and brother-in-law.

The Braxtons were the wealthiest family in Gunnison County and one of the wealthiest families in the state. As such, Hardy had been able to purchase a mile of riverfront along the Gunnison River. Then, with the help of Jason, they'd created a mile-long walkway, complete with picnic areas and an open-air amphitheater for concerts and other events. The walkway was a huge hit with the townspeople, and Buck was proud of how it represented Lucy.

Everyone enjoyed the breakfast Buck had prepared, and when it was over and while Cassie led the cleanup team, Buck sat on the floor under the tree and played with his youngest granddaughter.

It was just past nine a.m. when his phone rang. He unclipped it from his belt and looked at the number. He had a feeling that the Christmas festivities   for him, at least—were over. It seemed like everyone in the house stopped and waited. It was time for Buck to go to work.

Chapter Nine

Buck answered the phone. "Merry Christmas, sir. What's up?"

"Hey, Buck. I hate to do this on Christmas morning, but I need all hands on deck," said Kevin Jackson.

Kevin Jackson was the director of the Colorado Bureau of Investigation and Buck's boss. He had been the youngest person ever appointed to head up the CBI when Governor Richard J. Kennedy tapped him to run the agency. He'd spent the early part of his career on the Colorado Springs Police Department's administrative side and was well regarded by the law enforcement community. He was not only an effective manager but a seasoned investigator in his own right. Buck held the man in high regard.

"No problem, sir. What's happened?"

"We're getting reports of at least seven bombings, all around the state. Hold on a minute."

Buck could hear talking in the background, and he wondered if the director was in the office.

"Sorry, Buck," said the director. "Eight bombings now, and this one may be the worst. We're getting reports of a massive explosion at a mosque in Avon. Sounds like a mass casualty event. I need you to head to Avon. I've got Bax and Paul heading to several other sites, and I'm rolling everyone in the Denver and Pueblo offices. This is gonna be one shitty Christmas, Buck. Sorry I have to do this to you."

Buck waved to David to turn on the TV. "News," was all he said. David reached for the remote.

"No problem, sir. I'll leave right now. Can you have someone text me the address of the mosque? What about forensics?"

"Max is sending out her teams. The team from Grand Junction will meet you in Avon. I've spoken with Hank Clancy at the FBI and Rich Garland at ATF, and they'll be dispatching their teams as well. What a mess."

"Don't worry, sir. I'll check in with Bax and Paul when I get to Avon and put the forensic team right to work."

"Thanks, Buck. Call me later and fill me in."

The director hung up, and Buck joined his family in front of the TV. Buck watched as the news anchors tried to gather information from the field, but at this point, there was little information to share. The story was breaking so quickly that they didn't have time to gather their experts, to speculate on what was going on.

A reporter broke in and reported two more bombings, bringing the total to ten. Buck wondered how many more there would be before it was all over.

"Sounds like reports are coming in from all over the state," said David. "Where are you heading?"

"One of the explosions was at a mosque in Avon. Sounds like that may be the worst one so far. I'll call you tonight and let you know where I am and see if I can give you an idea of how long I'll be gone."

Buck went around the room and hugged each person, apologizing for leaving and wishing them each a Merry Christmas. They each, in turn, told him to be safe. He grabbed his coat off the stair rail and headed for the back door. As he passed through the kitchen, Judy handed him a bag of sandwiches and a small cooler filled with Coke bottles. She gave him a big hug.

Cassie followed him out the door and walked him to the Jeep. "Dad, please be careful."

"Don't worry, kiddo. You know me."

She smiled. "Yeah, that's what I'm afraid of." They both laughed.

They hugged for a long minute, and then Buck slid into the Jeep and backed out of the driveway. He had been hoping for a quiet Christmas, but in Buck's line of work, you never knew what to expect.

As always before he left on a new case, he thought about Lucy and wished she could have been there today to see how the grandkids had grown. Lucy would have been the life of the party.

Chapter Ten

If you asked Buck, he would tell you that he fell in love with Lucinda Torres the first day of their senior year in high school. On the other hand, Lucy always told people that Buck stalked her the entire senior year before she gave in to shut her friends up and agreed to go to the movies with him. She had always considered him just another jock, another football player who was too full of himself. What she found on that first date was a shy, unassuming gentleman, for lack of a better word, who, it seemed, cared more about pleasing her than bragging about his prowess on the football field. She would tell people it was love at first sight that had taken a year to accomplish. From that day forward, they were inseparable.

During senior year Buck had been approached by several college football scouts who wanted to sign him to play for their schools. Gunnison High School was a small school back in 1978, and Buck and his family were amazed at how many schools had recruited him, but for Buck, college just wasn't in the cards.

Buck hated school and spent a lot of time getting himself out of trouble instead of getting an education. When he found something that interested him, he had no problem learning all he could about the subject, but regular schoolwork just bored him. After several long heartfelt discussions, first with Lucy and then with his parents, he had decided to join the army after graduation. Surprisingly, no one was surprised.

Buck spent four years after high school in the army, and by the time his enlistment was up, he had been promoted to First Sergeant. He spent three years of his enlistment in the military police and really took to police work. That was when he decided to apply for a position with the Gunnison County Sheriff's Office.

Since he was already well known in the county, he had no trouble getting a job as a deputy. He proposed to Lucy on the night he received the call that he had gotten the position. His life and career were set. He made the most of his time with the Gunnison County Sheriff's Office, eventually becoming the undersheriff in charge of the Investigation Division and coming to the attention of the Colorado Bureau of Investigation.

Buck had worked with the Colorado Bureau of Investigation on several cases inside the county and had earned the respect of the investigators he had worked with.

As twilight started to fall on Buck's career, he

knew that unless he wanted to go into politics and run for sheriff, he had reached the highest position in the sheriff's office that he could obtain. He loved his job, but when the first offer came in from the CBI, he sat down with Lucy and had a long heart-to-heart talk.

He'd spent seventeen years in the sheriff's office and had always figured he would retire from that job. They had three children, two in high school and one not far behind, and he was a well-respected member of the community. Did he have the right to disrupt all their lives and pick up and move someplace else and start all over? The kids had friends, Lucy owned a small deli/ice cream parlor, and they had a nice life.

He could stick it out for another ten years and retire, and they could travel and see the world like they had always planned. Twice he turned down the offer from the CBI, although more and more, he felt like he was trapped behind a desk instead of doing what he loved, which was investigating crime.

The final offer came directly from Tom Cole, then-director of the Colorado Bureau of Investigation. Buck always remembered that day. The Denver Broncos had just lost another game, the third one in a row, and his friends had all packed up and headed home when there was a knock at the front door.

Now, anyone who lives in a small community knows that no one ever uses the front door, and no one ever knocks. So, who could this possibly be this late on a Sunday evening?

Buck answered the door and was surprised to see the director of the Colorado Bureau of Investigation standing on his front porch. The director smiled and said, "Before you close the door in my face, please listen to my offer."

Buck invited him in, and he and Lucy sat on the couch and listened as the director laid out his plan. He was opening a new branch office in Grand Junction, Colorado, that would house five agents and a small forensic unit. Buck could continue to live in Gunnison but would have to report to the office in Grand Junction twice a month. Otherwise, he would be free to work out of his house. There would be no disruption in his life other than having to spend some time on the road as his investigations warranted. He would work alone, but he would have all the branch office's resources at his disposal.

Before Buck could say a word, Lucy said, "Buck, this is what you have been waiting for, a chance to be a real investigator again. You have to take this." That was one of the things that made him love Lucy every day. She always knew what he was thinking, and she always understood what drove him. She had nailed it this time. Buck looked at the director and replied, "Well, I guess it's settled; looks like you have a new investigator on your team."

That was twenty-four years ago, and Buck had never looked back. He had made the most of those years and was one of the most respected and feared investigators in the state, but all that work couldn't make up for the loss he suffered.

Lucy was diagnosed with metastatic breast cancer following a routine mammogram, and they set off together on their next adventure: the quest to beat the dreaded disease. After a double mastectomy and five years of chemo, they knew their time was drawing to a close when the cancer returned several times to her brain and was no longer controlled by the radiation.

They made the decision together to stop all treatments, even though they had always told the family that the decision was Lucy's alone to make. Lucy spent the last couple of months of her life taking care of her small business and spending as much time as she could with her children and grandchildren.

The end came quietly one spring night. Lucy had been sleeping on and off for twenty or so hours a day in the end. The night she died, Buck had been lying in bed next to her, reading a report, when she snuggled into his arms and rested her head on his shoulder. Sometime during the night, Buck had fallen asleep. When he woke up, Lucy was gone, and his world was shattered.

They say that time heals all wounds, but Buck wasn't sure that was the case when you lost your closest friend. And even now, all these years later, he missed her more and more each day.

Buck always thought back to that Sunday morning when the family had gathered for a private ceremony at the little dock along the Gunnison River to scatter Lucy's ashes. Each family member got to say a few words about Lucy, and when they finished and turned to go, they were stunned to see several hundred of their neighbors and friends standing silently behind them in the park. Word had gotten out about their private service, and everyone turned out to pay tribute to Lucy. The affair turned into a huge party, with plenty of food and drinks. Lucy never wanted any kind of service, but Buck figured she would have loved this spontaneous outpouring of love.

Chapter Eleven

Buck made good time getting to Avon, which, considering the amount of snow the mountains had received the day before, was an impressive accomplishment. With only a minor delay just over the top of Monarch Pass for a small avalanche, once he passed the slide area, the drive was smooth.

Avon, Colorado, was one of several municipalities in Eagle County and had a population of about 6,500. For years, Avon and the neighboring town of Edwards were where the people who worked at the ski resorts of Vail and Beaver Creek had lived since they couldn't afford to live at the resorts.

Over the last decade or so, these towns had seen an influx of wealthier people moving in, pricing out the workers, who kept moving farther down the valley. As a result, the town had grown up a lot since the last time Buck was here.

The director had texted him the address for the mosque, but it turned out that with all the emergency equipment around, it was easy to find the location. Buck could see the destruction from the highway as he drove past.

The mosque had been a landmark in the Eagle Valley for over forty years, with its stone and tan stucco walls capped off by a beautiful gold dome and two towering spires. Its ornate design and large windows made the mosque not only a beautiful building but a great place to worship.

Buck couldn't believe the destruction as he pulled off I-70 and pulled up to the roadblock. A young Avon police officer approached his Jeep, and Buck held up his credentials. The officer took them and then keyed the mic hooked to a loop on the left shoulder of his uniform coat.

He listened carefully and handed Buck back his credentials. "You won't find any parking near the mosque, sir, so it's best if you pull into the Maverick parking lot and walk in."

Buck thanked the officer, drove through the first traffic circle, and pulled into the convenience store parking lot. He slid out of the Jeep, zipped up his insulated Carhartt ranch jacket and grabbed his backpack.

It was almost a mile to the mosque, and Buck stopped on a slight rise just before he reached the building and surveyed the area. The damage was incredible. One side of the mosque had collapsed into a pile of smoldering rubble.

The dome still stood, but Buck could see cracks

in the stucco. All the windows had been blown out, and one of the spires was now a long row of rubble running through the parking lot. Several dozen cars sat under the rubble in various states of destruction. There were firefighters from several municipalities working on remaining hot spots, and there were more emergency vehicles and first responders than Buck had seen in one place in a long time.

Buck spotted the Eagle County Sheriff's Office mobile incident command trailer and headed that way. The trailer was a buzz of activity as Buck walked through the door. Eagle County Sheriff Al Hartman stood next to a large table covered in blueprints talking with a guy wearing a white hard hat. Sheriff Hartman spotted Buck and waved him over.

Al Hartman had been the Eagle County sheriff for going on fifteen years. He was six foot two and weighed probably two forty. His gray hair was thinning on top, and he sported a gray mustache. He could usually be found in his department uniform, but today he wore jeans and a flannel shirt. His badge was pinned to the left pocket of the shirt.

Buck walked towards the table and reached out his hand. "Al, good to see you. What can I do to help?"

Buck wasn't an imposing figure, but when he was on a crime scene or running an investigation, there was little doubt to anyone around who was in charge. At six feet tall and one hundred eighty-five pounds, Buck was in the best shape of his life. He looked like he could still play football for the Gunnison High School Cowboys.

He wore his salt-and-pepper hair, which had a lot more salt than pepper in it, longer than the style of the day, and considerably longer than when his wife of thirty-four years, Lucy, had still been alive. Today he wore a T-shirt and jeans. His jacket was unzipped, and his gun and CBI badge were clipped to his belt.

Sheriff Hartman shook Buck's hand. "Director Jackson called me to tell me you were coming down. Glad to have you here."

He turned around and introduced Buck to Rich McKenna. "Rich is our county engineer, and he's worried that more of the building might collapse before we can get in there to search for victims. I've got public works bringing in some heavy equipment and materials to shore up the rest of the building, but that's going to take time."

"What do we know so far?" asked Buck.

Sheriff Hartman swiped his hand across the tablet that was sitting on the table. He lowered his reading glasses. "Explosion happened right at seven a.m. They were having a sunrise unity celebration and had about one hundred fifty people in attendance. The synagogue in Beaver Creek was damaged in a fire about a month ago. The mosque had reached out and offered them a place to worship. They decided a week ago to hold this celebration to honor their continuing friendships."

Buck interrupted. "Any chance the fire at the synagogue could be part of this?"

"Fuck, Buck. I was trying not to go there, but I guess it's possible. Fire marshal ruled the fire as accidental. Some kind of electrical short, but in this crazy world we live in, who knows?"

Sheriff Hartman looked down at his tablet. "Eyewitness accounts say the explosion happened in the kitchen area, but from what we can tell so far, it blew through the wall and into the common area. We've identified about a hundred survivors, many with broken bones and a lot of contusions from shrapnel. It appears the bomb was filled with screws, nuts and bolts. We can't work our way into the heart of the building until the debris cools down. Shit, Buck. There could be fifty men, women and children still in there dying, and we can't do a damn thing to help them."

The sheriff's face showed his anguish. "Who the fuck does something like this on Christmas morning? There were kids inside the building, for Christ's sake."

Buck patted him on the shoulder. "It's okay, Al. We'll figure this out. Is Vail PD running the explosion in Vail, or are you guys on that one too?"

"PD has the lead on that one. One of my bomb squad guys is there. We're giving mutual aid to the locals, and I heard the FBI is on the way, but so far, only Ashley Baxter is there. She's one of your people, right?"

"Yeah," said Buck. "Bax will take good care of them, and she knows how to work with the Feds."

Buck looked at McKenna. "What can you tell me about the condition of the building? Can we risk sending in a search team?"

McKenna removed his hard hat and smoothed his dark brown hair. When he spoke, his voice was soft and calm. "I understand the urgency, but I wouldn't recommend it. One wall is completely gone. Parts of two adjacent walls are gone. There's a steel beam holding up the dome, but the walls supporting the beam are damaged. One spire has already crashed into the parking lot, and the other one has a fifteen-degree tilt to it. In my opinion, Agent Taylor, I would not recommend entering that building until we can shore up the damage."

Chapter Twelve

Buck stepped over to the table and looked at the blueprints for the mosque. "Al, can we determine where most of the remaining victims might be based on information from the survivors?" asked Buck.

The door to the trailer opened, and in walked the man who might be able to answer that question. The Avon fire chief was a slight man who wore glasses and stood less than six feet tall. He had on a huge yellow raincoat and a white chief's hat. He stepped up to the table and introduced himself to Buck. "Mark Shepard." He stuck out his hand, and Buck was amazed at the man's grip. Buck asked the chief the same question.

Chief Shepard pulled the blueprints around to better orient himself. He set his helmet on the edge of the table and looked at Buck. He pointed to an area on the plans marked Kitchen.

"At this point, our best guess, and this is only a guess, is that the bomb went off in the kitchen, here. The problem is that we have victims with serious damage from all over the building."

Buck looked at the blueprint. "If you were going

to pick a spot to start looking for victims, where would it be?"

"If I had one spot to choose, I would start in the kitchen."

McKenna spoke up. "Agent Taylor, I know what you're thinking, and it is foolhardy. There is no way to guarantee anyone safety once you step into that building."

Chief Shepard cut him off. "Come on, Rich. My guys walk into situations every day that are not safe. There's never a guarantee of safety. People are dying in there, that we might be able to save, but we need to move now. The hot spots are out, and we're wasting time. That's why I came in here just now. To let Al know we were going to start searching."

McKenna let out a sigh and walked away from the table. Buck looked at Chief Shepard. "Do you have a helmet I can borrow?"

Chief Shepard looked surprised. "As Rich said, I can't guarantee your safety."

Buck smiled. "If you told me you could, I wouldn't go. I need to start searching for the source and see if there is anything left of the bomb that could help us identify the bomber."

Sheriff Hartman walked over to a closet at the back of the trailer and pulled out two white helmets.

He handed one to Buck and put the other on his head. "If we're gonna do this, then let's go before I change my mind."

Buck took the helmet and stepped out of the trailer, followed by Chief Shepard and Sheriff Hartman. McKenna, wearing his hard hat, followed close behind. Buck pulled out his phone and stepped to the side. He pushed a button and speed-dialed Melanie Hart.

"Hey, Buck. Merry Christmas, I think. What can we do for you?"

"Hi, Mel. Can you and George start running some things down for me?"

George Peterman and Melanie Hart were the CBI cybersecurity team based out of Grand Junction, Colorado, and they couldn't be more different.

George Peterman had joined the CBI after retiring from the navy, where he'd spent his entire career working in cybersecurity. As far as Buck was concerned, George and his partner, Melanie Hart, were two of the best computer people he knew. Paul Webber was good. Ashley Baxter was better, but these two were world-class.

Melanie was about five foot two, with shoulder-length black hair; she wore black jeans, dark gray hoodies and had several piercings. Anyone meeting her for the first time would think she was a high school kid, but she had received her doctorate in computer science from MIT about a dozen years before. She'd joined CBI right out of college.

George Peterman, on the other hand, could have passed for her father. George was about the same height as Buck, a shade under six foot, but where Buck still weighed what he'd weighed when he played football in high school, George had added a few pounds over the years.

"You bet, Buck. The director said that whatever you need is now top priority."

"Thanks, Mel. Start compiling a list of all the bombings and all the victims—deep background. Pull phone logs, social media, anything you can find. Look for connections. If nothing shows up, go deeper, look for extended family, and look at any connections there. There has to be a reason these people were chosen. Also, have George hit the internet and the dark web and let's see if anyone is claiming responsibility. Let's look for large purchases of high explosives. Lastly, hit the databases and look for similar-type attacks, and put together a list of recent bombings over, say, the past ten years."

"You know the FBI isn't gonna like us messing in their files, since they are probably looking for the same information."

Buck laughed. "Then let's make sure the FBI doesn't know you're in their files. Besides, they move too slowly—too much bureaucracy. You guys are a lot quicker. So, let's get ahead of them and see what they bring to the table."

"You got it, Buck. Where are you heading?"

"Hopefully to rescue some people."

Buck didn't elaborate, and Melanie told him to be safe. Buck walked towards the group of firefighters that had formed at the edge of the collapsed kitchen wall. He was amazed at how many had volunteered to join the search.

Chapter Thirteen

Bax pulled onto the street the director had texted to her and parked behind a Vail Police Department SUV. She climbed out of her Jeep, grabbed her backpack and approached the crime scene tape. The scene was chaotic, with police cars, fire engines and ambulances scattered along the street, with their lights flashing. She held up her credentials for the Vail police officer who was manning the tape and signed the clipboard he was holding.

CBI Agent Ashley Baxter worked with Buck on many interesting cases, in between working on her own cases. At thirty years old, she was one of the youngest agents in the Grand Junction Field Office, and she valued the time she got to spend with Buck because she learned so much about running an investigation. She stood about five foot six with blue eyes and blond hair she often kept tied in a ponytail, usually hanging through the hole in the back of her CBI cap. She had been with the Colorado Bureau of Investigation for seven years, and she had earned Buck's respect.

Bax was also a whiz at doing deep background searches—a talent Buck did not share—so he relied on Bax to help him out. They worked well as a team and had found themselves collaborating more and more as the years rolled by.

"Chief's inside," said the officer as he raised the tape so she could pass under it. She thanked him and approached the house. From the outside, the house was a beautiful mountain mansion, complete with huge timber posts, a stone façade and a huge carved front door. There was no evidence of any damage, and she wondered to herself how intense the explosion had been.

She pushed open the front door and was met by a completely different scene. The entire back wall of the great room she entered was blown out, and the debris covered the treed slope behind the house. She could see what looked like the remains of a Christmas tree lying on the back deck. Most of its larger branches were stripped bare of needles, and tattered strings of lights still hung from the burned-up branches.

Broken toys, smoldering furniture and debris were scattered everywhere. It looked like a bomb had gone off, which was precisely what happened.

Bax spotted Vail Police Chief Hank Crawford standing in the middle of the room, talking with a couple of firefighters and a tall, bald black man wearing an Eagle County Sheriff's Office patch on the sleeve of his khaki jumpsuit. Bax walked over, introduced herself and shook hands all around.

Chief Crawford made a poor attempt at a smile. "Hell of a Christmas morning, huh, Bax? Last we heard, there had been twelve explosions around the state, plus the mosque. Sounds like it might be damn terrorists to me."

The comment surprised Bax. Chief Crawford didn't look that much older than she was, but he sounded like a grizzled old veteran. She looked at the sheriff's deputy. Carlton Hickman had spent most of his life working in army explosive ordinance disposal. He had joined the Eagle County Sheriff's Office after retiring from the army, so he could keep his many skills relevant.

"Carlton, have you been able to confirm this was a bomb?" she asked.

Carlton looked at Bax. "Not officially. No." He walked her towards a gaping hole in the middle of the floor that looked down into the basement. Debris filled the hole. "Right now, I'm thinking the bomb was sitting here," he said, pointing towards the hole. "Since there's no gas lines or anything like that visible under the floor, it's unlikely it was anything but a bomb. Now that the fire guys are moving out, we can start to search for pieces of the bomb."

"I spoke to my office on the way up, and forensics should be here within the hour," said Bax.

"Chief, can we get everyone out of the house until the forensic team arrives?"

Chief Crawford, looking none too happy, yelled for his people to clear the house. He walked over to Bax and Carlton. "How big would this bomb have to be to cause this much destruction?" he asked.

Before Carlton could answer, they had to step out of the way as two firefighters carried out a black body bag. From the size of the bag, it appeared to be a child. Bax noticed Chief Crawford wipe a tear from his eye.

Bax pulled a notebook out of her pocket and opened it to a clean page. "Chief, let's step outside and let the firefighters bring out the bodies."

She led him towards the door, followed by Deputy Hickman. They stepped onto the driveway and out of the way as four more body bags were carried out.

"Chief," said Bax. "What can you tell me about the family?"

Chief Crawford pulled a notebook out of his back pocket but rattled off most of the information without looking at the page he had opened.

"House belongs to Jackson Logan and his wife, Carly. They've lived here for probably ten years, on and off, but I heard they just moved up here full time after they retired. They are both involved in local civic groups and have led several fundraisers for children with disabilities. One of their grandkids has a disability. Not sure what one, but it probably doesn't matter anymore. Funny how tragedy can follow a family."

"How's that, Chief?" asked Bax.

"They are the owners of Logan's Bar and Grill in Denver."

Bax cut him off. "Didn't that burn to the ground last month?"

"Yeah. One of the oldest bars in Denver. For the past ten or fifteen years, it's been a huge entertainment venue. All the big names in music and comedy have appeared there. Jacky was heartbroken and had promised to rebuild."

"I wonder if the two events are related?" asked Bax.

"I guess it's possible, but why? And if someone wanted to take out Jacky, why would they kill his family?"

Bax thought about that for a minute and then put the thought aside.

"Any idea how many people were in the house this morning?" asked Bax.

Chief Crawford looked at his notes. "From what we can tell and from the cars in the driveway, it was Logan and his wife, their daughter Gillian, her husband and their four children. Their housekeeper might have been there too. Been trying to reach her since we got here with no luck."

Bax was about to say something when a white van with government plates was passed under the crime scene tape and pulled up to the curb.

"Looks like the FBI has arrived," she said.

A tall blond man wearing a white jumpsuit with the letters FBI stenciled on the back and over the left pocket exited the van and walked up to Bax and Chief Crawford. He didn't extend his hand or remove his sunglasses.

"I'm Jake Morrison, FBI evidence response team from Denver." He looked at the house. "We'll take over from here, Chief, and we'll let you know if we need anything."

He walked off, followed by six similarly dressed technicians. Chief Crawford looked from Bax to Carlton. "Looks like we've been dismissed." He turned and headed for his SUV, shaking his head as he went.

"Let's stick around and see what they find," said Bax. Carlton nodded, and she pulled out her phone.

Chapter Fourteen

Paul Webber turned left off Highway 50 onto Holman Avenue, followed Holman as it turned into Airport Road and then turned right onto Silver Springs Drive. He followed the cul-de-sac around until he was stopped by a Salida police officer standing at a barricade. Paul could see several emergency vehicles ahead.

Paul presented his ID to the officer at the barricade and was waved through as the officer pulled the barricade out of the way. As he approached the end of the cul-de-sac, he noticed many broken windows in the surrounding houses.

The cul-de-sac was part of a well-kept subdivision with tree-lined streets and well-tended lawns. Despite the cold and the fact it was Christmas morning, many of the neighbors were standing behind a couple of barricades, watching the activities. Several fire engines and ambulances were in the cul-de-sac, and paramedics were working on people with cuts and scrapes.

Paul spotted Salida Police Chief Everett Langford standing next to what appeared to be the remains of a community mailbox. He was talking with another man wearing a badge on his coat. Paul grabbed his backpack and stepped up to the two men.

"Chief, Merry Christmas."

"Yeah," said Chief Langford. "Not very merry for these folks. Paul, good to see you again. Glad you're here."

Paul was over six foot four with a muscular physique. He had joined CBI four years earlier after spending ten years with the Dallas, Texas, police department. His last post had been as a homicide detective. Paul may have seemed like a giant, but those who knew him knew he was a pussycat. He was one of the most soft-spoken guys Buck had ever met.

Chief Langford pointed towards the man standing next to him. "Paul, Jim Fisher, U.S. Postal Inspector. Jim, Paul Webber, CBI."

Paul shook Jim's hand. "So, what's the Postal Inspection Service's interest in this bombing?"

Jim Fisher pointed to what remained of a steel post, bent and twisted, sticking out of the ground. "This, up until this morning, was one of our community mailboxes. Now it's just twisted junk metal. Chief Langford called our office as soon as he heard that the bomb might have been inside the mailbox."

Paul looked at the twisted metal and nodded. He pulled a notebook and pen out of his pocket and opened to a clean page. "Chief, want to give me the rundown?"

"About seven A.M.," said Chief Langford, "nine-one-one started receiving calls about an explosion. We dispatched fire and police, and when they arrived on the scene, this is what they found." He waved his hand around. "Folks were just opening gifts or having breakfast when the mailbox exploded. Most of the injuries are from flying glass and shards of metal. Most of the houses in the immediate vicinity had their front-facing windows blown out, and a couple of cars and trucks took the same kind of damage. Thank god no one was seriously hurt. Looks like the mailbox contained the worst of the explosion. Sure made a hell of a mess."

He looked at Paul. "What the hell's going on? We heard the reports about the other explosions, twelve homes all over the state and that mosque up in Avon. If it was only the mosque, I'd think this was a terrorist attack, but that doesn't make much sense."

"Well, Chief. Right now, you know as much as we do," said Paul. He turned to Jim Fisher, who was just disconnecting a call. "Jim, any way to tell which box had mail in it?"

Jim Fisher looked at the notebook in his hand.

"That was the route driver on the phone. Every personal box had just the usual assortment of mail. He mentioned that the box for address one three seven four had a lot of mail in it like they hadn't picked up mail in a couple of days. He also said that same address had a large package in one of the package boxes that hadn't been picked up in three or four days."

Paul looked down the street. "Chief, we'd better go check on that address."

Paul, Chief Langford and Jim Fisher stepped away from the mailbox post and walked three doors down the street. Paul walked up the front steps and knocked on the door. He put his ear close to the door, listened and knocked again.

He looked at the chief. "I think we need to check inside. Exigent circumstances."

Chief Langford nodded, and Paul removed a small leather pouch from his back pocket. He looked at the front door lock and pulled two lockpicks from the pouch. He squatted in front of the door, and in ten seconds, the door was unlocked. He put the picks back in the pouch, and with his hand on his pistol, he pushed open the door. "Police," he yelled. "Anyone home?"

They all stepped through the door and fanned out, Paul to the left, Chief Langford to the right and

Jim Fisher up the stairs. "Clear," came from each of them, and Jim Fisher came back down the stairs and met them in the kitchen.

"Looks like they must be gone for the holidays," said Chief Langford.

"Probably saved their lives," said Paul as he looked at the family photos taped to the refrigerator door. He looked at a few pieces of mail on the counter, pulled out his phone and sent a text with the family name and address to George Peterman, with a request to see if he could locate a cell phone. He asked Chief Langford to check with the neighbors and see if anyone had a cell phone for the family.

They walked out the door, and Paul locked the door behind him. Chief Langford was standing on the front sidewalk talking with a man in a bathrobe and slippers who was flipping through his phone. He held the phone up so Chief Langford could read something, and the chief entered the information in his phone.

Chief Langford dialed a number and, for the next few minutes, had a conversation with whoever answered on the other end. He disconnected the call and walked back to Paul and Jim Fisher.

"Just spoke with Mark Bellingham, the owner. The family left five days ago to spend the holidays at his in-laws' house in Dayton, Ohio. They are due back in two days. Said he didn't know anything about a package in the mailbox and didn't think they were expecting anything."

"Jim," said Paul. "Can we find out the return address or the postmark on the package that was in the box?"

"I've already called in that request. If it were sent priority or first class, there would be a record of it. Any other class, and it is doubtful we would have a record."

Paul handed Jim Fisher one of his business cards and asked him to please send him whatever he might find. He spotted a van pulling into the cul-de-sac, and he excused himself and walked towards the van. Several techs stepped to the back of the van and started putting on Kevlar jumpsuits and booties.

Paul spotted a short Asian woman with long black hair that she was tying up in a bun on the top of her head. "Hey, April. Long time."

April Wang was the senior evidence tech based out of the State Crime Lab in Pueblo, Colorado. She turned and looked surprised. "Paul. My god, how long has it been?" she said. "Must be what, five years since we worked a scene together." She hugged Paul.

"Hell of a way to spend Christmas morning, huh?" she said. "At least I got to see the grandkids open their gifts."

She pulled the hood from her jumpsuit over her hair bun and zipped up the suit.

"Want to show me what we've got?" She looked around the cul-de-sac at all the activity. "Now that half of Chaffee County has walked all over my crime scene."

Paul took her to the twisted metal post sticking out of the ground. "We believe this is ground zero. We think the bomb was in a package section of the community mailboxes. That might have helped contain some of the blast."

April Wang looked at the nearby houses with their blown-out windows and frowned. "Could have been a lot worse."

Paul nodded, and April headed back to the van to give her team their marching orders. Between the size of the area they needed to search, the snow from the night before and the mess created by the first responders, she knew she had her work cut out for her.

Her team stood together while she briefed them, and then each member took their evidence kit and headed in different directions. When she was finished, April Wang headed back towards ground zero. It was going to be a long, tedious day, and they needed to start before the repair crews showed up to start boarding up windows.

Paul, Chief Langford and Jim Fisher stepped away from ground zero and walked towards the barricades. They each pulled out their phones and started dialing. The investigation was now in full swing, and Paul wondered where they would end up when they were finished, and if there were more bombings to come.

Chapter Fifteen

Buck walked from the incident command center to the edge of the rubble pile. Steam rolled off the debris, and ice formed on the tops of the puddles. He snugged up his jacket and tightened the strap on his white helmet.

Fire Chief Mark Shepard was addressing his team and laying out the game plan as Buck walked up. He turned to Buck and then back to his team. "Guys, this is Buck Taylor, CBI. Buck, anything you want to say before we start?"

"Thanks, Chief. Our priority is finding and recovering victims. Secondarily we are looking for evidence of the bomb. If you see something that looks out of place, let out a yell, and the sheriff and I will mark it, photograph it and bag it. Don't pick it up yourself. This building is unstable. If you hear Chief Shepard yell to get out, that means now. We have enough people hurt. No one else gets hurt today."

Buck and Sheriff Hartman turned to head towards the area where they believed the bomb had been planted when a black SUV pulled up to the incident command center.

Franklin Williams, the lead forensic tech based out of the CBI office in Grand Junction, slid out of the SUV and walked towards Buck. Franklin was a distinguished-looking black man who stood about four inches taller than Buck, but weighed about the same. He had short gray hair and a gray goatee. He stepped up to Buck, and they shook hands. Buck introduced him to Sheriff Hartman and Chief Shepard.

Franklin looked past Buck at the destruction. "Looks like quite a mess, Buck. How do you want to handle this?"

"We are just getting ready to search for victims. We have no idea right now how many we are looking for. The building is unstable, so hard hats are a must. Why don't you come with the sheriff and me so we can start looking for bomb parts? Have the rest of your team follow the searchers. We've told them to call out if they see something that's out of place. Let's bag everything we find, no matter how insignificant."

"Okay, Buck. I'll get my team sorted out and suited up, and I'll come find you once they're situated."

Franklin walked off to join the other three members of his team, who were already pulling on Tyvek jumpsuits and rubber boots. Franklin filled them in and then started pulling evidence kits out of the back of the SUV.

Buck and Sheriff Hartman started making their way slowly through the debris, picking and choosing a path that disturbed the least amount of rubble. As they walked, they kept an eye out for victims and stopped several times to call for a firefighter.

They knew they had reached the kitchen when they started finding torn-up pieces of stainless steel. They could make out some shelving and pieces of what looked like sinks. Sheriff Hartman pulled the blueprint floor plan out of his back pocket, opened it and scanned the area. He pointed to some blackened pieces of debris.

"Looks like a possible place to start."

As they stepped towards the area, Buck pulled out his cell phone and started videotaping their progress. The debris in this part of the kitchen was burned worse than the surrounding area. Buck pulled a flashlight out of his backpack, tightened the beam and started looking through the debris.

He stopped when he heard Franklin walking behind him. "This could be ground zero. Let's start looking but be careful. This whole building could fall on us." Franklin nodded and looked at the partial roof above his head. He focused on the ground and started removing the darkened debris. He put a sample of the blackened debris in an evidence bag.

Sheriff Hartman had moved beyond Buck by some twenty-five feet when he stopped and called out. Buck and Franklin headed in his direction. The whole time they searched, they heard several of the firefighters call out that they had either found a victim or found a piece of odd debris. Despite the creaking of the building, everyone worked like a well-oiled machine.

Buck and Franklin caught up with Sheriff Hartman, and Buck shined his light where the sheriff was pointing. Franklin took a picture of the object and then pulled it out from under the debris.

The object looked like a piece of computer chipboard with two wires sticking out of it. "Could be someone's cell phone, or it could be a piece of the timer," said Franklin. He put it in an evidence bag.

Buck picked up a small section of wall and found a flat piece of stainless steel with the remains of some rigid foam insulation glued to it. He took a picture, then lifted the piece and handed it to Franklin. Sheriff Hartman was the first to comment.

"Looks like a piece from an insulated cooler or refrigerator."

"Sure does," said Franklin. "I wonder if the bomber used an old refrigerator to bring in the bomb."

Buck was just about to comment when they heard one of the firefighters yell, "Got a live one!"

Several firefighters raced towards their colleague and started removing debris as two paramedics raced into the crowd. The paramedics called for a backboard and did a cursory examination while they waited. The board arrived, and they loaded the victim, a young girl, onto the board. Then, with the help of several firefighters, they carried the board towards the waiting ambulance. Everyone cheered and applauded as the board was carried by.

Buck, Sheriff Hartman and Franklin continued their search, and over the next several hours, they found several more charred stainless steel cooler pieces. Buck was pleased that they found as much as they did. Several more pieces of refrigerator and another piece of what might be the timer were found by the firefighters and collected by Franklin's team.

Buck looked at his watch as the shadows got longer and stopped and drank from his now-warm bottle of Coke. They worked until late in the evening and then headed back to the command center. They were all dog-tired, but it had been a productive day. They'd recovered the remains of thirty-four individuals. They'd also recovered several additional body parts, but more importantly they'd recovered seventeen live individuals, who were transported to local hospitals and airlifted to several Denver area hospitals.

Sheriff Hartman put down his digital notebook. "As of now, we've recovered or accounted for everyone we believe was in the building at the time of the explosion. It was a hell of an effort."

Buck felt exhausted but rewarded. This was a horrific day, but they had done what they started out to do. He shook Sheriff Hartman's hand and stepped out into the frigid evening. He caught up with Franklin just as he was closing the rear hatch of the SUV.

"You done?" asked Buck.

"We'll be back at first light. We've got a lot of pieces to look at and a lot of material to send to the State Crime Lab. Have you opened an investigation file yet?"

"Soon as I get to the hotel. Thanks, Franklin. You guys did great. I'll send the link for the file tonight. Get some rest."

They shook hands, and Franklin slid into the SUV and the techs headed for their hotel. Buck stood for a minute and looked at the mosque, lit by several huge work lights. The public works crew was in the process of bracing the weak parts of the building, and Buck was impressed by the amount of activity.

Buck turned and walked the mile back to his Jeep. He slid in and headed for his hotel. It had been a long day, and the investigation was just beginning.

Chapter Sixteen

Jacky III walked out of the Eagle County morgue, stopped and lit a cigarette. Standing next to him, his wife was inconsolable, and the tears flowed from her bloodshot eyes and down her red cheeks. She wiped her face with the back of her hand as Jacky paced back and forth, finally throwing the cigarette onto the sidewalk.

Jacky III had been called to the morgue and asked to identify his father, mother, younger sister, her husband and their four children. The detective standing next to him in the viewing area held back the vomit rising in his throat as the coroner pulled back the cover on the table.

Jacky III couldn't believe his eyes. "What is this, some kind of fucking joke?" He looked at the young detective, fire burning in his eyes.

The table contained bits and pieces of charred remains, all that was left of his family. His next comment was, "How in the hell am I supposed to identify this pile of stuff? It doesn't even look human."

Sensing his frustration, the coroner pointed to a diamond pinky ring attached to what looked like a hand. Jacky III looked closer. He had seen that ring all his life. His grandfather had given it to his father when the senior Logan retired and turned everything over to Jacky Jr.

His father had been planning to give him that ring at Christmas dinner tonight, a family tradition. It would signify that Jacky III was now in charge. Tomorrow night, at another dinner in Denver, the lieutenants and the big earners would have kissed the ring and pledged their allegiance to the new boss.

Jacky III, wiping tears from his eyes, said to the detective, "I want that ring, now."

The detective was about to say something, but he stopped short and looked into Jacky III's wet, black eyes. He walked around the corner and entered the morgue. He stepped up to the table, and, wearing a pair of nitrile gloves, he picked up the remains of the hand and removed the ring. Pieces of charred skin and tissue fell onto the table. The coroner took the ring over to the sink and washed away the debris. He handed it back to the detective.

Back outside, the detective took a deep breath to try to clear the burnt skin smell from his nostrils. He walked back around the corner and handed the ring to Jacky III. Jacky slid it on his pinky, and it fit like it was made for him. He turned and walked down the long, sterile hallway to where his wife was standing.

Dee Logan could tell from the look on his face that it was his family, and she started crying into the handkerchief she held balled up in her hand. Jacky took her by the arm, and they headed for the entrance.

Jacky III stepped on the cigarette he had dropped on the sidewalk and pulled out his phone. Well, not his phone, but a burner he had taken out of the safe in his house. He dialed a number and waited.

"Is it true?" asked the voice on the other end when the phone was answered.

"Yeah," said Jacky III, choking back tears.

"Oh my god, Jacky, I am so sorry. Whatever you need, just ask."

"Call everyone—my house tomorrow morning at ten. And I mean everyone. No one skips, or they'll have me to deal with."

Jacky III hung up the phone, placed it in his pocket, walked over and wrapped his arms around his wife. "It's okay, Dee. We'll get through this."

"My god, Jacky, the kids. They were just kids." She stopped, and a look of fear came over her face. "That could be us lying on that table. If Mary

Katherine hadn't gotten a stomachache last night, we would have been at your dad's house this morning opening gifts along with everyone else." Tears flowed down her face.

"Don't think about that, Dee. We're alive, and the motherfucker who did this will regret the day he was born. Let's go. I want to swing by the house. I need to see the damage for myself. Then we'll call Father Donovan and start making the arrangements."

They walked across the parking lot and slid into Jacky III's Cadillac SUV. He pulled out of the parking lot and headed for what was left of his dad's house. He looked at the ring on his pinky. His smile was almost indistinguishable.

Chapter Seventeen

Connor O'Connor had been watching the news all day. He could do little else, as it took all of the energy he had left to just climb out of bed to take his meds and fix himself something to eat. The pain in his abdomen was getting worse, and the oxy he had scored from the kid in the apartment in the back couldn't keep the pain at bay.

As he lay in bed eating a baloney sandwich and drinking his last cold beer, the news coverage confused him. He put the beer on the table as another fresh-faced reporter took up the center of the screen with another casualty report. Connor O'Connor listened carefully.

The reporter stood in front of what looked like a picture from the Middle East of some kind of bombed-out building. The reporter earlier had said it was a mosque. "Why is this mosque getting all the attention, and who would blow up a spiritual building?"

It was like the news people weren't even talking about the other bombings. "Of all the crap," he thought. "Someone else planted a bomb, and now they are getting credit for my bombings. How the hell did that happen?"

He clicked the remote and switched stations to the local NBC affiliate out of Grand Junction. The talking heads were describing the scene at one location.

"The mailbox was destroyed," they were saying. It sounded like one of his bombs went off in a mailbox. "What the hell?"

Another talking head came on and started a recap. This is what he was waiting for.

"The governor's office has confirmed that twelve residential bombs exploded this morning at around seven a.m. So far, we've been able to confirm at least forty people dead and another thirty-five injured, some more serious than others. The biggest part of the story is the bombing of the mosque in Avon. The latest count we have from the Eagle County Sheriff's Office is seventy-five dead and at least ninety people injured, with twelve of those in intensive care, having been transported to several hospitals in the Denver area. A tragic Christmas morning. This is Jeffrey Turner reporting live from Avon. Back to you, Jenny."

Connor O'Connor zoned out the rest of the news. He was confused. They had mentioned twelve bombs, plus this mosque. "What happened to the thirteenth bomb?" he said out loud. "I mailed thirteen bombs, but only twelve went off. And I had nothing to do with the mosque bombing."

The pain in his abdomen hit like a freight train, and he doubled up on the bed. The baloney sandwich fell on the floor, and he was lucky enough to grab the small trash can before he vomited up everything he had eaten since breakfast. He waited it out, tears flowing down his cheeks until the pain subsided.

He grabbed the plastic bag off the nightstand, pulled out another pill and popped it in his mouth. He knew it was stupid to be washing the pill down with the last of his beer, but he had given up caring. After all, what was drinking a couple of beers gonna do, kill him?

He lay back on his pillow and wiped the sweat from his eyes. None of the news stories had mentioned the names of any of the dead, but then it was probably too early to have a full list. His mind was still focused on the missing bomb and on the bomb that blew up a mailbox.

Kind of embarrassing, a man with his skills to have two mistakes like that. He clicked the off button on the remote, and his room was drenched in darkness. The last thought he had before he closed his eyes was, "Will I wake up in the morning?"

Chapter Eighteen

Professor Eldridge Parker slammed the lid of his laptop shut. He was pissed. Someone was getting credit for his bombing, and he didn't like it one bit.

Everything had gone as planned once he reached the mosque in Avon. There were no cars in the parking lot, and all the parking lot lights were off except for one in the far corner. The building sat in complete darkness. He had waited and watched to make sure no lights came on, and once he felt confident that there was no one in the building, he backed the truck up to the back door.

He assumed the door would lead him into the kitchen. He had gotten a rough floor plan of the mosque off the internet, but it didn't give a lot of detail. Scanning the area once more, he took out his lockpick tools and went to work on the lock and the dead bolt. Now, he just had to hope there was no alarm on the back door.

His lockpick tools weren't working correctly, and it took him longer to unlock the door than he had planned. He decided he would order some new tools once he got back home. It never occurred to him that it was his skills that had deteriorated.

He pushed the door open a little at a time and waited for the alarm, but nothing happened. He opened the door and looked into the dark space. He pulled a small flashlight from his pocket and shined the light inside.

The first thing he saw was a row of stoves and fryers. He was in luck. The door opened right into the kitchen, just like he had planned.

He propped the door open with a small triangular-shaped piece of wood lying on the floor, turned back to his truck and opened the tailgate. He removed the blanket and lifted the small refrigerator from the truck bed and set it inside the door.

He closed the door and entered the spacious kitchen. He spotted a small stainless steel rolling table parked along one wall, dragged the refrigerator over and slid it under the table. It fit like it was made for it. He plugged the cord into the wall receptacle, even though he had removed most of the refrigeration equipment from the back to give him more room. The plug in the receptacle would make the scene look more believable.

He looked around the kitchen at all the equipment and got even more pissed off. He wondered how these Muslims could afford all this stuff when they used all their money to support terrorists. He decided that most of the equipment must have been stolen. His friends and followers around the country would be so proud of him for what he was about to do.

He pulled out his phone, pulled up the timer app and set the alarm for seven a.m. His bomb was now active. In just five short hours, he would be famous. He locked the bottom lock and shut the kitchen door. He couldn't relock the dead bolt from outside, but he hoped no one would notice. He slid into his truck and pulled out of the parking lot, leaving his lights off until he was on the main street heading back to the interstate.

Everything had gone perfect, except some fool was taking credit for his bomb. He wondered what the world was coming to that someone would blow up a bunch of people opening Christmas gifts. "What a sick world we live in," he said out loud to the empty room.

He wondered why none of the news channels had mentioned his manifesto. He had sent a copy to all the national news outlets, the FBI, and the Colorado Bureau of Investigation. Yet, no one had said a word about it. He vowed to find out who'd screwed up his bombing by planting other bombs, and he would send that person a nice letter bomb.

He decided he would send follow-up emails to everyone he'd sent his manifesto to, so he opened up his laptop, connected to an Australian VPN and opened his email. He sat for a minute, staring at the screen. The email he had sent to all those groups containing his manifesto was sitting there.

"What the hell?"

He couldn't understand how the email had come back to him when he knew he had sent it before he left the cabin. He figured it was some electronic glitch, so he hit send, and the email disappeared.

He opened up a can of beef stew, put the can on top of the woodstove and waited till it started to bubble. He ate like a man who hadn't eaten in days. After finishing the meal, he felt good. He stood up, made sure the doors were locked and the IEDs set and lay down on his bed. He was confident that when he woke up, the internet would be full of praise for him and his work.

Chapter Nineteen

Buck pulled into the Valley View Motel parking lot and spotted Bax's Jeep Grand Cherokee parked in front of room seven. She had texted him that she had checked him into room eight and that she had the key and would be waiting in the restaurant attached to the motel. Buck parked next to her Jeep, grabbed his backpack off the passenger seat and slid out of his Jeep.

He was stiff, and he knew he would be sore in the morning. It had been a long day, and he was glad to see that the restaurant was open on Christmas. He didn't realize how hungry he was until he saw the restaurant sign. He hadn't eaten anything since the breakfast he made for the family. That seemed like a long time ago, after a day of pulling dead and mutilated bodies out of a bomb site.

He opened the door to the restaurant, and the smell of bacon hit him in the face. He almost drooled on himself. The restaurant was more crowded than he would have expected for Christmas night. He saw several families sitting at the tables and booths and several long-haul truckers sitting at the counter. He spotted Bax sitting in the last booth along the row of front windows and headed her way.

"Jesus, Buck," she said as she lifted her eyes from her laptop. "You look worn out. You okay?"

Bax was what some would describe as husky, or what used to be called having a "mountain girl" figure. She wasn't gorgeous, but she was pretty enough to turn men's heads when she walked into a room, at least until they spotted the badge and gun clipped to her belt. Tonight, her long blond hair was tied in a ponytail that was sticking through the back of her CBI ball cap.

Buck sat down, and the waitress brought over a glass of Coke and a menu. "I've already eaten, Buck, so dig in," said Bax.

Buck ordered the half-pound burger with everything on it and a side of house fries. The waitress left, and Buck pulled out his laptop and set it on the table.

Bax smiled at him. "How many calls and messages did you miss today?" she asked. "My phone has been ringing off the hook with people looking for you. I feel like your secretary." She laughed.

"Yeah, sorry about that," he said. "Once we started finding live bodies, we didn't want to stop, and with the noise of the heavy equipment trying to shore up the building, it was almost impossible to hear anything."

Bax's eyes softened. "Must have been rough. How many live victims?"

"Lost count, but maybe seventeen. Doesn't make up for the forty or more dead ones." He paused. "I've seen a lot of death and destruction in my life, Bax, but the mutilation and the damage caused by the explosion was something I hope I never have to see again."

The waitress placed his burger and fries down on the table and headed off to another table. Buck dug into the burger while Bax filled him in.

"I opened up an investigation file for the mosque and the Vail bombings. Paul opened one for the Salida bombing, and the director opened the rest. He is taking charge of the overall investigation, and all our files are interconnected. We have more than forty of our agents working on this. The State Crime Lab and the FBI crime lab are working overtime, sifting through the evidence we've recovered so far. I also think the FBI is going to try to take control."

CBI had gone digital a couple of years back, so instead of having a blue binder for each case, Buck just had to open a program on his laptop. The new case was automatically assigned a case number, and

Buck would list everyone who needed access to the file and send them email invites. All evidence, lab reports, photos, etc. that were part of the case would be uploaded into the file, and anyone who needed access just had to open the file. That was a lot better than the old system, where everything had been placed in the binder by hand, and Buck would spend half his time trying to track down who had the binder.

For a tech dinosaur like Buck, this made his life so much easier, and he had ready access to anything he needed. Buck clicked on the file and opened the chronology page, which was the first page in the file. Nothing was ever entered into the file without a note being entered in the chronology first. The chronology kept track of everything that happened in the investigation. Buck was meticulous about his case files and had never lost a case in court in all his years in law enforcement because something was missing from his files. Next, he clicked on the email addresses of everyone he wanted to have access to the file and hit send.

Buck took a bite and put his burger down. "How so? I thought the director said the governor had reached out to the FBI for forensic help, not to run the investigation?"

"Maybe they didn't get the memo. The guy who led the team at the Vail site pretty much ordered me and the chief of police off the site. I stuck around for a while, but the guy in charge refused to share anything they found. Instead, he told me we would be copied on anything they felt was relevant. Director Jackson told me that the same thing happened to several of our agents at other sites."

"Tell me about the Vail bombing," said Buck. He clicked on the Vail investigation file and started looking at the photos Bax had uploaded. He would upload his photos to the mosque file later tonight.

"Victims were Jackson Logan, his wife, Carly, their youngest daughter, Gillian, her husband, Sean Carmichael, and their four children, Rachel, age four, Cameron, age seven, Rebecca, age nine, and Michael, age eleven. Bodies, such as they were, were identified by the older brother, Jackson Logan III."

Buck stopped her. "This is Christmas. Why wasn't the older brother at his parents' home?"

"Fate, luck. Call it what you will. His daughter developed a stomachache last night, so they decided to drive up first thing this morning instead of spending the night. Saved their lives."

Buck studied her for a minute. "Anything funky about that story?"

"When we spoke to him at police headquarters, Jackson was seriously broken up, as was his wife. I didn't sense any weird vibe. Why do you ask?"

"Just curious," said Buck. He looked at a picture of the back of the house facing the mountain. "Tell me about this picture," he said as he turned his laptop to face her.

Bax looked at the picture for a minute. "Best guess right now is that the bomb was in a Christmas gift. No other explanation for it. From what we could tell, the family was close to the package when it went off. The explosion left the front of the house intact but blew the back wall and the Christmas tree onto the deck and the mountain behind it. I know what you mean about devastation. There was almost nothing left of the family to identify, except for some charred remains."

"What do we know about the family?" asked Buck.

Bax pulled up her notes. "The older Logans recently retired. They owned an entertainment venue in Denver. Logan's Bar and Grill. I understand it's a popular nightspot with a lot of name entertainment. Funny thing. The venue burned to the ground about a month ago. It had been in the family since the earliest days of Denver."

Buck stopped eating his fries and looked at her. "That Jacky Logan?"

She wasn't sure what he was asking. "You know him?"

Chapter Twenty

Buck took a sip from his glass and set it back on the counter. His face got serious. "The Logans have run the Irish mob in Denver since the year Denver was founded. Logan's Bar and Grill was their headquarters, even after they turned it into the entertainment venue you're talking about. Everybody and his brother have investigated them over the years, but nothing ever stuck. They are a tight-knit family, and they protect each other. And they are damn careful who they allow into the inner circle."

"You think this is retaliation? But what about the other bombings tonight? Can't be a coincidence," she said.

"Not sure what to make of all the bombings. It's odd that Jacky Logan is one of the victims, and his place burned down a month ago. Call George in the morning and ask him to do a deep background check on Jacky, his wife and the daughter's family. Also include the son. My guess is, he'll be the one taking over the business."

"Should we share this with the FBI?"

"I'll bet they already have it. Might be why

they're closing ranks and pushing their way into the investigation. Might be just what they need, since retaliation is in order if the next Jacky Logan finds out who blew up his family."

"You're thinking a mob war?"

"Not necessarily. Their real enemy is the Italian mob, and a Christmas day hit would be extreme even for them. The problem with all this is what about the other eleven bombings and the mosque? Were they all to cover up the hit on Jacky Logan, or is Jacky a random victim?"

"Twelve other bombings," said Bax.

Buck looked at her. "What are you talking about?"

"If you checked your messages once in a while." She laughed. "The director sent out a message letting us know that the FBI has a bomb that didn't go off. He didn't have many details, just that a family in Englewood received a package two days ago, addressed to them, with a note attached to a wrapped gift inside the box that said not to open until Christmas. They didn't know who sent it, but when they opened it, they found all kinds of wires and explosives, so they put it in the middle of their backyard and called the Englewood Police."

"Where is the package now?" asked Buck.

"The FBI lab, and they are being tight-lipped about what they found. That's all the information the director could get out of them."

Buck thought for a minute. "Okay, so let's see what we have. Someone sent out thirteen bombs wrapped up as Christmas gifts to thirteen random families all over the state. They might be random, or they might be to cover up a hit on Jacky Logan. One bomb blew up a mailbox, which, when I talked to Paul on the way over here, he said was because the family had been out of town and hadn't received the package. A second bomb didn't go off. Why, we have no idea, and the FBI isn't telling. Lastly, we have a mosque that gets blown up at the same time. What does all this tell us?"

Bax stared at him. "Our bomber was very good, and he wanted to hurt as many people as he could?"

"No. Think more outside the box. We know what the thirteen bombs have in common. They were all sent to different people and families, but they were all most likely delivered through the mail as Christmas packages. Now, look at the mosque. We found stainless steel fragments with Styrofoam attached to some of them. We think the bomb was either in a metal cooler or possibly inside a refrigerator, which makes sense. A refrigerator in a commercial kitchen would not have looked out of place. The thirteen bombings were personal. The mosque bombing was a widespread terrorist event designed to hurt as many people as possible."

"Two different bombers?" asked Bax. "What are the odds?"

"Astronomical would be my guess. But it makes sense."

"Couldn't it still be one bomber?" asked Bax.

"Of course," said Buck. "But I will bet that when the lab results come back, we are going to find two different signatures."

Buck was about to say something else when his phone rang. At the same time, both his and Bax's laptops chimed, signaling an incoming message.

Buck looked at the number. "Yes, sir."

"Buck," said Director Jackson. "Sorry about the late hour. I just forwarded a lengthy treatise that we received this evening to all the teams. Our friends at the FBI and several national media groups, including Facebook, also received copies. This thing is over six hundred pages long. What I've read so far makes no sense. It just rambles from one subject to the next."

"Do you think it's from the bomber, sir?"

"The big brains at the FBI seem to think so. I

want you guys to give it a read, and let's gather all our teams together at noon tomorrow. I'll send out a web invite. We are going to need to brainstorm this before I can confirm one way or the other that this is our guy."

The director hung up, and Bax swung her laptop around so Buck could see the screen. "This thing goes on forever. I just read the first five pages, and my head wants to explode. What I've read so far is incoherent and just rambles."

Buck picked up his phone and speed-dialed a number. George Peterman answered right away.

"Shit, George, don't you ever sleep?" he asked.

"You wouldn't have called me if you didn't expect me to answer." George laughed.

"Okay, you got me there," said Buck. "Did you get the email from the director with the treatise attached?"

Another voice came on the line. "Hey, Buck. It's Mel. We got it, and it's not a treatise. You remember a while back when the Unabomber was active? He sent out the same kind of thing. This thing is a manifesto. It contains ramblings on all kinds of subjects. Just from what we've read so far, I would say this is something our bomber has been working on for years. There are also some interesting comments that might lead us someplace else, but I'm not ready to talk about that yet. Gonna need to read a lot more of this crap."

Buck looked at Bax, the unasked question in his eyes. "Okay, can you guys do your magic and find out where he sent this from? Might give us a lead on where to look."

George came back on the phone. "That was the first thing we did. All the metadata has been scrubbed from the email string. We've been trying to backtrack the signal, but so far, it's been routed through four different servers all over the world."

"Do you think you can track it?"

Mel came back on the line. "Short answer is yes. No one can hide from us for long. The more realistic answer is, it depends on where he takes us and how many servers he's patched through—one thing to note, Buck. As you read this, you may want to believe that this guy is stupid or uneducated. Don't be fooled. My take is he or she has an extremely high IQ."

"Okay, Mel. You guys call me when you have something; in the meantime, thanks."

Buck hung up and looked at Bax. "Interesting," was all she said. Buck nodded his head. "We'd better try to get some sleep. Tomorrow is gonna be another long day.

Chapter Twenty-One

Buck tried to sleep, but his mind was wide awake, so at four in the morning, with snow flurries coming down, he found himself standing in the middle of the Eagle River with his fly rod. There was just enough light from the streetlamps along the road that ran next to the river that he could make out subtle movement in the riffles.

He laid a tiny bead head nymph into the riffle and watched it sink out of sight. He barely felt the tug on the line as the twelve-inch cutthroat trout sipped the nymph into its mouth and hooked a cheek.

Buck lifted his rod tip ever so slightly, and the bend in the rod and the tremor at the tip told him the fish was on. Trout in cold weather don't typically fight that hard, but once hooked, this guy wanted to dance, and Buck was ready for him. He worked him out of the main current and brought him to shore. He kept him in the water while he pulled out the hook and watched him slide off towards some safer refuge.

Fly-fishing was Buck's way to clear his head. He had learned a long time ago that once you set that fly where you want it, you have to turn all your focus on that fly. For that period of time, there is only you, the fly and the fish. Nothing else matters, and to be successful, it takes all your focus.

Buck fished for about two hours and headed back to the motel as the eastern sky started to lighten. The snowflakes had disappeared, the clouds had broken up, and it looked like it might be a decent day.

Bax was just heading for the restaurant when she saw Buck pull into the parking lot. He stopped, slid out of the Jeep and walked up to her.

"Couldn't sleep?" she asked.

"Needed to clear my head, so I spent a little time on the river."

"Come up with anything that might help us?" she asked.

"Yeah. We need to get hold of the bomb that didn't go off."

He pushed the door and stood back as Bax walked past him. She looked at him and smiled. "Did a little fishy tell you that, or did you think of that all on your own?"

"No. The little fishy told me I was nuts to be standing in a frigid river at four a.m. while it snowed."

They both laughed as the server led them to the empty booth in the corner. Bax slid in and pulled out her laptop. Buck grabbed the seat on the other side and slid in. They looked at the menu and gave their orders to the server, who left and came back a minute later with coffee for Bax and a large glass of Coke for Buck.

"How much of the manifesto did you read last night?" Buck knew she hadn't gone to sleep after they left the restaurant. He knew her too well.

"Got through about half of it before my brain shut down and took my eyes with it. I can see why Mel thinks this guy, or gal, is brilliant. If you can move past all the bullshit, there are some interesting thoughts in there. The rest is just mind clutter. Random thoughts and passing ideas. It's like this person wrote down whatever came into his mind at that moment."

"That's a sound assessment," said Buck, as the server set their scrambled egg platters down in front of them and refilled Bax's coffee. "Once you dig deeper into it, the writer starts talking about other bombings. I need to check out a few things, but I think this is the ravings of the Mountain Bomber."

"The guy who sent out a bunch of letter bombs over the last decade. He killed, what? Seven, eight people, injured a bunch more. We haven't heard from him for like two or three years. Everyone in

Colorado law enforcement figured he was dead. Why now? Besides, these bombings seem way out of his league. How much of the manifesto did you read last night?"

Buck smiled. "Read the whole thing."

"No wonder you needed to clear your head on the river. Fuck, Buck. Did you sleep at all?"

"Not really." He ate another forkful of eggs and washed it down with a sip from his glass. "Have we gotten any reports back from the State Crime Lab on the pieces from the mosque or the other bombings?"

Bax opened the investigation files on her laptop. "Nothing yet. I doubt we'll see anything from the Logan bombing. FBI didn't seem eager to share anything they found."

Both their phones chimed at the same time. They picked up their phones and looked at the message.

"Video conference call at ten," said Bax.

"Great. Maybe we can find out what the FBI knows about the bomb that didn't explode."

Buck's phone rang, and he looked at the number and answered. "Hey, Paul. How are things going?"

"Good, Buck. Did you guys get the link for the conference call?" asked Paul Webber.

Buck and Paul had first worked together on an arson fire that had almost cost Buck his life when the case got bigger than just a fire. Paul had also been instrumental in helping Buck unmask a decades-old serial killer in Aspen a year ago. It had been Paul's diligence that led to the information that revealed that the old serial killer's granddaughter, Alicia Hawkins, had taken up her grandfather's cause. Paul was instrumental in tracking down Alicia Hawkins when she'd returned to Aspen a few months back to fulfill a sick promise she had made to her dying grandfather. A promise that would embolden her and secure both their sick legacies.

"Yeah, we just got it. You still in Salida?"

"Yes, sir. The family that didn't get blown up decided to cut their Christmas vacation short, and they are driving back from Ohio. They were planning to arrive sometime after lunch. I wanted to be here to see if there is anything they might be able to tell us." Paul hesitated.

"What is it, Paul?"

"I read through some of the investigation files from the other bombings last night, and it got me to wondering if we are dealing with one bomber or multiple bombers. The twelve bombings sound similar, but then I can't see how the mosque bombing fits in."

"Bax and I were talking about that too. Doesn't make sense. The smaller bombings seem personal, but the mosque is more political. I've been having George and Mel monitor the internet, but no one is claiming credit for the mosque, except for possibly that manifesto we got. He never comes right out and says he planted the bomb, but his writings are more politically motivated. Hopefully, the FBI will have some answers during the call that might give us some insight. Let us know what you find out from the family."

Buck disconnected the call and looked across the table at Bax. The server came and picked up their plates and dropped the bill on the table.

"Looks like Paul is thinking different bombers too," he said. "What are you doing this morning?"

"I called Carlton Hickman before I left my room. He's one of the Eagle County Sheriff Office's bomb techs. I asked him to meet me back at the Logan house to see if maybe the FBI missed something. You?"

"I'm heading back to the mosque. Franklin and his team will be there, and I want to check in with him. Let's meet back here at lunchtime, and we'll discuss the conference call."

They each dropped a twenty-dollar bill on the table, and Buck waved to the server and pointed to the money. The server nodded, and they grabbed their coats and backpacks and headed out the door.

Chapter Twenty-Two

Bax pulled up in front of the Logan house. The Vail police had moved the barricades and yellow police tape back to the property line and had reopened the street so the neighbors could get in and out. There was still a lot of traffic since everyone wanted to see the damage. The problem was that the front of the house was undamaged, so there wasn't much for the curious public to see.

Carlton Hickman, wearing his green sheriff's department jumpsuit, stood at the top landing of the front steps. Bax signed in with the Vail police officer at the barricades and walked up the steps.

"Agent Baxter, nice to see you," said Carlton.

"Good morning," said Bax. "Thanks for meeting me."

"No problem. The sheriff said to give you all the help you need. So, what are we looking for?"

"Anything the FBI Evidence Recovery Team might have missed."

"Those guys have their act together," said

Carlton. "They don't miss much." The grin on his face said he didn't really believe that statement.

They each took a pair of Tyvek booties out of the box next to the door and put them on, along with an N95 face mask and a pair of blue nitrile gloves. Carlton pushed open the front door, and they stepped inside.

With better lighting, Bax could see how much damage the explosion had caused, and she was amazed that it didn't take out the entire house, instead of just the family room. What the fire hadn't destroyed, the water from the firefighting effort had.

There were piles of smoldering debris and large puddles of water, and the carpet that had been part of the family room squished as they walked across it.

Taking out flashlights, they narrowed the beams and started focusing on the floor as they walked. The narrow beam focused their attention on just that tiny area that the light hit, and they started a methodical search.

Bax had moved off towards what she assumed was the kitchen, just off the family room. It no longer looked like a kitchen, with all the appliances and furniture smashed up against the wall. She moved so as not to disturb too much of the crime scene.

She was about to give up when she spotted what looked like an opening in the paneling, next to the built-in refrigerator. The refrigerator looked to be about three times the size of the one in her apartment, and there was a freezer, the same size, right next to it.

"Carlton. Can you come here for a sec?" she called out.

Carlton stood up from where he was looking at something on the floor, and he walked over.

"Can you give me a hand? There's a loose wall panel, and it looks like sunlight is shining through the opening."

Carlton saw the spot she was talking about and helped her slide the refrigerator out of the way. Bax pushed against the panel, and it moved. She looked at Carlton, and he placed his hand on his pistol. She shoved at the panel, heard a click and the wall panel pushed open to reveal a butler's pantry.

The pantry appeared to be intact, the wall and the moveable wall panel taking the brunt of the explosion. Bax stepped into an almost pristine environment. She turned to see where Carlton had gone and saw him looking at the latch on the panel.

"I think this is a safe room," he said.

In addition to the latch that held the panel in place, there was also a wheel, similar to one you would find on a ship or submarine, that, when turned, latched three large steel rods into holes in the wall.

Bax looked around, and beside canned goods, she spotted another refrigerator, a second stove, a cell phone in a charger and a bank of monitors mounted to the wall. She hadn't spotted sunlight coming through the wall panel, but the reflection from one of the monitors still on and displaying a local news program.

"This room must be on a generator. The power is off to the house, but this room has power. What were these people so afraid of that they would need a room like this?" she said.

"Whatever they needed it for, it's lucky for us," said Carlton, as he reached under the table and pulled out a cardboard recycling container. In it was a medium-sized shipping box. "I think I found the box the bomb package came in."

Bax walked over and looked at the box. She pulled out her camera and took several pictures of all sides of the box, and then Carlton set it on the counter.

"I think we hit pay dirt," he said. "Once this

is tested, we should find explosive residue, and it looks like the postmark is intact." Then he looked around sheepishly. "What about the FBI? Should we call them?"

Bax looked at the shipping label. "There's no return address, but this package was shipped from Delta, Colorado." She pointed to the red stamp under the address label. do not open until christmas was stamped on three sides of the box.

Bax thought for a minute. "Let's ship this to the State Crime Lab first, and if anything comes out of it, we can give it to the Feds. I wouldn't want them to get too excited if it proves to be just a box from a food delivery or something."

Carlton nodded his head. "You're right. We wouldn't want to look foolish if it's nothing." The grin reappeared.

Bax looked at her watch. She didn't realize how much time they had spent searching the house. "I've got a conference call with the FBI. Once that's done, let's see if there is anything else the FBI missed before I send this to the lab."

Bax headed outside to her Jeep while Carlton continued his search. She pulled a large evidence bag out of the back hatch, placed the box in it and signed and dated it. Then she took a picture of the sealed bag and placed it in her Jeep.

She slid into the passenger seat and pulled out her laptop. She had two minutes until she needed to connect for the meeting. She sat back and took a deep breath. If that was indeed the box that the bomb package had come in, that could be pivotal in solving this case. She also wondered what these folks did that they needed such a sophisticated safe room.

She knew Jacky Logan was considered one of the bosses of the Irish mob in Colorado, but she also knew, if rumors were correct, that he had stopped running the organization several years back and had just announced his retirement.

She checked her watch and clicked on the meeting link. She entered the password she had been texted and joined what must have been several hundred people on the call.

Chapter Twenty-Three

Buck pulled his Jeep up to the Eagle County mobile command trailer and parked next to several black SUVs with U.S. government plates. He spotted Franklin and his team standing at the edge of the destruction and walked over.

"What's going on?" Buck asked as he watched a dozen people, some wearing Tyvek coveralls and some wearing suits, walk around the site. The Eagle County Public Works Department had done an excellent job supporting the damaged parts of the mosque.

"Feds," said Franklin. "Showed up this morning and asked—no, check that, told us to get off the site."

"What about the evidence pieces we collected yesterday?"

Franklin smiled. "Sent those to the State Crime Lab this morning before we came back to the site. Feds didn't get those, but they grabbed everything we found so far this morning. Who invited these guys to play?"

"Not sure," said Buck. "Any idea which one of these guys is in charge?"

"Yeah, he's in the trailer, probably telling the sheriff to get his people off the site."

Buck turned and walked towards the trailer and was almost to the stairs when the door opened. A downtrodden-looking Sheriff Hartman walked down the stairs and stopped in front of Buck.

"Who the fuck do these people think they are, telling me to get my people out of here?" Sheriff Hartman did not look happy. "We've been here all night working our asses off, and they waltz in here like they own the place."

Buck held up his hand to tell the sheriff to wait a minute and walked up the steps. He opened the door and stepped inside. Three suits were standing around the plan table, and they all looked up when Buck opened the door.

"Who's in charge?" asked Buck as he walked towards the trio.

"Who the hell are you?" asked one of the suits.

"Buck Taylor, CBI. Your people are walking all over my crime scene, and I'd like to know why?"

The mouthy suit was about to say something else

when the bald-headed suit in the middle held up his hand and silenced him.

"Agent Taylor, your reputation precedes you. Special Agent Tom Whitmore and my colleagues, spec—"

"I asked you why your people are walking all over my crime scene?" Buck interrupted the introductions.

Special Agent Whitmore looked like he wasn't used to being questioned by locals. He stammered a little and then regained his composure.

"We were assigned to take over this site by Deputy Director Felix Marshall. Those people, as you call them, are highly trained in evidence gathering and the latest investigative techniques. We . . ."

"Please have them remove themselves from the crime scene until my forensic team completes their investigation."

Buck picked up several evidence bags off the plan table and turned towards the door. He stopped, turned and looked at a dumbfounded Special Agent Whitmore. "Leave your card on the table, and I will make sure you get a copy of the report when our crime lab is finished with these."

He pushed open the door, walked down the

steps, past Sheriff Hartman, and handed the bags to Franklin. "Get these to the lab right away."

He walked to the edge of the debris pile, stepped up on a piece of broken concrete, placed his two pinky fingers in the corners of his mouth and gave a whistle that was so loud and shrill that it must have sent shivers down the spines of anyone within hearing distance. All the federal investigators stopped and looked.

Buck held up his badge. "You are all interfering with an active crime scene. You will step back the way you came and try to do as little damage as possible. Anything you have collected, you will hand to Agent Williams on your way out."

Buck turned as Agent Whitmore and the other two suits stepped out of the trailer. He turned back towards the Feds in the mosque. "I will not repeat myself. MOVE!"

The Feds looked unsure of what to do until Buck saw Special Agent Whitmore, in his peripheral vision, wave his team towards their SUVs. Special Agent Whitmore walked past the sheriff and slid into the rear of one of the SUVs, followed by his team. No one said a word as they walked past. Franklin collected a handful of evidence bags as the FBI team walked by him. He looked at Buck and smiled.

Sheriff Hartman walked up to Buck. "Well, that took some balls. You didn't make a friend out of Agent Whitmore."

Buck laughed. "Yeah, sometimes it just takes a little bravado."

"Franklin," said Buck. "Wrap this up as soon as you can, because they will be back."

He started to walk towards the area where they'd found the refrigerator pieces when his phone rang. He looked at the number and answered.

"Yes, sir."

"What the fuck, Buck?" said Director Jackson. "Did you just throw a team of FBI agents off the mosque site?"

"Yes, sir. They rolled in here, ordered everyone off the site and then proceeded to walk all over the areas where we were gathering evidence. They also walked all over the people who have been working here since yesterday. I needed to preserve the integrity of the site. If I'm not mistaken, sir, this is still a Colorado crime scene until you order me off the site. Since that hasn't happened, I asked them politely to leave."

"You know they'll be back," said the director. "My guess is this guy, Marshall, is gonna go straight to the governor. I'd love to be a fly on the wall during that conversation. I almost feel bad for Marshall."

Buck laughed, knowing from firsthand experience how much the governor hated the people in Washington, DC. "Who is this Deputy Director Marshall, sir? Where's Hank Clancy? This is his region."

"I don't know much more than you do. I was surprised when he called me. What I've heard is he's some hotshot anti-terrorist guru from Washington. Runs a special task force looking at domestic terrorists. I heard his team is handpicked from all over the country, and he was sent here by the director of the FBI and the U.S. Attorney General. Maybe we'll find out more during the conference call. How long does Franklin need to wrap this site up?"

"Couple more hours should do it, sir."

"Okay, Buck. I'll get with the governor, and we'll do what we can to hold these guys off till you get finished. And Buck. Let's try not to piss off the FBI any more today."

"I'll do my best, sir."

Buck disconnected the call and looked at Sheriff Hartman and Franklin. "Be thorough, but let's get done and get out of here." He looked at his watch.

"Sheriff, we've got a conference call in ten minutes. Let's not keep the FBI waiting."

They both laughed as they climbed the stairs to the command center. Once inside, Buck pulled his laptop out of his backpack, clicked on the email he had been sent earlier and entered his password into the meeting site.

He hoped he might get some answers to some of the questions crashing around in his head. The little bug that was always stomping around in his brain during an investigation was dancing an Irish jig while wearing combat boots.

They both looked at the screen. At this moment, all that was visible was a wood podium in the center of the screen with the FBI logo emblazoned on the front. Behind the podium were eight American flags, all folded precisely as they hung from their poles.

Buck made himself comfortable as he leaned against the plan table. He couldn't wait for the meeting to start. The FBI was going to put on a show.

Chapter Twenty-Four

Paul had been at the Salida bomb site since well before sunrise. His North Face insulated jacket was zipped up to his neck to fight off the cold breeze that had arrived sometime during the night and brought with it a fresh coating of snow.

The new layer of snow and the Christmas lights hanging from the gutters that the explosion hadn't damaged gave the street a festive look. If you had just arrived on the street for the first time, you might have missed all the destruction the bomb had caused. But there was an eerie silence on the street.

All the houses were now boarded up, but there was no one around except for Paul, the forensic team and two Salida police officers stationed at the entrance to the cul-de-sac. All the residents of the cul-de-sac had been evacuated to several local hotels and motels.

The crime scene was huge, and even though it was the day after Christmas, Paul couldn't take any chances. It was hard enough looking for evidence under the new snow without working around the bystanders.

He hated moving people out of their houses on

Christmas, considering that most of the families had yet to open all their gifts, the morning's festivities having been interrupted by the explosion.

He poured another cup of coffee from his thermos and watched the forensic team move into the next house. He wanted to get as much done as quickly as possible so he could get the families back into their homes.

April Wang looked beat as she walked up and eyed his coffee. He opened the thermos, topped off the cup and handed it to her. The first thing she did was warm her hands on the sides of the stainless steel cup. The smell seemed to perk her up.

"I think we have about four or five more hours, and we should be able to wrap up the site. Most of the damage to the houses we are moving into now was caused by the pressure wave and not by shrapnel," she said.

"Anything we can identify as coming from the bomb?" asked Paul.

"The good news is that the community mailbox contained a lot of the explosion. We found some pieces of the timer and the packaging in the area of the mailbox. The paper and cardboard survived because there wasn't much in the way of fire. There's no doubt that this bomb was powerful, but it wasn't incendiary. With a little luck and a lot of science, the lab should be able to tell us what kind of explosive was used. Might even get a signature from the timer pieces."

"Okay. Let's get the samples back to the lab as soon as possible. I'm hearing rumors that the FBI is playing heavy-handed at several crime scenes when it comes to evidence. Since they haven't shown up here yet, I don't want to take the chance."

"Any word on someone claiming responsibility?" she asked.

"Nothing yet, but we have a conference call at ten. Maybe we'll get some information from the FBI. We'll see."

Paul walked towards his Jeep. He had a few minutes to get ready for the call. Hopefully, the homeowners he was waiting for would get home by the time the call ended. With any luck, they might be able to give him some insight into why they had been targeted. There had to be a reason, and even they might not know what that reason was yet.

He set his laptop on the center console, clicked on the meeting link and entered the password he had been sent. He unzipped his coat, picked up his coffee and waited for the show to start.

Chapter Twenty-Five

The man behind the podium was impeccably dressed in a navy-blue pinstripe suit, white shirt and red, white and blue government-issue tie. His gray hair was neat as a pin without a hair out of place. There was a slight New York accent if you happened to have an ear for accents. Otherwise, his voice was firm and commanding.

"Good morning, ladies and gentlemen. Thank you all for taking the time to join us this morning. Although I prefer face-to-face meetings, we have investigators at multiple crime scenes, and logistically, that would be impossible to achieve.

"I am Deputy Director Felix Marshall with the FBI. I have been asked to take charge of this investigation—an investigation involving multiple law enforcement agencies across the state of Colorado and beyond. My team and I bring valuable experience to this investigation since we have dealt with almost a thousand terrorist acts since nine-eleven. Until yesterday, none of those acts have succeeded, a record we are very proud of. We intend to find out why this one succeeded and to hold those people responsible.

"We have accumulated vast amounts of

evidence, which is now in the hands of the FBI crime lab as well as other labs around the country. This is a monumental effort, which will be all the more easily accomplished if you refrain from running our forensic teams off the crime scenes. Our people are trained professionals who know how to gather evidence.

"That being said, with permission from Director Jackson of the Colorado Bureau of Investigation, FBI special agents will be reviewing all your investigation files and any evidence that was discovered before the FBI arrived on the scene.

"This investigation is proceeding along several fronts, and we will keep you apprised, as best we can, of any evidence that leads to a suspect or suspects. All information you develop as part of your investigations will be channeled through the FBI and compiled in our database. That information will be shared on a need-to-know basis.

"Speaking of evidence, and in keeping with the spirit of cooperation between the state and federal governments, you may have heard that we recovered an unexploded bomb. This information is correct. The bomb materials are being analyzed as we speak. We are confident that fingerprint and DNA analysis will lead us to one of several militia groups that will undoubtedly claim responsibility for these heinous acts of cowardice.

"Please know that we are confident we will bring these killers to justice and that we are already working through a database of all known militia members with bomb-making experience. We will find the bastards that did this. We will be reaching out to the various investigation teams as we have questions or require additional information. Please respond with the utmost haste. We realize this investigation will take time, but we have assured the public that they have nothing to fear, and that the FBI has the situation well in hand. Since a meeting like this is not conducive to asking questions, please hold your questions for the special agent assigned to each crime scene. They will be contacting their teams before the end of the day today.

"One word of caution. In the climate in this country today, misinformation and falsehoods run rampant, and once unleashed, they are hard to control. Please do not speak with anyone from the media about anything your investigation reveals. I would prefer you keep whatever information you have as close to your chest as possible. Once we have moved onto any suspected domestic terrorist cells, we will bring in the media.

"In the meantime, stay vigilant, stay safe and contact us if you need anything. Thank you."

Chapter Twenty-Six

Sheriff Hartman looked at Buck. "You buy that bullshit about a militia group being behind this? Doesn't sound like they are even considering other options. He sure got his dig in at you though."

Buck closed his laptop. "You think his comment about running people off was directed at me?" Buck held his hands out in front of him with his palms facing the sky. "Why?" Buck laughed.

"Right. But in all seriousness," said Sheriff Hartman. "Where do you think they got the idea this was militias?"

"Not sure. I read some of the reports last night from our teams, and there was nothing in those reports to indicate militia involvement. Maybe something from the unexploded bomb gave them that idea. I was hoping he would go into a little more detail about that bomb," said Buck.

"You said you read some of that manifesto that was sent to you guys and the media. Anything in that says militia?"

Buck thought for a minute. "Not really. Whoever the author was, he was all over the board, but the impression I got was a lone individual, not a group. Let's go find out how Franklin is doing before our friends from the FBI come back."

"Yeah," said Sheriff Hartman. "It will be interesting to see how far their spirit of cooperation goes."

Buck placed his laptop back into his backpack, and they headed for the door.

Franklin and his team were standing in a group near what remained of the kitchen wall as Buck and Sheriff Hartman walked up.

"Guys, what's going on?" asked Buck.

Franklin lowered his mask. "We've reached an impasse. We covered this whole area, and we were just talking about a strategy. We haven't found anything that we think is bomb-related in the past couple of hours, and we're deciding if it's worth it to keep looking or if we call it a day."

"That's the problem with bombs," said Sheriff Hartman. "They tend to destroy all the evidence."

An idea came to Buck. "Did we find the kitchen door?"

"No," said Franklin. "What are you thinking?"

"I'm wondering if the bomber thought the same

thing, that his bomb would destroy all the evidence. Maybe because of that, he was careless and left us a little something on the doorknob."

Sheriff Hartman ran back to the command center and came back with a set of blueprints, and they all gathered around. He laid the plans out on a pile of debris and opened to an interior floor plan. He turned the plans until they were positioned the way he thought they should be.

"If this is correct," he said. "Then we should be standing about here." He pointed to a spot on the floor plan and then checked the nearest dimension to the back door. "That would put the back door about forty feet in that direction." He pointed to a possible location.

Franklin pulled out a tape measure, and with the help of one of his team, they marked off forty feet. He stopped and looked around.

"Should be right about here," he said.

They all spread out and headed towards where Franklin was standing. The debris pile was large, with huge chunks of concrete and roofing. Buck walked around the site to where a backhoe operator was removing some of the heavy debris. They spoke for a minute, and then Buck walked back, followed by the backhoe. He pointed to several of the largest pieces of debris, and the operator nodded. The operator set the scoop just above the ground and slid under the largest piece of debris.

He removed the debris and then gave Buck a salute and headed back to where he had been working. Franklin and the rest of the team started removing the smaller pieces of concrete until they uncovered what looked like a twisted metal door. Franklin signaled for everyone to stop digging.

He removed the rest of the debris and, with the help of one of his team, pulled the door from the pile. The door was twisted and pockmarked from shrapnel, but Franklin had one of his guys run to the SUV and get the fingerprint kit.

Buck wasn't hopeful. The problem was, how many people had touched the door or the knob between the time the bomb was planted and the time of the explosion? Franklin dusted the edge of the door and the outside knob. He blew away the residue, and several prints appeared. He used a loupe from the kit and looked at the prints.

"Multiple prints here. It's going to take a while to sort them out."

He accepted the digital camera with the macro lens from his team member and took some high-def close-up photos. "We'll load these onto the computer and try to separate them into individual prints. We'll run anything that looks promising."

"Thanks," said Buck. "Let me know if you get a hit."

Buck and Sheriff Hartman stepped away from the group. "How did your canvass of the neighbors work out?" asked Buck. "Any cameras overlooking the parking lot?"

"None that we could find," said Sheriff Hartman. "I have a couple of deputies still looking, but it's not promising."

Buck stopped walking. "There are two ways to get onto this frontage road, right? If you come in on the highway, you have to take one of two exits to get here. Any chance we might find a camera at either end?"

"Don't know," said Sheriff Hartman. "We've been working on the houses, apartments and commercial buildings that look onto the parking lot."

"I'm gonna go check the Maverick station at the traffic circle, where I parked yesterday. Why don't you check the other exit. Maybe we'll get lucky."

They split up and slid into their respective SUVs, Buck heading west and Sheriff Hartman heading east.

Buck entered the traffic circle, followed it around and pulled into the Maverick's parking lot.

He slid out of his car and headed towards the building. Once inside, he asked to speak to the manager. The kid behind the counter yelled for Kathy, and Buck turned to see a portly woman with arm tattoos and short pink hair walk up to the counter. Buck introduced himself.

He asked if she had security cameras and would she be willing to let him look through the views from Christmas Eve night and early Christmas morning.

Kathy told him to follow her, and she led him to a small office in the back of the building.

"This about the bombing?" she asked. "What a tragedy. A lot of those folks are regular customers."

She sat at the desk and called up the camera feeds. She explained that she had several cameras, but only one that might give him a view of the traffic circle. Buck gave her the times he was interested in and sat next to her and watched the screen.

Traffic on the circle and the frontage road was slow on Christmas Eve night, and the picture was from a good distance away. Buck spotted several cars and an old pickup truck go by between ten and midnight. Then, just after midnight, he saw several cars exiting the frontage road onto the traffic circle.

He wondered if those were the last of the people from the mosque leaving.

He asked Kathy to slow down the feed, and at about three fifteen a.m., he spotted what looked like the same pickup truck exiting the frontage road, entering the traffic circle and following the road towards I-70 Eastbound. He asked Kathy to rewind the images and go through them frame by frame. When he got the clearest image, he asked her to stop.

Buck asked her to print off the still image, and then he asked her to rewind to when he'd first spotted the truck. Kathy stopped the image when they spotted the truck and Buck compared the two pictures side by side.

"There's something in the back of the truck in the earlier image," said Kathy, pointing to the bed of the truck and a square something sitting in the middle of the bed. The item did not appear in the second image, but Buck was convinced the images were of the same truck.

Buck pulled out his phone and dialed Sheriff Hartman. "Al, any chance you can run by the courthouse and get a warrant for a video from the Maverick station?"

He explained to Sheriff Hartman what he'd found on the tape, and the sheriff told him to sit tight, and he would get there as soon as possible. Buck hung up and explained the warrant to Kathy. She seemed fine with what he told her, and she suggested that while they waited, she could download a copy of the video and email it to him.

Buck accepted her offer, sat back and waited for the email. The little bug in his brain started dancing around again.

Thirty minutes later, Sheriff Hartman pulled into the parking lot and entered the building. He walked back to the office and handed the warrant to Kathy. She locked it in her desk and reran the video for Sheriff Hartman. He got right up next to the screen, took out a pair of glasses and looked at the thing in the bed of the truck.

"Sure, looks like a box of some kind, but I can't tell what it is. It's also not in the later image. Wish the image was closer or clearer. We might be onto something."

Buck pulled out his phone and called George at the office. "George, I'm sending you a video of a possible truck at the mosque bombing. It's not a great video, but we think we spotted a pickup truck with something in the bed that was there earlier and not there in a later frame. See if you guys can enhance the images."

"No worries, Buck," said George. "By the way,

was that you that FBI deputy director was talking about this morning on the conference call? Did you run their guys off the mosque site?"

Buck filled him in, and George laughed. "Fuck, Buck. You must have balls made of steel. Would have loved to be there to see the look on the agent's face when you told his team to leave."

Buck laughed, thanked George and hung up. He thanked Kathy for her help and told Sheriff Hartman he would let him know what they found, if anything, once they tried to enhance the video.

Buck checked his phone and saw he had two missed texts from Bax. On the second one, she told him to meet her at the Valley View Restaurant, so Buck slid into his Jeep and headed back towards the motel and restaurant. He hoped that Bax had had some luck at the Logan site. He felt good about the day so far, but things were about to get interesting.

Chapter Twenty-Seven

Paul sat in his Jeep in front of the Bellingham residence. He had spoken with Mark Bellingham an hour ago, and they were expecting to arrive back in Salida about now. He set his laptop aside and looked at the sky. Dark clouds were starting to appear over the mountains to the west, and a few snowflakes landed on the windshield. He started the Jeep and turned on the heater to warm his feet.

He spotted a white Chevy Suburban making its way down to where he was sitting, and the SUV pulled into the Bellingham's driveway. Paul turned off the Jeep, slid off the seat and grabbed his backpack and laptop. He slid the laptop back into his backpack and slung it over one shoulder.

Mark Bellingham was tall and lean, with short blond hair. He moved with the grace of an athlete, and Paul wondered if he was a runner or a biker. Several kids jumped out of the back of the SUV, grabbed backpacks that Mark had set on the ground by the rear hatch and headed inside the house.

Mrs. Bellingham was shorter than her husband by about a foot, but she was also lean and moved with a certain grace. She had long blond hair tied in a ponytail and wore jeans and a flannel shirt under her down vest. She looked up and down the street and watched as workers boarded up the broken windows on her neighbors' houses. She turned as Paul walked up and headed inside.

Paul stepped up to the back of the SUV and reached out his hand. "Mark. Hope you had a good drive. Thanks for taking the time to meet with me."

Mark Bellingham shook his hand, closed the rear hatch and suggested that Paul follow him inside and out of the cold. Paul was more than happy to oblige. The house was warm, and Paul removed his jacket and laid it over the back of the couch. He introduced himself to Mrs. Bellingham, Veronica, and she asked him if he would like some coffee. She had the glass coffeepot full of water in her hand and filled the coffee maker as they spoke.

Paul took a seat at the kitchen table and pulled his laptop out of his backpack. With the coffee maker brewing and the kids secreted away in some other part of the house, the Bellinghams took their seats opposite him and, suddenly, the strain of what had happened on their cul-de-sac sunk in.

"How many people were injured?" asked Veronica.

"Seventeen people were treated at the scene and released," said Paul. "Seven people were hospitalized, and two are still in intensive care. The doctors think the strain was too much for one of your neighbors, an elderly gentleman named Sanchez, who had a heart attack that afternoon. Luckily, if there is such a thing in a situation like this, it happened in the hospital, so he got immediate care."

"The damage doesn't look as bad as we expected," said Mark. Veronica nodded in agreement.

"The mayor ordered a bunch of the town employees to come by yesterday afternoon to help clean up, and the neighbors on the surrounding streets pitched in. It was an interesting way to spend Christmas Day, and not what most of those folks had planned. Besides, the mailbox knocked down the force of the explosion, which mitigated a lot of the collateral damage."

Paul gave them some of the details about the explosion and what they suspected had been a Christmas package that hadn't been removed from the mailbox.

Veronica looked concerned. "If we hadn't decided to drive to Ohio for Christmas, we might all be dead." Her hands shook as she poured the coffee into three mugs.

Paul decided that the statement was more

rhetorical, so he chose not to burden her further with an answer.

"Do you have any idea who might have sent you a package for Christmas?"

Mark answered first. "We discussed that all the way home and even called some of our relatives to see if anyone sent any gifts to us. Nothing comes to mind. I wish we could help more."

"Veronica," said Paul. "What about something you ordered online that was delayed or maybe something from one of the kids' teachers, your pastor or a friend?"

Veronica looked startled. "You can't think that someone we knew tried to kill my family on Christmas Day?"

"I'm sorry, Veronica," said Paul. "I didn't mean to imply that, but I have to ask the hard questions." He waited while she sipped her coffee. "What about threats, either in person or online? Threatening emails or texts. Any confrontations with people you either knew or didn't know? Maybe a road rage incident."

They both shook their heads no.

"What is it you both do for a living?"

"I'm the manager of a tire store in town," said Mark.

"And I'm a fifth grade teacher," said Veronica.

"Okay," said Paul. "So, no problems at work or any issues with anyone in town? That helps, because it eliminates a lot of people." Paul sipped his coffee. He was starting to warm up, and it felt good.

"What about relatives, maybe a black sheep or maybe someone who was supposed to be staying with you over the holidays until you decided to head for Ohio?"

Neither Mark nor Veronica could think of anything like that. None of this made any sense to them.

Paul asked if he could use the bathroom, and Mark pointed down the hall towards the living room. Paul excused himself. He didn't need to go, but he wanted to give them a chance to talk amongst themselves now that he had put some ideas or questions in their heads.

He stepped into the living room and looked around. The house was furnished for comfort, and even though the furnishings were old, they were still in good shape. He spotted several framed pictures on the fireplace mantel, and he walked over to take a look.

The pictures were typical family photos—school pictures of the kids, a couple of family portraits taken over several years as the kids grew and a couple of pictures of older relatives. One picture caught Paul's attention, and he stepped over to the bookcase that surrounded the fireplace.

The picture showed a man in a suit standing outside a marble building with lots of stairs. It looked like it had been taken a long time ago, but what caught Paul's eye was the newspaper the man was holding. It was a copy of the old *Rocky Mountain News*, and the headline read guilty in large letters. Paul couldn't make out anything else, so he picked up the picture and headed for the kitchen.

"Guys. Who is this a picture of, and what was the occasion?" asked Paul.

Veronica took the frame, and a sad smile came over her face. "That was my dad. It was taken back in the seventies. He passed away two years ago this coming summer."

"I couldn't help but notice the headline on the newspaper. Was your dad convicted of a crime?" asked Paul.

Veronica smiled. "No, he was on the jury. This was back when we lived in Denver. I have a scrapbook with more information if you're interested."

Paul told her he would love to see it, and she stepped away from the table and headed for the living room. She returned a minute later carrying an old, worn photo album. She sat in the chair and opened the album on the table. She flipped through a couple of pages of old pictures and then stopped. The page she had turned to had a larger version of the same picture, and under one of the plastic page covers was the original front page of the newspaper.

She slid the album over to Paul.

"My dad came to the U.S. in the late fifties and settled in Denver. He worked for the railroad for almost fifty years. He became a citizen in nineteen seventy. He was proud of that accomplishment, but the two things he always told us that made it special were being able to vote and serving on a jury.

"His wish to serve on a jury was fulfilled in nineteen seventy-six when he was called to serve on a murder case. You might have heard about the case. A woman and her daughter were blown up on Pearl Street with a car bomb. The bomber was some IRA fanatic, and he was caught a day or two later. The bomb was meant for her husband or boyfriend, who was a newspaper reporter. The trial made all the national news programs, and he was convicted and sentenced to life without parole.

My dad was thrilled to be on the jury. One of his proudest moments."

Paul's interest was piqued, and he removed the newspaper page from the album and read the article. He stopped reading and looked at Veronica and Mark. "Did anyone threaten your dad while he was on the jury?"

Mark looked at Veronica and then back to Paul. "You can't possibly think this old case and the bomb meant for us could be related. That was over forty years ago. That doesn't make any sense."

"Right now, it's just a thought, but it is an interesting development. Do you know what happened to the bomber?"

They shook their heads. Veronica said, "I don't think we ever talked about it after the trial was over. I would think he's either dead or still in prison."

Paul pulled out his phone and took a picture of the newspaper page and a picture of the photo of Veronica's dad. He dialed a number, and Melanie answered.

"Hey, Paul. What's up?"

Paul explained what he was looking for, and he texted her the two pictures. She told him she would get on it as soon as she had a free minute, and she hung up. Paul sat there staring at the newspaper.

His mind was racing at a hundred miles an hour, thinking about various scenarios, none of which made any sense, but it was a lead, and it needed to be followed.

He finished his coffee and thanked Mark and Veronica Bellingham for their hospitality. As Mark walked him to the door, he asked, "Do you think we are in any danger?"

Paul handed him one of his business cards. "I don't know, Mark, but if you have any questions or concerns, you give me a call. I'll stay in touch as the investigation progresses."

Paul shook Mark's hand, thanked him again for the coffee and the conversation and headed for his Jeep. He had a lot to think about, and he wondered if he might have just stumbled on the motive for the bombings. But how did the mosque bombing fit in? That was still a puzzle.

He slid into the Jeep, set his backpack on the seat and started the car. He pulled out his phone and dialed. He had a lot to think about, but he needed to fill Buck in and see what he might think about his crazy idea.

Chapter Twenty-Eight

Buck and Bax were just digging into their cheeseburger platters when his phone rang. He checked the number and answered.

"Hey, Paul. What's up?"

Paul filled him in on his conversation with the Bellinghams and the bombing case Veronica Bellingham's dad had been a juror on back in the seventies. The fact it was a bombing case was the only thing even remotely related, but it was a place to start.

Buck listened without speaking. "So, this may sound crazy," said Paul, "but what if the personal bombings are related to this bombing case her father sat on? It's been over forty years, and I have no idea why, after all this time, someone would want retaliation, but the more I think about it, the more I think there's something there."

Paul talked nonstop for a few more minutes. Bax looked at Buck with questioning eyes, but he held up one finger to indicate he would fill her in when Paul finished talking. Paul finally took a breath, and Buck hesitated a minute, gathering his thoughts.

"That's a crazy theory for sure, but what you're saying makes some sense. Besides, we're running up against a brick wall, so let's play it out and see where it goes. Get on to the state prison in Florence and figure out if this O'Connor fella is still an inmate or if he's passed on. Then call the Denver courthouse, ask for Candace Madison in the court clerk's office and see if she can track down the trial transcripts. If they're digitized, have her email them to us. If not, you may have to go to Denver and dig them out of a basement somewhere. Candace can help you with that. Also, try to get us a list of jurors." The little bug in Buck's brain went into overdrive.

"Paul, great job. We may have our first break."

"What about our friends at the FBI? Should we let them know?" asked Paul.

"Let's keep this in house for the time being until we can develop this further. We wouldn't want to waste their time until we're more certain of our theory."

Paul hung up, and Buck put his phone down on the table. He leaned in closer to Bax, so the other patrons wouldn't be able to hear him.

Buck relayed the conversation to her almost verbatim. The more he told her about Paul's theory, the more it started to work for him. Bax looked puzzled.

"But why now?" she asked. "Forty years is a long time to hold a grudge. For all we know, this guy O'Connor is dead and buried. What happened now that made this such a priority?"

"That's what we'll need to work on. Right now, all we have is a theory with no facts. We need to get some facts."

Buck stopped for a minute, and a thought crossed his mind. "Here's another interesting fact, which Paul isn't aware of. The family mentioned that the defendant in the case, this Connor O'Connor, was an IRA bomber back in the day. Who do we know who was running the Irish mob in Denver and was also the victim of a bombing?"

"Fuck, Buck," said Bax. "Jackson Logan."

"Right. So that's two people who were victims, or potential victims, of the bombings who could be connected to O'Connor. It's a stretch right now, but I'll bet you dinner that Connor O'Connor and Jacky Logan's paths crossed someplace along the way."

"I need to go to Denver and talk to Jackson Logan, the surviving son," said Bax.

"Good idea," said Buck. "But you need to tread carefully. If Jacky Logan III is now running his father's operations, and he's figured out that the bombing was directed at his family, he is going to have his guard up, and his security is going way up. These guys don't mess around. I will also bet that they are one step ahead of both us and the FBI. It wouldn't surprise me if they already have an idea of who's behind this, and if they do, bodies are gonna start dropping. Disappearing a cop will not be a concern for them if they're on a vendetta."

"Okay, Buck. We need to move quickly in case the FBI is already talking to him. He may not want to talk to me, and I don't want him to lawyer up. I might try a little mutual cooperation since we could potentially have the same goal in mind."

Buck laughed. "If Jacky Logan finds out who killed his family before we do, he will not have the same goal as us. That you can take to the bank. These people may look legit on the outside, but they still rule their world with an iron fist, and they will do whatever they need to make this right. This is a bad time for them. Their longtime boss is dead, and his son, the heir apparent, is going to be tested by all the guys who have been loyal to his father. Jacky Logan III is going to have to prove to his people that he is in control, and that is going to mean swift action."

Bax finished her burger and placed a twenty-dollar bill under the edge of the plate. "Then I'd better get moving. I'll keep you posted every step of the way." She grabbed her down vest off the seat, picked up her backpack and headed for the door.

Buck called to her, "Let the director know when you get to Denver, so he can set up backup if you need it. Be careful."

Buck sat for a minute and finished his burger and Coke. This case had just taken an interesting turn if the information Paul discovered proved out. His mind was running in circles, but he still kept coming back to the why. Why now? This guy had been convicted over forty years ago. He received several life sentences and would be in jail for the rest of his life. Why retaliate now? Who was he going after, how were the other victims related and how could he accomplish this from prison?

Then, once again, the numbers hit. If the bomber were targeting the jurors in the original bombing case, that would mean twelve bombs for the jurors. If you added in Jackson Logan, that made thirteen, which was the number of bombs they were aware of. What didn't make sense was that in a retaliation scenario, why not target the judge and the lawyers as well? And how did the mosque fit into this? Or didn't it?

Buck picked up his phone and hit the speed dial button. Director Jackson answered on the second ring.

"Hey, Buck. Making new friends at the FBI, I see." The director laughed.

"Yeah, sorry about that, sir. It needed to be done. They were walking all over a crime scene that was already complicated."

"No worries, Buck. You work for me, not them. So, fill me in."

Chapter Twenty-Nine

While the FBI web meeting was taking place on a secure website, the Denver Irish mob began gathering at Jacky III's house in the upscale Denver neighborhood of Cherry Hills. Family, friends, business associates, sports and entertainment figures, and local politicians had been showing up since right after breakfast to pay their respects and offer condolences for the loss of Jacky Jr.

From the beginning, Jacky III fit right into the neighborhood. He was a successful businessman with his hands in entertainment venues, auto dealerships, sports and entertainment management. His neighbors liked him and his family, and no one ever questioned what he did for a living. Had they known about his extracurricular activities, some of them might have been a little taken aback, except that Jacky III and his wife threw some fabulous parties.

That was why no one questioned the arrival of several luxury cars just before ten a.m. That is, no one except for the FBI surveillance van that was parked down the street, taking pictures of all the license plates and everyone arriving at the front door.

The FBI agents were not trying to be subtle about being there, and at one point, Jacky III's wife, Dee, walked down the long driveway carrying a platter of scrambled eggs, bacon and assorted pastries, which she handed to the agent who opened the back door of the van.

It was comforting for Jacky III's wife, knowing that the FBI was keeping watch on her house. After all, if it weren't for a stroke of luck and a sick kid, they would be lying on a slab next to her in-laws. Worst of all was knowing that whoever killed them was still running around, and she was concerned for her own family's safety.

The cars carrying Jacky III's associates pulled around the back and entered the house through an entrance that led directly to the lower level. Jacky III had had the place swept for bugs before his family was even out of bed, but he still took no chances. Once everyone arrived, he started the white noise generator, which filled the entire lower level with a cloud of noise that he had been assured by the installer would block any listening devices.

Besides the huge buffet upstairs, there was another complete buffet set up on the long bar downstairs, and while everyone grabbed a plate of food, Tommy O'Hara did the honors behind the bar.

Fed and supplied with drinks, everyone gathered

around the table in the middle of the room and sat quietly as Jacky III gathered his thoughts.

"First, I want to thank you for coming on such short notice. This is a tragic day for my family and having you all here with us means a lot. Dad would have been proud. Dee and I will be meeting with Father Donovan later today, and I will keep you all apprised of the arrangements."

Jacky III told them not to spend their money on flowers for the funeral but instead to donate to their favorite charity in his father's name. He knew it wouldn't matter because the funeral home would be filled with flowers when the time came.

"Whatever arrangements you had with my dad will stay in force. Since the bar burned down, take your weekly earnings to Toby Mclean's garage. He'll take your collections each week—a word of advice. I am not as tolerant as my father was. If you're short, I want to know about it before the drop is made.

"Next, I want everyone, and I mean everyone, out looking for Connor O'Connor. Talk to your snitches, your junkies, anyone you do business with. I want that son of a bitch in my hands as soon as possible. Anyone gets good information, let Jimmy Sullivan know, and we'll take it from there. No one is to take any action on their own. Don't try to impress me by going rogue."

Jacky III stopped talking, and Jimmy Sullivan stood up and walked around the table. "We know the motherfucker is out there, somewhere. Somebody has to know something. Somebody had to help him get supplies. You don't just walk out of prison after forty years and buy explosives on a street corner. Do we have any idea what he's using for money?"

Gabe Murphy held up his hand, and Jimmy Sullivan looked down the end of his nose at him. "Fuck, Gabe. This ain't school. You got something to say, speak up."

"Sorry, Jimmy. I went by the O'Connor's old house yesterday, and someone opened a hole in an old chimney in the basement. That hole wasn't there a couple of weeks ago. Looks like he might have had a stash."

Jimmy smiled. "Good, Gabe. Let's see if we can find out what was in there."

He looked around the table. "We talked to his parole officer. He hasn't checked in since he was released, but with the holidays, the asshole wasn't concerned. Figured he'd show up after the New Year. We also had one of our people talk to the prison doctor. There's a damn good chance that Connor O'Connor is lying dead somewhere. They only gave him a couple of weeks to live. Talk to our contacts at the hospitals and funeral homes and find out if any dead homeless people have shown up in the past couple of days."

Jacky III stood up. "Dead or not, I want to know where this fuck is. I either want the satisfaction of killing him myself, or I want to piss on his grave. So, talk to everyone you know. There's fifty grand for whoever brings us a lead that helps us find O'Connor, and there might be a spot at this table for the person bringing us the information."

Jimmy sat back down. "Stop upstairs before you leave and pay your respects to the family. There's also a donation jar to help pay for the funeral expenses. Don't let me find out you were cheap."

Jacky III laughed. "And don't forget to smile for the FBI as you leave."

Jimmy got serious. "Jacky Jr. is gone, and Jacky III is now wearing his ring. So, it's now time to proclaim your loyalty."

Everyone got up from the table and stacked their plates and glasses on the bar. Following Jimmy Sullivan, each man in the room walked up to the end of the table, knelt and kissed the ring. They all headed upstairs, except for Tommy O'Hara, who had answered his phone and was listening intently.

"Okay," he said. "Take him to the garage. I'll meet you there. And I want him to be able to talk, so be gentle."

Jimmy Sullivan and Jacky III turned from the stairs and came back down to where Tommy O'Hara stood. The looks on their faces called for an explanation, which Tommy O'Hara provided.

"We might have found someone who gave O'Connor the lead on the explosives. Two of my guys picked him up this morning, and I'm gonna meet them at the garage. You want in?"

"I can't leave just yet," said Jacky III. "Call Jimmy when you know something, and we'll come by. Do not kill him. I want to talk to him myself."

Tommy O'Hara put his phone back in his pocket, reached out and took Jacky III's hand, kissed the ring and headed upstairs. Jimmy Sullivan turned to Jacky III.

"Might be nothing, but I'll make sure he can still talk once Tommy is finished with him. I'm gonna pay my respects to Dee and follow Tommy. You need anything, you call."

Jimmy hugged Jacky III and headed upstairs. Jacky III sat back down at the table. Every man in the room had expressed loyalty. It was not a bad way to start this next chapter in his life. He smiled and headed upstairs.

Chapter Thirty

Buck hung up with the director and merged onto I-70 East. After a few miles, he exited onto US 24 at Minturn and headed south. He was just passing Camp Hale National Historic Site when his phone rang.

At over nine thousand feet in elevation, Camp Hale was built in 1942 as the training camp for an elite army unit that would become the 10th Mountain Division. Soldiers at Camp Hale were trained in mountain climbing, skiing, cold weather survival and mountain warfare techniques. At its peak, the camp saw over fourteen thousand men training there, and later, it held over four hundred of the most hard-core German soldiers from the Afrika Korps. In 1945 the camp was decommissioned and was used until 2003 by various agencies before being dismantled.

Buck looked at the number that popped up on his dash screen. He hit the green button.

"Hey, Paul. What's up?"

"I just got off the phone with the warden at the state prison in Florence," said Paul. "Connor

O'Connor was given a compassionate release just before Thanksgiving of this year."

"I thought the newspaper article said he was given multiple life sentences without the possibility of parole. What happened?"

"Pancreatic cancer," said Paul. "Stage four. According to the prison doctor who had been treating him, they figured he was down to his last few weeks when he was released."

"Who let him out?" asked Buck.

"One of those do-gooder organizations that takes on special cases. They took it to the state supreme court, and they granted the release. The governor had no choice but to sign the release. Bet he wasn't happy about it."

"I also called the parole officer he was assigned to. O'Connor was last seen by the prison guards getting on the Denver-bound bus. He checked into the hotel they set up for him, spent a couple of days there and disappeared. He never checked in with his parole officer. He pretty much dropped off the face of the earth."

"Shit," said Buck. "Now we have a bomber on the loose who may have already caused a shitload of damage. That's wonderful. How the hell do we find this guy? Any family in Denver?"

"The warden said he has no living family, anywhere. That's why he was sent to a hotel near University Hospital, so someone would be able to take care of him during his last days."

"Any chance this was some kind of fake-out? Maybe he's not as sick as they thought?"

"I didn't get that sense. Everyone at the prison knew about the cancer, and they all said he was in significant pain. The doctor figured he might last a month, but that would not be a month he would want to wish on anyone. I asked him to email me his medical file."

"Okay," said Buck. "Let's think about this for a minute. We have a bomber who was trained by the IRA and was convicted for killing a woman and her daughter when he was supposed to be killing her husband, a reporter. He gets multiple life sentences, and after forty-some years, he's released because he's dying."

"Sounds about right," said Paul.

"So where does he get the explosives? And if the theory is correct, and he somehow went after the jurors from his trial, how did he get their names or the names of their families? That would take a lot of internet work, and unless I'm mistaken, prisoners are not allowed free use of the internet in Florence, which brings up the other part of that. How do you find contacts with explosives after forty years? He couldn't just ask some guy on a street corner where he could buy explosives. No, if this is our guy, he had help on the outside. Besides, where would he get the money? He would have left prison with maybe a hundred bucks in his pocket."

"All good questions, Buck. I think we need to dig deeper into Connor O'Connor, determine who his friends were and who he worked for back in the day. Maybe some of his old friends, old being the optimal word here, or their offspring might have helped him."

"Good idea," said Buck. "Call Denver homicide. See if any of the cops who worked the original case are still alive, and let's start to get some answers."

"I'll stop by DPD when I get to Denver. I called your friend at the courthouse, and she said the files for that case had not been digitized, and I'd have to go to the court archives warehouse and search for them. So, I'm heading that way now."

"Good," said Buck. "Call Bax. She's heading to Denver to talk to Jackson Logan. When she's done, she can give you a hand at the archives and with DPD. You might want to have her hold off on visiting Logan until you get there. You can back her up."

"You think Logan might try something?"

"I have no idea, but let's not take the chance. Call me later and fill me in."

"Where are you heading? Sounds like you're driving."

"Heading to Leadville to work on this militia angle the FBI is pushing. Got someone there who might be willing to talk to me."

"Okay," said Paul. "Be careful."

"You too."

Buck hung up as he passed the entrance to Ski Cooper, one of the smaller, less expensive ski resorts in Colorado. Very few amenities, but awesome snow. He drove in silence the rest of the way to Leadville.

Chapter Thirty-One

US 24 became Front Street as Buck entered Leadville and continued south. Leadville was an old mining town with a population of somewhere south of three thousand people; it had once been a thriving community during the heyday of the mining era.

Front Street of today was lined with restaurants, bars and quaint shops, and the snow was piled high along the sides of the highway. It reminded Buck of his hometown of Gunnison. One of Leadville's claims to fame is Leadville Regional Airport. At an elevation of over 9,900 feet, it is the highest public use airport in North America, a stop along the way for many airplane and helicopter pilots training for high-altitude mountain flying.

Buck continued through town and pulled into a small industrial park at the south end of town. His destination was a small auto body and repair shop called Miller's Garage. He pulled up in front of the open garage door and slid out of his Jeep.

Glancing across the street at a small storage facility, he spotted the black SUV with dark tinted windows, parked and facing the garage. The FBI was on the case. Buck laughed to himself, and then he did something a little unusual. He checked his hip to make sure his pistol was in place, and he unsnapped the thumb break on the holster. He unzipped his jacket and headed for the open garage door. He never knew what kind of reception to expect from the militia guys.

Buck stepped through the open door and into a noisy, active workspace. The noise from the compressors, grinders and a loud radio in the back somewhere was almost deafening. A Mutt and Jeff team approached him, one short and bald, one tall with long hair pulled back in a ponytail. Both had tattoos visible under their open-collared work shirts. The taller one carried a large crescent wrench. They spotted the badge on his belt.

"You lost, Officer?" asked the shorter one.

"I need to talk to your boss," said Buck, keeping an eye on both men as they stepped closer.

"Sorry, pal. Boss ain't seeing visitors today, so why don't you turn around and leave before you get hurt. There's lots of things in the garage that can poke ya."

They both laughed, but Buck held his ground. "Look, guys. I'm not here to bother you, but I need your boss, now. We can do that the easy way or the hard way. Doesn't matter to me, but it will matter to you."

The shorter one took a step forward. "Look here, old man. We told you to leave. You can decide if that's walking or crawling." He reached his hand behind his back, and Buck grabbed the grip on his pistol.

"Billy, back off." The voice boomed from the small office above the shop. "You want to fuck around with this guy, you'll be dead before you even get your piece out."

The shorter one, Billy, glared at Buck but brought his hand back around to where Buck could see it. Then he stepped back a couple of steps and waited.

Carl Miller was of average height and about Buck's age. His gray hair was cut "high and tight," and his muscles put a strain on the polo shirt he was wearing. He stepped up to Buck and reached out his hand.

"Buck Taylor. It's been ages."

Buck shook his hand. "Carl, it's good to see you. We need to have a conversation."

Carl looked at him and jutted his chin towards the storage facility. "Not here. You got your gear? Just your rod and one fly. Let's go have some fun."

Buck nodded and walked back to his Jeep and opened the rear hatch. He pulled out a case containing his ten-foot Tenkara rod and chose his favorite dry fly from the fly box. Carl walked out carrying a lightweight fly rod and pointed towards the ATV parked alongside the garage.

They climbed in, and Carl headed across the field behind the shop. Buck glanced back towards the storage facility and saw the two FBI agents outside the SUV, one with a pair of binoculars and one holding his phone up to his ear. They looked like they were unsure of what to do.

Carl raced across several fields and down a couple of unused service roads until he came to a small section of the Arkansas River. He stopped and looked at Buck. "Sorry for the cloak-and-dagger, but this is all private property, and I knew my shadows couldn't follow me back here."

"How long they been there?" asked Buck.

"Showed up the day after Christmas. What's going on, Buck? Am I about to get raided?"

Buck thought for a minute. He knew if he wanted some straight answers from Carl, he would need to be straight with him. Carl had retired from the army as a full colonel, and he didn't deal in bullshit.

"It's possible. I'm not sure what the FBI is up to, but let's just say that you guys are in their crosshairs."

"Why us?" Carl Miller asked as he cast his fly behind a rock in the river and got an instant hit, pulling in a small rainbow trout.

Buck unhooked his second small trout and looked at him. "What do you know about the Christmas Day bombings?"

Carl Miller stopped short with his next cast and looked at Buck. "That's what this is about? They think we had something to do with that?"

Buck cast into a small pocket and watched his fly drift. "The FBI doesn't screw around with shit like this. They must have some kind of evidence that put the militias on their radar."

"That's nuts, Buck. None of our groups would pull a stunt like that. Whoever did that killed women and children. That's not our style." Carl Miller looked astonished.

Buck hooked another small trout and pulled it to shore. "Come on, Carl. We both know you have some real wackos in your groups. You can't control everyone."

"Buck. On my mother's grave, rest her soul. None of our groups would have done that. I have no idea what kind of evidence they might have, but it wasn't us. Nothing happens in this state that I don't know about, and I would never condone killing women and children. Our fight is with the government and fascist groups trying to destroy America. Not with women and kids, on Christmas morning. Do they think we did the mosque in Avon too?"

Buck cast into the pocket again. "Don't know for sure. They seem to think both events were a package. You know something different?"

"Come on, Buck. We're not bombers of innocent people. We're soldiers protecting our homes. We're all God-fearing people, and from everything I read, so were those folks. Sure, they didn't worship our God, but they still worshipped some God, even if it's the wrong one, but we can respect that. Everything I heard about the mosque bombing, those folks were being peaceful and not causing anyone any trouble. What reason would we have to attack them?"

Carl Miller was disturbed by the idea that they had any part in the bombings. However, Buck also knew Carl Miller well enough to know that Carl's people would not have done this. Yes, there were some splinter groups out there that had their own agendas, but Carl Miller and the other militia leaders around the state that reported to him did their best to keep those groups in check.

Carl pulled in another trout and watched Buck do the same. "What do we do, Buck?"

Buck thought for a minute as he closed up his rod and placed it back in the carrier. "My suggestion. Get on the phone with your people, make sure you are good and put your lawyers on standby. This is going to happen. Once the FBI latches on to an idea, they will do everything necessary to move on it. So let your people know not to resist. The FBI is going to come in hard when they do. Be ready."

Carl Miller looked at Buck and nodded. "Okay, Buck. I hope you find the bastards that did this."

Buck and Carl Miller climbed back into the ATV, and Carl headed back towards the garage. Buck couldn't help but wonder how this was going to end.

Chapter Thirty-Two

Bax was parked down the street from Jackson Logan III's house in Cherry Hills Village, a suburb of Denver, when Paul pulled up behind her. He climbed out of his Jeep, walked up to hers and slid into the passenger seat.

"Hey, Bax," said Paul.

"Paul. How're you doing? Did Dad send you to keep an eye on me?"

Paul laughed. "You know how Buck is. He likes to make sure we're safe. Besides, I noticed the other two cars around the corner. Looks like we have all the backup we need. They ours?"

Bax shook her head. "FBI would be my guess. Since Logan was supposed to die Christmas morning, my guess is they're keeping an eye on him to see what happens now."

"Okay. So, what's the play here?" he asked.

"Fill me in on this Connor O'Connor character. He's missing, right?"

Paul gave her the same information he had given

Buck. When he was finished, Bax had everything she would need to talk to Jackson Logan III. Her plan was for this to be a casual conversation. She would try to get him to cooperate since she was trying to find his family's killer. She hoped it would be enough.

"Good," said Paul. "Keep your phone on and in your pocket. Geronimo is the trouble word. Let's hope we don't need it."

She smiled, and he slid out of her Jeep and went back to his, answering her call as he went. He slid into the driver's seat and placed the phone in the holder mounted to the dash. Now came the waiting part.

Bax pulled her car into the circular driveway and noticed several expensive cars pulling out as she pulled up to the front door. She thought she might have recognized some of the passengers. If she was correct, Jacky Logan III had some influential friends.

She slid out of her car as two guys in poor-fitting suits approached. "What can we do for you, lady?"

The second guy ran his eyes up and down her body like he was buying a car, his eyes locking on the badge clipped to her belt. He tapped the other guy.

"Cop," he said.

The other guy's eyes dropped to her badge, and he smiled. "Sorry, honey. What can we do for you, Officer?" He smiled through crooked teeth, and it took all her strength not to drop this guy onto the pavement.

"I'm here to see Mr. Logan. Please step aside so I can pass," she said, forcing a smile.

"Sorry, lady, Mr. Logan ain't seeing nobody today. So, turn your pretty ass around and head back out the way you came."

Bax balled her fist and took a step back with her right foot. The way these two idiots were sneering at her, they would never know it was happening until it was over.

"Hey. What are you two jackasses doing?" The voice came from a man standing at the front door.

They both looked over. "We were just explaining to this police officer that you ain't taking no meetings today."

"From where I'm standing, it looks to me like you two were just about to get the surprise of your lives. Let her by."

"Yes, sir, Mr. Logan." The two guys stepped to either side, and Bax walked past them and up the four steps to the front landing.

"Mr. Logan, Agent Ashley Baxter, Colorado Bureau of Investigation. I'm working on the murder of your family. My condolences, sir, and I apologize for the intrusion, but I was hoping you could spare me a few minutes."

A woman wearing black jeans and a black sweater stepped onto the landing and wrapped her arms around herself. "Jacky, invite her in; it's freezing out here." She turned and walked back inside. Jacky III stepped aside and waved his hand towards the door. Bax stepped into a marble foyer that was one of the most opulent spaces she had ever been in. A woman in a maid's dress stood next to the door and held out her hand. Bax took off her coat and handed it to her.

Jacky III led her towards a room off the corridor, and Bax walked into a wood-paneled office that was bigger than her apartment. He pointed towards a leather chair, walked around the massive desk and sat down.

"Can I get you anything, Agent Baxter? We've gotten a ton of food from people today, offering their condolences. The last of our well-wishers just left. How about a drink—water, soda, coffee?"

Bax thanked him and pulled out her notebook. She was about to ask her first question when Jacky III raised his hand. "May I ask you a question first, Agent Baxter?"

Bax nodded.

"Were you really going to take on the two guys in the driveway? I recognized the stance; my son takes tae kwon do."

Bax smiled. "I wouldn't have hurt them bad. Just a little lesson in respect."

Jacky III laughed and raised a glass half-full of amber liquid in a small salute. "Agent Baxter, I like your style. Now, how can I help you find out who murdered my family?"

Bax pulled a notebook and pen out of her back pocket. "Mr. Logan, have you had any threats towards you or any members of your family?"

Jacky III thought for a minute. "Nothing recent. I'm in the entertainment business, Agent Baxter. Someone's always unhappy, but not enough to want to kill my family or me."

"The fire at your bar. Tell me about it."

Jacky III looked at her. "Do you think the two things are connected? The fire marshal said it was faulty wiring. That was an old building. I'm just glad it happened when we were closed, so no one got killed. I think you're barking up the wrong tree, Agent Baxter."

"Strange that it happened two weeks after your

father announced his retirement and four weeks before someone murdered your family," said Bax.

Jacky III got a shocked look on his face, and he stared at her. "Agent Baxter, now you're scaring me. I'm just a businessman. Why would someone want to destroy me?"

"Any bad business deals?" she asked.

"Nothing that would make someone want to kill me."

Bax thought Jacky III answered a little too quickly. "Mr. Logan, do you recognize the name Connor O'Connor?"

Jacky III was thinking about how to answer the question when Dee Logan stepped into the office, introduced herself and sat down next to Bax.

He took a drink and set the glass down. "That's not a name I recognize. Is he connected to the case?" Bax could tell from looking in his eyes that he was lying.

Bax checked her notes. "Mr. O'Connor was someone who might have known your father a long time ago."

"How does that connect him to the bombing?"

"Well, sir. We don't know if it does. Mr.

O'Connor spent the last forty years or so in prison for a bombing that went wrong. The wrong people got killed. He was released just before Thanksgiving, right around the time of the bar fire, and we haven't been able to find him. Thought perhaps you crossed paths."

"I can assure you, Agent Baxter. I do not associate with people like that. My father and his father may have been involved in some shady deals back in the early days, but I'm into only legit enterprises."

They spoke for a few more minutes, then Bax put her pen and notebook away and stood up. She shook both their hands and started for the door. She turned abruptly.

"I'm sorry, sir. One more question. Why wasn't your family at your father's house in Vail for Christmas morning?"

Dee stood up. "We were supposed to be," she said. "My daughter had some kind of twenty-four-hour bug, so we decided to open presents here first and then head to Vail after breakfast. I have never been so grateful that one of my kids got sick, but it probably saved our lives."

"Thank you folks," said Bax. "I appreciate you taking the time, and again, my deepest condolences." She dropped her card on the desk, headed for the foyer, retrieved her coat from the maid and headed for the car. She was glad that the two goons she'd met earlier were nowhere to be found. She slid into her Jeep, pulled out her phone and told Paul she was done and would meet him at the Denver courthouse. She headed down the driveway.

Chapter Thirty-Three

Jacky III finished his drink and was just about to say something to Dee when his phone rang. "Talk to me."

He listened for a minute, disconnected the call and stood up. "I need to go out for a while. I shouldn't be long."

Dee nodded. He walked into the foyer, grabbed a coat out of a closet that was hidden in the corner of the room and stepped into the cold, buttoning his coat as he went. He walked over to a black Range Rover, slid into the driver's seat and pulled out of the driveway.

He turned south, heading for University Avenue, and spotted the black SUV sitting on a side street around the corner from his house. He had no way of knowing if they were there for his protection or if he was under surveillance. The SUV that was usually parked across the street from his driveway had not been there when he pulled out. He wondered why.

Jacky III headed for the garage in Denver's Five Points neighborhood, just around the corner from the burned-out shell of what was once his father's bar. He already had plans in the works to build a huge entertainment venue in its place. It would be the centerpiece of his entertainment empire. He pulled into the fenced lot, and the gate closed behind him. The garage was dark except for one light above the roll-up door.

He parked next to the three other cars in the lot and slid out of the Range Rover. He scanned the area, walked over to the side door and stepped inside. He nodded to the guy standing just inside the door and headed towards the back of the building. The garage space was quiet as he walked through, and he headed for the light in the supply room.

Jimmy Sullivan and Tommy O'Hara turned as he entered the space. They stepped aside, and Jacky III got his first look at the guy they were questioning, and he was momentarily stunned. Sitting naked and taped to a metal chair was a man whose injuries made him almost unrecognizable. His face was bruised and bloody, and it looked like he had been burned with a torch.

Jacky III walked to the body, and the two guys standing next to the guy in the chair stepped aside. He reached out and lifted the guy's chin, and he saw the recognition in the poor soul's eyes.

He turned away and looked at Tommy O'Hara.

"He don't look too good," he said. "What's the story?"

"Guy works for an excavation company on the western slope, out near Nucla. Sandoval Earthworks. Company does major excavations. These are the guys you call if you want to take down a mountain or move a giant boulder—big explosives outfit. One of my guys got a tip that they might be missing some plastic explosives out of their inventory. Not sure how it came up. Didn't ask. Anyway, this guy here is their lead explosives guy."

"Has he said anything?" asked Jacky III.

"Nothing yet, boss, but we have a little bit of time while he's still able to answer. We'll get it out of him," said Tommy.

The guy standing next to him got the nod from Tommy, and he slammed his fist into the guy's chest. The guy in the chair slumped over and gasped, trying to catch his breath. Jacky III held up his hand and stepped closer to the man in the chair. He looked into his face.

"What's his name?" asked Jacky III.

"Perez," said Tommy O'Hara. "Mike Perez. Spent some time in Afghanistan with an army EOD unit. Been working at Sandoval for the past four, maybe five years."

"How sure is your information?" asked Jacky III.

"Rock solid. Guy we got it from works there too. Drinks with one of my earners in Montrose. Said this guy is always selling plastic explosives to the local militia guys. You know them wannabe soldiers that get together on weekends and make like they're in the Green Beret. Like to blow shit up and shoot at stumps.

"I guess the company shuts down from before Thanksgiving until after the first of the year, but the guy we got this from comes in during that time to do inventory. Found a discrepancy in the plastic explosives inventory. Since we had put out the word and offered a nice cash award, he called my guy, and I had this moke picked up last night."

Jacky III leaned in closer to the man in the chair. "Who'd you sell the explosives to?"

The guy raised his head and started to whisper something. All Jacky III heard was, "Sorry, Mr. Logan. I didn't say . . ."

Jacky III cut him off. "I asked you who the fuck you sold the explosives to? Tell me now, and I can make all this pain go away."

The man in the chair started to mouth some words, but Jacky III stood up.

"What he say?" asked Jimmy Sullivan.

"Sounded like he said, Tony Ryan."

Tony Ryan had been a minor rival of Jacky Jr.'s as they were coming up in the mob. He was as old as Jacky Jr. was and had been cutting into Jacky Jr.'s profits in the southern suburbs of Denver. This was a chance to get rid of a small branch of the organization, even though he knew Ryan had no part in this.

"Son of a bitch," said Tommy O'Hara. "Your dad always thought Ryan was trying to make a move on us. I'll bet his crew burned down the bar too. What do you want to do?"

"They still got that social club on South Broadway?" asked Jacky III.

Tommy O'Hara nodded.

"Good. Let's send a message that no one fucks with us and send someone to Ryan's house. Someone we don't know. Use the Italians. I want it to be public."

Jimmy Sullivan stopped for a minute. "What I don't understand is how he connected with O'Connor. And why did O'Connor kill all those other people, including the Muslims?"

"Who knows," said Tommy O'Hara. "Maybe his

mind went south after forty years in the joint. Who cares. We got a chance to make this right for Jacky Jr."

Jimmy Sullivan didn't look convinced, and he was concerned that Jacky III was making decisions based on anger and not on good business sense. Tony Ryan had never been late with his contribution to Jacky Jr. while he was alive. He thought they had buried the hatchet a long time ago. This didn't make sense, but Jacky III was now the boss, so he would make it happen. But it made him wonder.

Jacky III asked everyone to step out of the storage room for a minute. He wanted a minute with the guy in the chair. After they all left, he walked back to Mike Perez. He stood behind the chair and took a pair of blue nitrile gloves out of his pocket and put them on. He walked around and knelt next to the chair.

Mike Perez looked at Jacky III through his one good eye, and Jacky III saw the fear in his face. "I'm sorry, Mike. Never meant—well, it doesn't matter. You got sloppy."

Jacky III stood up, walked behind the chair, and pulled a twenty-two-caliber pistol out of his pocket. He leaned across the back of the chair and whispered into Mike Perez's ear. "I'll make sure your family is taken care of, Mike."

He stood up, placed the barrel of the pistol next to Mike Perez's ear and fired one shot into his brain. The body jerked and slumped forward.

Jimmy Sullivan and Tommy O'Hara ran into the room and looked at the slumped body. Jacky III placed the pistol back in his holster and removed the nitrile gloves. He took out a lighter, flicked it and held the flame up to the gloves, which melted onto the floor next to the chair.

"Get rid of him. Someplace public."

He headed towards the door, stopped and turned. "Get the word out—a hundred grand for Connor O'Connor. Tommy, make sure the guy we got the info from gets the fifty K." He turned and walked out of the garage.

Chapter Thirty-Four

Buck looked at his watch as he pulled into Avon and realized he hadn't eaten since breakfast. Bypassing his hotel, he continued into Avon and pulled into the Columbine Inn. The sign out front advertised live music, and Buck could use the distraction.

He could hear the country music in the parking lot as he slid out of his Jeep. As he entered the bar, the music almost knocked him over. The place was packed, but he managed to grab a seat at the end of the bar. The bartender stepped up and asked what he could get him, and Buck ordered a large Coke and a cheeseburger and fries. He left, and Buck turned slightly on his stool and watched the band.

The band consisted of a lead guitar, bass, drummer with a small drum kit and a female singer who was very good. Buck was no judge of music; he just knew what he liked. His son David played lead guitar in a country-bluegrass band and was the house band at the Cowboy Bar in Gunnison. The bar was owned by his brother-in-law, Hardy Braxton, and was a popular spot in town.

The bartender had dropped off a large Coke in a red plastic glass. Buck pulled out the straw and set it on the bar top. He took a big sip and sat back on the stool to listen to the band. He felt his mood lifting already.

He thought about his conversation with Carl Miller. Miller swore his people weren't involved in the bombings. He had had several conversations over the years with Carl Miller, and this was one time he believed everything Carl had said. His people had no reason to bomb the individuals or the mosque.

All that kind of action would do is bring down a heavy reaction from the government. And that was Buck's fear. He would hate for the FBI to come in hard, the militia guys to overreact and people on both sides to get killed. He hoped Carl would take his advice and let his people know not to resist.

He also wondered what was motivating the FBI into believing that this was the militia. Nothing he had seen so far said militia other than the mosque, which he admitted to himself could be white supremacists. But he just couldn't make the connection. The feeling he had was two separate bombers, one personal and one political.

He turned, dug into his cheeseburger and fries, which had suddenly appeared in front of him, and looked around the room. Out of nowhere, something grabbed his attention, and he wasn't sure what it was, but the little bug in his head had suddenly gotten active.

The band finished their last song and took a break, and the bar filled with normal conversation. He wondered what the bug was trying to tell him. He took another bite and looked at the people around the bar. His focus landed on one table: a two-top towards the back of the bar.

What was it about that table that caught his attention? The young woman was pretty enough, a little on the heavy side. She wore jeans and a flannel shirt. The guy was dressed like a tourist, silk shirt, one gold chain, a fancy watch and black dress pants. His hair was combed back, showing a lot of forehead. On the outside, they looked like almost any couple in the place. He was a little overdressed, but you can't arrest somebody for that.

Buck finished his burger and sat sipping his Coke. The band was heading back towards the stage, and he set his Coke on the bar. He looked over at the table with the young couple. The waitress had picked up the glass from in front of the young woman and headed for the bar. The guy looked like he wanted to stop her, but instead, he looked around.

The waitress set a new drink in front of the young woman and left. The young woman leaned across the table, whispered something in the man's ear and stood up. She had to grab the back of the chair to keep from stumbling backward, and then she straightened up and headed for the restrooms at the other end of the bar.

Buck watched the young man out of the corner of his eye. Something wasn't quite right. The young man reached into his pocket, looked around and then leaned across the table to pull the young woman's chair in closer to the table. As he did it, Buck spotted the move: the man's left hand hovered over the woman's glass, and Buck noticed the powder as it hit the top of the drink.

The young man sat back down and waited for his date. When she headed back to the table, she looked very unsteady, and she was very giddy, laughing each time she banged into a table or another person on her way across the bar.

Buck waved the bartender over. "What can I get you, sir?" he asked.

Buck unclipped his badge from his belt, and, keeping it in his palm, facing away from the tables, he held his arm out across the bar top so that the bartender could see the badge.

The bartender looked at the badge, and concern crossed his face.

"Without being obvious," said Buck. "Do you

know that woman at the table with the guy with the slick hair?"

The bartender took a quick sideways glance while wiping down the spot in front of Buck with the bar towel. "Yeah. She's a regular. In here a couple of times a week. Her name is Toni Fellows. Lives somewhere near here. What's your interest?"

"What about the guy? Ever seen him before?"

The bartender looked again. "Can't say I have. What's going on?"

"How many drinks has the woman had tonight?" Buck asked.

The bartender walked over and talked to the waitress standing at the bar. He walked back to Buck. "That's her second. She barely touched the first, so Carol picked it up and dumped it."

The band picked up their instruments, and the conversation slowed to a dull roar, except for Toni Fellows, who was whoopin' and hollerin' like she was watching the Beatles or Springsteen. Buck watched as she fell backward and landed hard in her chair, still laughing. The bartender looked at Buck.

Buck handed the bartender one of his business cards. "Use a phone in the back and call the Avon PD, give them my name and tell them I need backup for a drug bust. Tell them I said no lights or sirens."

The bartender nodded, and Buck stood up and clipped his badge back on his belt. The band was getting ready for the first song when Buck caught the attention of the singer. He pointed to his badge and raised one finger. The singer nodded and turned to the other members of the band.

Buck walked up to the table, reached out and picked up the woman's glass. The woman didn't notice, but the guy was starting to get out of his seat.

"Hey, what the fuck, old man, that's her drink."

Buck pulled his badge off his belt and shoved it into the guy's face. "Sit still and don't move."

By this time, the woman had noticed Buck holding her drink, and she started to say something, but the words were slurred. The guy started to move when two big pink rubber hands grabbed his shoulders and held him down. Buck and the guy both looked up.

Standing behind the guy, wearing rubber dishwashing gloves and a stained white apron, stood a big guy with huge muscles. Buck also noticed that he appeared to have Down syndrome. He smiled at Buck through a couple of crooked front teeth.

"The man told you to sit," he said while pushing down on the man's shoulders. The smile never leaving his face. The man started to protest, but the pink hands just pushed down harder.

In a sudden move, the man swung his arm out in an attempt to knock the glass out of Buck's hand, but Buck pulled his hand away just in time.

"What are you doing with my drink?" Toni slurred.

The man looked at Buck. "Do you know who I am? I will have your badge. What's the meaning of this outrage?"

Buck smiled. "Typically, when someone asks me if I know who they are, they are not as important as they think they are. Now, be good and just sit there before my friend here breaks your shoulders." The guy with the pink gloves smiled a huge smile.

Buck pulled a little package out of his pocket. He peeled off the aluminum foil cover, and, taking the straw from Toni's drink, dropped a few drops of her drink on the plastic tab. Then he waited.

A crowd had now gathered around the table, and the bartender and waitresses were holding people back. After thirty seconds, Buck looked at the disc. Two lines and the drink was fine, one line and the drink was drugged. The tab showed one line. The guy turned a shade of white that Buck had seen before.

The front door opened, and two female Avon police officers walked into the bar and noticed the crowd around the table. They headed towards the table, and Buck held up his badge.

"Officers Sanchez and Boone," said the blond officer. "We got a call you were involved in a drug bust." Just then, a sergeant walked through the door and headed towards the table.

"Agent Taylor. Sergeant McKenzie. What'd ya got?"

Buck explained about the spiked drink and the Rohypnol test he had performed. He handed the disc to Officer Boone. Sanchez was applying the cuffs to the man's hands when Toni's head started to drop towards the table.

"Sergeant, better call an ambulance for Ms. Fellows here. Let's get her blood tested at the hospital. In the meantime, find out where this guy is staying, get a search warrant for his room and car and lock his ass up."

Sanchez pulled the now-silent man to his feet. Buck smiled at the two officers and handed the drink glass to Officer Boone. "Please have this tested as well. I want you to coordinate your investigation with CBI Agent Ashley Baxter. She has been investigating the I-70 rapist. You may have just hit the jackpot, as far as arrests go."

Both officers looked pleased as they read the man his Miranda rights and then led the man through the bar. The sergeant looked at Buck.

"Will Agent Baxter be upset about losing the collar to my two officers?"

"Agent Baxter will be thrilled that, if this is the guy, he's off the highway. We think he's raped at least fifteen women in small towns along the interstate. I will call her and let her know what's going on. The arrest is theirs. Let me know what you get out of the search." He handed the sergeant his card, and the sergeant followed his officers out the door.

Buck then walked over and thanked the young man with the pink gloves on. "What's your name, son?" asked Buck. The man puffed up his already massive chest and grabbed Buck's hand.

"William Michael Loops, sir. Mr. Jerry said you might need some help."

"Well, William Michael Loops, I am grateful for the help. I couldn't have done it without you. Thanks."

The crowd surrounding the table cheered and applauded.

William Michael Loops headed back to the kitchen with the biggest smile Buck had ever seen. Buck shook the bartender's hand.

"Thanks for the assist," he said.

"Thanks for looking out for Toni. She may not remember it, but we sure will."

Buck nodded, dropped a twenty on the bar and headed for the door. It had been a long day, and he needed some sleep. Unfortunately, that wasn't going to happen.

Chapter Thirty-Five

Buck had just climbed out of the shower and was getting ready to crawl into bed when the phone rang. He looked at his watch. He knew calls at this time of night—or morning, as the case may be—were never good.

He answered, listened to the caller and got dressed. Then he headed downstairs to the lobby. Standing in the lobby were FBI Deputy Director Felix Marshall and four FBI special agents. Buck walked up to the group.

Deputy Director Marshall did not look happy. "Outside." He turned and walked away, followed by his clones. Buck put on his jacket and stepped through the door into the parking lot. Before he went through the door, he pulled out his phone, dialed Director Jackson and clipped the phone back on his belt.

Buck walked up to Deputy Director Marshall. "What's so important, it couldn't wait till morning?" asked Buck.

Deputy Director Marshall's face turned bright red like he was about to boil over. "You are fucking lucky I don't have you arrested right now for interfering with an FBI investigation. Are you bound and determined to destroy this investigation and make me look bad?"

"Make you look bad? Don't you mean make the FBI or the investigation look bad?"

"You think you're one smart-ass fuck, Taylor? Well, I have had my fill with you. First you run off the crime scene techs I sent to the mosque, then you give a heads-up to the very militia people we are investigating, and then you send Agent Baxter to interview a man we have already spoken with, who, in case you forgot, is a victim of this crime. What do you have to say for yourself, Taylor?"

Buck had made patience into an art form. There had been a story circulating the CBI offices for years about Buck getting a murderer to confess just by sitting at the table opposite him and not saying a word for four or five hours. Of course, the time got longer or shorter depending on who told the story, but it was always told as a sign of respect.

Buck let the moment of anger pass. "First of all, those clowns you sent to the mosque were walking all over a crime scene that my people were already working. Secondly, my meeting with Carl Miller this afternoon had nothing to do with you. For some reason, you are focused on forcing this crime onto the militias. I needed answers, so instead of just making shit up, I investigated, something you have forgotten how to do. Third, Agent Baxter is following up on a lead. You do remember what a lead is? Those pesky things that get in the way of supposition. Now, if you have a problem with any of that, I really don't care. We are interested in facts, not opinion, and we will continue to investigate these crimes as we investigate every crime."

Despite the cold temperature, sweat beads formed on Deputy Director Marshall's forehead, and steam was coming out from under his collar. His face was so red that Buck thought he was going to have a heart attack.

"Who the fuck do you think you're talking to? I've got twenty years in this job and hundreds of convictions. I'm running this investigation, and you don't get to question my methods. You may be some hotshot in your tiny little pool, but I'm the big fucking fish, and you will either get your shit in gear, or you are done."

Buck smiled. "You may be the big fucking fish, but your investigation stinks like a dead fish. You are stuck on one idea, that this is a militia thing, even though none of that makes sense, and you could care less about what anyone else thinks. My team will continue to investigate these crimes the way we always do. Since the FBI was only invited to this party to help with evidence gathering, perhaps it's you and your people that should bow out and go back to Washington and let us do our jobs."

"We'll see who's right once we start to interrogate the militia leaders we busted this morning," said Deputy Director Marshall. Buck looked at Marshall with confusion in his eyes. Marshall noted the surprise. "That's right, Agent Taylor. We have just concluded raids on six different locations while you were sleeping and having your people chasing their tails. We have your good friend Carl Miller in custody."

Buck wasn't listening to the rest. "Was anyone hurt in the raids?"

"What do you care? And yes, there were several injuries and one death amongst the militia people. If you must know, one of Carl Miller's guards, a Billy something, was killed when he drew down on our agents. By later today, we will have this all wrapped up."

Buck had heard enough. "You're a fucking idiot, Marshall. You have no idea how to run an investigation, and your incompetence has now gotten someone killed."

Deputy Director Marshall lost all control. "That's it, Taylor. You are off this investigation, and when I get through with you, I will have your badge, and I might still arrest you."

Buck laughed, and the other agents standing around looked stunned. "Two problems with what you just said. First, I don't work for you, so you don't get to throw me off anything. Keeping me out of the loop is the best thing you could do for me. At least I won't have to be embarrassed when the real truth is revealed. Second, you wouldn't know what to do with my badge if you did take it because only real investigators get to carry this badge, and you have already proven that you are not a real investigator."

Deputy Director Marshall was about to say something else when Buck turned and walked back into the hotel lobby. He could still hear Marshall yelling for him to come back as he stepped onto the elevator and headed to his room. He unclipped his phone.

"You there, sir?" asked Buck.

Director Jackson laughed. "He won't have to try to figure out how you feel about him. That's for sure."

A second voice came on the line. "Buck, it's Richard Kennedy." Buck was surprised that the governor was on the line at this time of the morning.

"Director Jackson woke me when this rampage started, and I'm glad he did," said the governor.

"How certain are you about these bombings not being a militia thing?"

"Sir, nothing is certain, but it just doesn't work. We have a theory we are looking at, and I have Agents Baxter and Webber in Denver right now chasing down leads. We believe this is the work of two different bombers with different agendas. When I spoke with Carl Miller, the militia leader, yesterday, he was surprised that they were being looked at. He swears they have no involvement, and my senses said he was telling the truth. We'll know more once I have a chance to talk to my team."

"Okay, Buck. As far as I'm concerned, this is still a state investigation, and you work for me. You keep running down your leads and keep Director Jackson in the loop."

Buck heard one line go dead. "You heard the man, Buck. Keep doing what you're doing. Feed information through me, and I will try to keep the FBI apprised. And stay away from Marshall. What went down in Avon tonight? The Avon police chief called me to tell me how grateful he was that you gave a potential major arrest to two of his officers."

Buck filled him in on the arrest and how it might be connected to the I-70 rapist.

"Great job, Buck. Keep Bax in the loop on the

rapist. Go get some sleep, and we'll talk in the morning."

Buck disconnected the call and called Bax. He was going to leave a message, but she answered on the second ring.

"Hey, Buck. What's up?"

"How did your meeting with Logan go? Does he know this O'Connor guy?"

"I think he lied through his teeth. I saw some tells while we talked that he knows more than he's saying. He's good, Buck, but his eyes gave him away. I was surprised that he would hold back information, since we are trying to solve his family's murder. It made me wonder if he is a step or two ahead of us."

"Okay. Tell me you guys aren't still at the Denver Court archives?"

"We are getting some good stuff, Buck. We didn't want to stop. Paul's taking a nap in the chair right now. We were able to find the juror list, and we've been going through the trial transcript. Some interesting things happened. As soon as we finish here, I will try to track down the original detective on the case. Paul's going to DPD to find out if they have the original murder book. We'll keep you posted."

Buck told her about his run-in with Deputy Director Marshall.

"No shit. He threw you off the case. He doesn't have the authority. Smart move, keeping your phone on. Bet the governor was livid."

Buck laughed. "It's all good. This will allow me to move around without their scrutiny. Hey, one more thing. We may have solved your I-70 rapist case; well, at least we have a strong suspect."

Buck told her about the incident at the bar. "When you get some time, touch base with Sergeant McKenzie and Officers Bloom and Sanchez. They were getting search warrants for his car and wherever he was staying. I got a strong feeling this is your guy."

"No problem, Buck. I'll call when I'm done here and see how their searches went. That is great news if he's our guy. A lot of women will sleep better tonight. I'll make sure the two officers get all the credit with an assist from CBI."

Buck disconnected the call and looked at his watch. If he went to sleep now, he'd just feel crappy in an hour or so. He decided, instead, to grab an early breakfast and organize his day.

Chapter Thirty-Six

Bax disconnected the call and looked at her watch. It was just about sunrise, but it was hard to tell in the basement of the Denver Court warehouse. It had been a productive night, and they had a lot of information that they would now have to sift through to figure out if any of it made sense based on the events of the past couple of days.

She woke Paul and filled him in on the conversation she'd had with Buck and about Buck being pulled off the case.

Paul laughed. "He called the deputy director of the FBI a fucking idiot? Guy must have really gotten under his skin. It was a smart move on his part to get the director on the line before he had the confrontation. I'm curious how the governor will react. He hates everything Washington."

"Great news on the rapist bust. That should free up some of your time. Buck is always in the right place at the right time to just fall over a crime."

"Yeah," said Bax. "I'll call Avon PD and follow up with them after we're done here."

Paul put the last of the files back in the banker's

box and set it on the rolling cart. He pushed the cart out of the way, sat at the table and finished his cold coffee. He looked at Bax.

"We got a lot done, now what?" he said.

Bax pulled up the notes she had been taking on her laptop. "The list of jurors will help if our theory is right. I emailed the list to George and Melanie. They have the list of all the families that were attacked on Christmas morning. Maybe they can find a connection between our bombing victims and the jurors."

"The trial," said Paul, "was pretty straightforward. But, after reading the transcript, the one question I had was what led the cops to Connor O'Connor in the first place? The evidence they presented at the beginning of the trial was pretty weak.

"They had O'Connor's criminal record," he said, "which started pretty early, but there wasn't anything significant in it after he got back from Ireland. The prosecution had almost nothing on O'Connor other than stories and speculation. Even the British government couldn't say for certain what crimes he had committed over there."

"He was never investigated for any specific crimes, let alone bombings, after he came back to this country. There was almost no evidence presented that could lead directly back to him. That's what I don't get. It's like he fell out of the sky and landed in the laps of the police."

Bax looked up. "Keeping with that same thought. How did they know about his relationship with Jacky Logan Jr., if he even had one? They must have known each other. Jacky Logan ran everything Irish in Denver. So, their paths would have had to cross at some point."

"Which brings us to the eight-hundred-pound gorilla in the room," said Paul. "If O'Connor worked for Jacky Logan, why would Logan turn on him? Logan Jr.'s testimony was damning, as was the testimony of Carly Ryan. It came out in cross that she was his girlfriend, but why did she turn on him? I thought in organizations like the Irish mob, friendships ran deep? Connor O'Connor was convicted by hearsay and innuendo. It will be interesting to get a look at the actual evidence if it still exists."

Bax thought for a minute. "We have the names of a couple of the detectives that worked the case. I'm gonna call a friend of mine. She works in Denver Homicide. Maybe she can put me in touch with one of the investigators. In the meantime, why don't you head over to DPD and see if the evidence from the case is still around."

Bax grabbed her phone and dialed a number from her contact list.

The phone rang a couple of times, and Bax was about to hang up when a voice came on the line. "Blackburn."

"Hey, Marcie, it's Bax. Hope I didn't wake you?"

"Hey, Bax. Been up for hours. It's even a little early for you."

"I'm in Denver working a case and wondered if you might have time to grab some breakfast. I need your help. Name the spot."

"I'm working a case behind Coors Field. Should be wrapped up in an hour or so. Hey, why don't you come by the scene? It'd be like college. We can grab breakfast after. There's a dynamite Mexican joint down the street. Best breakfast burritos in town. Your treat."

Bax laughed. "Okay, text me the address, and I'll see you in a few."

Bax hung up and helped Paul put the court files back in their proper place on the shelf. They picked up all the documents they had photocopied and put them in Paul's backpack.

"Call me when you're done at DPD, and we'll meet up to compare notes," she said.

Paul nodded, and they left the room and checked out with the guard at the desk. Bax's phone chimed, and she looked at the message. They headed for the elevator. Once outside the warehouse, they split up, and Bax headed to her Jeep. The sun was just coming up, and it looked like the clouds and snow showers were making way for a bluebird day.

Chapter Thirty-Seven

It was about a fifteen-minute drive from the warehouse to Coors Field. Bax parked her Jeep in the lot across the street from all the police activity, grabbed her backpack and slid out. She stepped up to the officer with the clipboard stationed at the barricade, presented her ID and asked for Detective Marcie Blackburn. Marcie was easy to spot in the crowd, and Bax spotted her before the officer pointed her out.

Marcie Blackburn was six feet tall and thin as a post, and she had an incredible head of dark auburn hair that glowed in the early morning sun. Friends since college, they had a lot in common, but their friendship had grown around running marathons and rock climbing. Both of which they excelled at.

Marcie spotted Bax at the crime scene tape and waved her over. The young officer lifted the tape, and Bax headed over.

"Hey, Bax. Welcome to my crime scene."

A voice came up behind her. "Our crime scene." A tall Hispanic male stepped up to Bax and Marcie and reached out his hand to Bax. "Detective Mike Ibarra. You must be Bax. Am I right?"

Bax nodded and shook his hand. Detective Mike Ibarra was about their age, with a full head of wavy black hair. He stood four inches over Marcie Blackburn. Bax, at five foot six, felt small standing next to them.

"Heard a lot about you," said Mike Ibarra. "Marcie's always bringing up your name. It's a pleasure to finally meet you."

"Nice to meet you as well," said Bax. "So, what are you guys working on?"

Marcie told Bax to follow her, and they walked towards one of the entrances into Coors Field. Propped up against a bronze statue of a baseball player was a body covered with a white sheet.

Marcie walked over, looked around to make sure no civilians were watching and pulled down the sheet. It was obvious from the start that this young man had been brutalized. His face was beaten to a pulp, both eyes were bloodied, and his nose appeared pushed to one side in an unnatural manner, but it was his chest that Bax was focused on.

Besides the black-and-blue marks all over his chest and arms, it looked like he had been burned in multiple places, and not with cigarettes. Whatever burned this poor fellow was hot enough to scorch huge patches of skin. This guy had been tortured.

Bax moved around to the side and looked at the blood coming out of his left ear. It was cold enough that most of the blood on the body had hardened.

Bax looked up at Marcie. "Twenty-two?"

Marcie nodded. "That's our guess, the coup de grâce. The lab will let us know for sure, but it looks like someone put this poor guy out of his misery. They sure did a number on him before that."

Bax looked down at his shoulder and spotted what looked like the edge of a tattoo. She asked Marcie for a glove, and she leaned the body slightly forward. The tattoo was a red seven, dripping blood, with two crossed swords penetrating it. She leaned the body back.

"You ever seen that tat?" asked Mike Ibarra. "We sent it to our gang unit to see if they could identify it."

Bax stood up and pulled off the glove. "They may not have it in their files. It's a Seventh Brigade tat. Small militia group based out of the Colorado–Utah border around Nucla."

"Wonder what he was doing here that got him into trouble?" asked Marcie.

Bax shook her head. "Doesn't look like your typical street crime. Any idea who he is and why someone would go through this much trouble?" She pointed to his chest. "This took a lot of time."

Marcie pulled the sheet back up and waved over the guys from the medical examiner's office. "Okay, fellas, he's all yours." They stepped away from the body.

"Guy's from your neck of the woods," said Mike Ibarra. He pulled a notebook from his pocket. "He had his driver's license in his pocket. Michael Perez. Lives on Valley Road in Nucla. We've got the office calling out that way to get someone to give us a hand."

"Nucla doesn't have a police department," said Bax. "Call the Montrose County sheriff. They have a substation in Nucla. They can help you out."

They stepped away as the body was being placed on the gurney.

"See, Mike, I told you she was good."

Bax just smiled, but something was nagging at her. "You guys mind if I run some background on this guy? I'd like to understand why he would come all the way to Denver to get himself popped."

"You think he's involved in something?" asked Marcie.

"Don't know, just some tingling."

Mike Ibarra handed her the evidence bag with the driver's license in it. She pulled out her phone, activated the camera and sent a text to Melanie in the office. She put her phone back in her pocket.

"Now," said Marcie. "How can we help you?"

Bax pulled out her phone and opened up a notebook app. "I need to find a couple of detectives from long ago." She looked at her notes. "Ivan Sharp and George Ramos."

Marcie looked at Mike. "Didn't Ivan die a couple of years ago?" she asked.

Mike Ibarra thought for a minute. "Yeah, I think you're right. Heart attack. They had a big funeral procession for him."

"I don't know the name George Ramos, but let me make a call. Why you looking for these guys?" asked Marcie.

"They investigated a bombing about forty-five years ago that might have some connection to the Christmas Day bombings," said Bax.

"Shit, Bax," said Marcie. "That's a long time to hold a grudge. You'll need to tell me more. Let's walk down the street for breakfast while I make the call."

Once they reached the restaurant, Bax and Mike

Ibarra grabbed a table while Marcie stayed outside talking on the phone. Marcie walked in just as the waitress was setting three cups of coffee on the table.

"Talked to Chief of D's Fletcher Grimes. Ramos retired about ten years ago. Moved to Sun City, Arizona. He still stays in touch with the chief. Grimes was going to give him a call and tell him to take your call. Now, tell us what's going on."

Chapter Thirty-Eight

Buck was just getting out of his Jeep when his phone rang. He always hated early morning phone calls, and when he looked at the number, he knew this one wasn't going to be good.

Buck answered. "Hey, Hank."

"Fuck, Buck. Are you trying to get yourself arrested or are you just out to make my life miserable?" asked Hank Clancy.

Hank Clancy was a deputy director with the FBI and oversaw the Denver Field Office and the seven states surrounding Colorado. He and Buck had been friends a long time, and Hank had been instrumental in helping Buck eliminate a Mexican drug cartel trying to set up shop in Durango, Colorado. That investigation led to one of the largest drug busts ever and helped put Hank Clancy on a fast track to his current position.

They had also worked together to bring down Alicia Hawkins. Alicia Hawkins was a serial killer. One of the best and most brutal serial killers ever, male or female. While in college, she'd found out that her grandfather had been a serial killer in Aspen, Colorado, in the early sixties. Buck had been instrumental in finding the bodies of his victims, fifteen in all, in an old mine and solving that crime, but Alicia had taken up his calling.

She was finally brought down by a team led by Hank and Buck while attempting to kill her sixteenth victim: a woman who had escaped being Alicia's grandfather's sixteenth victim—by accident, literally. An accident that had crippled her grandfather and ended his reign of terror. Alicia had planned to kill that same woman to honor her grandfather and cement both their legacies. It never came to pass, thanks to Buck, Hank and their team.

Buck didn't trust many people from the government, but he trusted Hank. And it came as no surprise that Hank would be calling this early in the morning.

"Guess you heard, huh," said Buck.

"Heard. I'm lucky I'll ever be able to hear another thing. I've had the director of the FBI screaming in one ear and the United States Attorney General screaming in the other. Your governor woke them both up this morning and blasted them. What the hell happened?"

"This guy Marshall came in and ran roughshod over everyone. His investigation is a farce. He's so completely focused on this being militia that he can't see that it's not. So, he tried to intimidate me this morning, and I told him where to stick it," said Buck.

"Did you really call him a fucking idiot?"

"Yeah," said Buck. "He kind of got under my skin, so I let him have it. That's when he threw me off the case, which was okay by me. This is still a state case, and our people are working on real evidence, not speculation."

"Well, your governor threatened to throw the entire FBI out of Colorado. We all know he can't do that, but he was pissed. How did he know what happened?"

"Yeah, that. When Marshall called me down to confront me, I dialed the director and left the phone on my belt. Once he heard what was going down, he woke up the governor and got him to listen in. Hank, this is crazy. Nothing points to any militia groups or white supremacists or anything like that. We think there are two bombers operating here; one of the events was personal, and one was political. We are looking into this information as we speak."

"Look, Buck. There's more at play here than what you are aware of."

"What is Marshall's problem, Hank? Why the fixation with militias? It feels like a vendetta."

Hank was quiet for a minute. "Between you and me, right? No one else."

"Of course. What's up?"

Hank was quiet again like he was trying to figure out how to properly word what he was about to say.

"Marshall was a special agent based in Memphis about ten years back. He was working some local militia activities and thought he had enough to round up all the local militia guys. Well, it went bad, and three FBI agents were killed."

"I remember reading about that. It was a bad day for the FBI," said Buck.

"What you didn't read," said Hank, "was that one of the agents killed that day was Marshall's fiancée. She was in hostage rescue and was first in line when the bullets started flying. Marshall has been on a vendetta ever since to squash the militias. This is one of those opportunities."

"So, he brought his personal baggage to Colorado. Why would your boss let that happen?" asked Buck.

"He runs a special unit that handles high-profile crimes. Incredible track record. These bombings are like a blessing in disguise. Might even be a little redemption for getting his fiancée killed."

"He's gonna screw this up," said Buck. "One person is already dead because of these raids he pulled last night. I don't want any of our people to die in the cross fire."

"The attorney general has asked me to keep an eye on this investigation," said Hank, "but Marshall is still running the show. I'll do what I can to keep him off your back, but you need to keep me in the loop. Marshall is not going to like this one bit, and I can't tell you how he's gonna react, but if I were you, I'd steer clear of him. You are not his favorite person right now."

"Okay, Hank. I'll play nice, but only to a point. I will try to keep you up to date on where we are, but you need to rein him in."

Hank clicked off, and Buck stood next to his car for a minute. He hated to see Hank get caught up in this kind of political bullshit. He would do his best to minimize any blowback on Hank, but he still had an investigation to run. He headed into the restaurant and ordered breakfast.

Chapter Thirty-Nine

Bax left the restaurant after picking up the tab for breakfast and walked to her Jeep. She slid in, pulled out her phone and dialed the Arizona number Marcie Blackburn had texted to her. She looked at her watch and hoped it wasn't too early. She could never remember which time zone Arizona was in at this time of the year, Mountain or Pacific.

The phone was answered by a man with a deep voice. "Ramos," he said.

"Hi, Detective Ramos, my name is Ashley Baxter, and I'm with the Colorado Bureau of Investigation. I hope it's not too early to call."

"Never too early to talk to a fellow investigator, but you can drop the detective part; George or Ramos is fine. What can I do for you, Agent Baxter? Fletcher wasn't too clear on what you were looking for."

"Please call me Bax. We're looking into an old case of yours. The Connor O'Connor bombing. Do you remember it?"

"Absolutely," said Ramos. "His bomb was meant for a reporter, and instead, he blew up the guy's wife and daughter. Sad case. But what's your interest now, after all these years?"

"O'Connor was released just before Thanksgiving."

George Ramos interrupted. "Wait a minute. Did you say O'Connor was released? He got two consecutive life sentences without parole. How did he get out?"

"Compassionate release. He was diagnosed with stage four pancreatic cancer. The doctors gave him a couple of weeks to live. I take it you weren't told?"

"Hell, no, I wasn't told. Pardon my French. That weak-ass liberal governor have something to do with that? Never liked that guy."

"No," said Bax. "It was one of those do-gooder organizations trying to right perceived wrongs."

George Ramos was quiet for a minute. "Okay, well, you didn't call to listen to an old man rant. How can I help you?"

"We read through the trial transcript, but we came away with more questions than answers. It didn't look to us like the prosecutor presented a lot of hard evidence. More like O'Connor was convicted on personal testimony."

"You're right about that, Bax. We had almost nothing on O'Connor. There was nothing that would have put him on our radar. Lots of stories and innuendo, but no one ever connected him to a crime."

"So, what tipped you to him?" asked Bax.

"We got an anonymous tip from someone saying he was the bomber and that he was staying in a flophouse off Lincoln Street in Five Points. So, we put together a team and hit the place."

"What about evidence?"

"That was a high-profile case. Everybody from the mayor and the city council all the way to the governor were on our backs. No one cared about evidence, only about an arrest."

"When the DA decided to pursue the case, we told him there was nothing except that phone call linking O'Connor to the bombings. He didn't care. He told us he had a couple of surprise witnesses."

"Jacky Logan Jr. and some woman named Carly Ryan," said Bax.

There was almost a sadness in George Ramos's voice. "Yeah. I guess the deal was that Jacky would testify against him, and he was free to keep running his businesses."

"Did they know each other, Jacky Logan Jr. and O'Connor?"

George Ramos laughed. "Those two were like brothers. They grew up together, and O'Connor worked as Logan Sr.'s enforcer. My partner and I were stunned when they called Jacky Jr. as a witness. Never saw a situation like that, one friend turning on the other. Logan provided the prosecutors with everything he needed. Evidence we never uncovered during the investigation."

"That's incredible," said Bax. "And no one questioned it, not even O'Connor's attorney?"

"O'Connor's attorney sat there and kept the seat warm. I remember at one point during another mob guy's testimony, the judge had to ask O'Connor's attorney if he was going to object. The guy was a waste of time. O'Connor would have been better off representing himself."

"Do you think money changed hands?"

"As they say today," said George Ramos, "that's above my pay grade. We never got a taste, but . . ." He stopped talking for a minute, and Bax thought she might have lost him.

"George, what about the woman who testified against O'Connor?"

"Carly Ryan, boy, she was a real piece of work.

Testified that she watched O'Connor build the bomb on her kitchen table. Destroyed his alibi. If Jacky Logan set him up, which was the speculation around the cop shop, and Jacky Jr. testified against him, then it was Carly who drove the final nail in his coffin."

"How did Carly Ryan know O'Connor?"

"She was his girlfriend. They were supposed to get married, but it never happened. Did you know that she married Jacky Logan Jr. a month after the trial ended?"

Bax was stunned. She finally gathered herself. "His girlfriend testified against him and then married his best friend, who also testified against him. No wonder O'Connor came out looking for revenge."

"What revenge?" asked George Ramos. "You said they let him out with stage four cancer. My dad had stage four liver cancer. You don't recover from that."

Bax told him about the Christmas morning bombings, their speculation that O'Connor was the bomber and how Jacky Logan III had lied to her about knowing him.

When she stopped talking, George Ramos was quiet. "I heard about the bombings but had no idea O'Connor might be involved, but you're on the right track with the revenge thing. Seems like Jacky Logan Jr. was the center of things. Man, imagine being O'Connor sitting in jail all those years thinking you were going to die there, without ever confronting Logan, and then getting the call that you were being released. Must have made his day."

"One more question, George. Did O'Connor have family in Denver or anywhere else in Colorado?"

"All he had was his mom. They lived in Five Points, just down the street from the bar. She died a few years back, and last I heard, some developer was going to tear down the house and several others and build fancy apartments."

"George. You've been a huge help. I can't thank you enough."

"No problem, Bax, it was nice talking about the old days; brought out some unpleasant memories too, but that's okay. Listen, you find that SOB, give me a call and let me know how things go down."

"You got it, George."

Bax disconnected the call and sat back in her seat. She thought about Carly and Jacky Jr. testifying, and the revenge thing became so much more real. A lot more real than the militia.

Her phone chimed, and she looked at the

reminder. She was expected to be on the FBI briefing call in ten minutes. Just enough time to get her head together.

Chapter Forty

"All right, settle down, people. We've made some real progress in the last twenty-four hours, so let's get to it."

Deputy Director Felix Marshall sat at the head of a large table surrounded by a team of FBI special agents. Bax was sitting in her car, as were many others who were involved in the case.

"Last night and early this morning, we raided the homes and offices of several members of various militia groups. The arrests went off without a hitch, and we are now interviewing those individuals. Once we finish with those interviews, we are expecting there to be many more arrests made.

"We also received word a few minutes ago that our lab in Washington was able to find a usable fingerprint on the package of plastic explosive from the unexploded bomb. That print belonged to one Michael Perez, a known member of a radical militia group known as the Seventh Brigade."

Bax was barely listening when she heard the name Michael Perez come out of Marshall's mouth. Was it possible? She set down the file she was reading and listened more closely.

Marshall was still talking. "We have an FBI SWAT team enroute to Nucla, Colorado, to arrest Mr. Perez, and we are working on his known associates in the Seventh Brigade. Mr. Perez spent several years in Afghanistan working with an army EOD team. He knows his way around a bomb, and we are certain he will lead us to the person who set this whole thing in motion."

Bax pushed the button on her screen to raise her hand.

"We have a question from Agent Baxter of the CBI. Go ahead, Agent Baxter."

"Would this Michael Perez be the same Michael Perez from Nucla who is in the Denver morgue?"

Marshall stumbled for a second. "I am not sure what you are talking about, Agent Baxter. Where did you get this information from?"

"I was at a crime scene this morning of a man who was tortured to death, and that man's name was Michael Perez, and he resides in Nucla, Colorado. Was wondering if it was the same guy?"

There was a mad scramble, and Bax could hear chairs around the table being moved and people leaving the meeting.

"We'll get back to you on that, Agent Baxter. We

will reconvene this meeting this afternoon at four p.m."

The screen went dead, and Bax smiled. Marshall looked so completely flustered that he didn't know where to go first, but she figured he was in the process of calling back the FBI SWAT team. She felt sorry for the people on his team who were supposed to liaise with the DPD. Someone was going to get blasted. She turned off her laptop and called Paul.

Chapter Forty-One

Buck spent the morning working out of the corner booth in the restaurant. First he completed filling out information from the past two days in the digital case file and made sure to include a detailed report of his conversation with Carl Miller. Then he created a separate document detailing his run-in with FBI Deputy Director Marshall. That document he sent to Director Jackson.

He read through Bax's interview with Jacky Logan III and came away with the same feeling she had. He was hiding something. Bax was right; his responses were odd. They were trying to find his family's killer, and he was cooperative, but only to a point. Buck agreed that Logan was working on something, and he was ahead of them.

Buck's computer chimed with an incoming message that a new file had been uploaded to the investigation file. He clicked on the tab and opened the latest document from Bax. He smiled.

The document contained information from her visit to the crime scene with Denver Detectives Blackburn and Ibarra. The part that made him smile was her note about the FBI conference call this morning and Marshall's reaction when she'd asked the question about Michael Perez. The deputy director appeared to be a little light on information. It must be embarrassing when you have to call and abort a SWAT mission because the person you were going to arrest is dead. Especially one where the end result would help prove your theory.

Buck pulled out his phone, scrolled through his contacts and called Chase Goodley, the Montrose County sheriff.

"Buck Taylor. Today is just full of surprises. What can I do for you?"

"I take it you heard about the aborted FBI raid in Nucla?" asked Buck.

"Yeah," said Chase Goodley. "Nice to find out about it after it was supposed to happen. I do hate the FBI, sometimes. So, what's your interest? This got something to do with the Christmas bombings?"

"It might have," said Buck. "What can you tell me about this Michael Perez?"

"Not much to tell. He keeps his nose mostly clean. Works for Sandoval Earthworks as a blaster. He spent time with the army overseas, doing the same thing. Good kid. Gets a little rowdy come payday, but nothing more than blowing off steam."

"Okay. Now tell me about the Seventh Brigade," said Buck.

Chase Goodley hesitated for a minute. "What do you want me to tell you, Buck? It's a bunch of guys from the area, and every couple of weeks, they dress up like they're in the special forces and head out into the canyons and shoot at trees and an occasional rabbit or prairie dog. They show up in town for parades and scream about the government ruining our lives and people trying to take their guns. The usual shit."

"The FBI thinks Perez was selling plastic explosives to the militias," said Buck. "They found his print on a brick of C-4 from a bomb that didn't go off. You think that's true?"

"There have been rumors," said Chase Goodley. "We've never been able to substantiate those rumors. Supposedly, there was a report filed that Sandoval's explosives inventory is light. They have guys over there right now doing another inventory, and our friends from the FBI showed up after the SWAT guys left town to watch the proceedings. They are also going through Perez's house."

"Okay, Chase," said Buck. "Are those guys the kind of people that would set off a bunch of bombs on Christmas morning?"

"In all honesty, Buck, most of them are dumber

than a box of rocks. They don't mind yelling about the government and shooting at rocks, but as far as bombing a bunch of women and children, I just don't see it."

"Thanks, Chase. And make sure you cooperate with the FBI."

Chase laughed, and Buck disconnected the call. He entered a transcript of the conversation into the investigation file.

He checked the investigation file to see if Bax had uploaded any information on her call with the original detective on the O'Connor case, but she hadn't entered anything yet. So he opened up her notes from the courthouse search and started reading the trial transcript.

The reading was slow going, and for a major trial, there was little hard evidence presented. The trial transcript was important, but what he was looking for was the list of jurors, which he found in the contact list. He looked over the list. There were a few names on the list similar to those on the bombing victims list. They would need to dig deeper.

Buck opened the evidence list, and to say he was stunned would be an understatement. Listed in the evidence log were O'Connor's clothes from the night he was arrested, although Buck couldn't find any reference to any lab tests having been done on the clothes to look for explosive residue.

There was some wire and pipe listed that the detectives had found where he was arrested. Those materials were similar to the wire and pipe used in the bomb. In addition, there was a bank statement showing that someone had deposited ten thousand dollars in his mother's checking account the day of the bombing. Buck sat back and scratched his head.

He wondered how they'd managed to convict this man of anything, let alone a bombing, and he was looking forward to seeing what the original detective had to say about the investigation. To Buck, it looked like no investigation had taken place.

He closed his laptop, took a sip of his Coke and picked up the menu. He called the waitress over and ordered a cheeseburger and fries and sat quietly thinking about everything he had read so far today.

His moment of quiet was interrupted by a thought, and he pulled out his phone and dialed George Peterman at the CBI office in Grand Junction, Colorado.

"Hey, Buck. We were about to call you. Heard you got into a tussle with the head honcho at the FBI. Good for you, because so far, they haven't been much help at all."

"Hi, George. Yeah, I am definitely off Marshall's Christmas card list. Hey, a couple of things. How did you make out running the victims' names for commonalities? Anything pop?"

"That's why we were going to call you. We ran their names through every database we have, and we came up with no connections. From what we can tell, none of these people have anything in common.

"That's what I meant about the FBI's lack of cooperation. We sent them the list as well, even though they already had it, but they haven't gotten back to us yet or shared any data, and we have to believe they are all over it, just like we are. Melanie called them this morning first thing, and they are still working on it. We were going to see if you could push them to get moving, but then we heard that was probably out of the question."

Buck laughed. "Yeah, I don't think they'll be taking my call anytime soon, but that's why I'm calling you."

Buck told George about the possible O'Connor connection and the trial. "Bax posted a list of the jurors from that trial. Just a quick read, and I recognize one or two last names as being similar to the bombing victims. Dig into those names and compare them to the victims' names and let's see if anything makes sense."

"You got it, Buck. Anything else?"

"Yes. Run a background check on Sandoval Earthworks. They're an excavation company out of Nucla. Find out who owns the company and take it as far as you can."

"You looking for anything in particular?" asked George.

"Not sure." Buck told him about Michael Perez and both his connection to the unexploded bomb and the fact that he was dead in Denver.

"Might be nothing there, but let's find out."

"Bax asked us to run a background check on Perez earlier this morning. Melanie's working on that now," said George.

"Thanks, George. Get back to me when you have something."

Buck disconnected the call and dug into his lunch. He felt like they were making progress on the individual bombings, but the mosque bombing was still an empty hole.

Chapter Forty-Two

Paul sat in the waiting area outside the Denver Police Department evidence archives. He'd known it would take a while to find the evidence, but he'd had no idea it would take as long as it did to get through the administrative portion.

He had presented the evidence request to one of the clerks, who then took it to her immediate supervisor, who then took it to the clerk supervisor. She looked at the request form and looked at Paul like he had two heads. She had a hard time believing that Paul wanted evidence from forty-five years ago, and it wasn't a cold case.

The next stop was the sergeant who oversaw the evidence archives, then his lieutenant and on and on until it hit the desk of the division captain, who finally signed the form. Then the wait began while they tried to find the actual evidence.

While he waited, he talked to Bax, who filled him in on what he might find in the evidence box now that she had spoken with the original detective. They had both read the trial transcript, so he wasn't expecting much, but you never know what evidence might have been logged that wasn't presented at trial for one reason or another.

"Agent Webber," came a voice. He looked up to see the clerk waving to him. He walked over, and she hit the electronic lock, letting him into the secure area. He told Bax he would call her back when he finished looking at the evidence and disconnected the call. The clerk led him to a small table and pushed the rolling cart to the side. Paul lifted the banker's box off the cart and was surprised at how light the box was.

"Good luck," she said, and she walked away with her rolling cart.

Paul pulled out his phone, opened the camera and started the video. He said his name, the date and the time and then positioned the camera to see the entire box. He pulled a pocketknife out of his pocket and slit the evidence tape, which crumbled as he ran his knife through it. He looked at the log that was taped to the top of the box. Most of the names were illegible from age. He signed his name to the log and set the top aside.

The first thing he removed was the clothes that were taken from O'Connor during his arrest. Paul looked for any evidence that the clothes had been sent to a lab to be checked for residue. There was none.

The next bag contained a ball of thin red electrical wire. The seal on the bag was signed by Detective Ramos on the day of the arrest and had never been opened after that. The seal was yellow with age.

The third bag contained a nine-inch piece of one-and-a-half-inch-thick steel pipe threaded at both ends. There were no threaded steel caps in the bag.

The next item contained a deposit slip for ten thousand dollars from a now-defunct bank. The slip was dated the day of the bombing.

The last item was a journal with a black leather cover and yellowing pages. The evidence slip was signed by Detective Ramos and dated a year after the bombing. Paul figured they must have taken it out of the bag to read during the trial. Paul took a close-up of the sealed bag with his camera and slit the seal. He put on a pair of nitrile gloves and gently pulled the journal out of the evidence bag. The pages were turning to dust.

Paul was surprised to see that the first entry in the journal was dated two weeks before the bombing. It looked like O'Connor had bought a brand-new journal just to record his observations of the reporter. That was odd.

The pages that Paul was able to open were short on details. The first entry on the first page indicated that the reporter had left for work at eight a.m. There were no other entries that first day. The next couple of pages were the same kind of vague entries.

Paul also noticed that the writing looked feminine. The cursive penmanship was neat and flowing, similar to the way his wife wrote. He took several pictures of the pages he could open. He placed the journal back in the bag, stripped a piece of seal tape off the roll hanging over the desk and resealed the bag. He signed and dated it, placed it back in the box and placed the other bags on top. He resealed the banker's box and left it on the desk.

As he approached the evidence clerk, she looked up from her computer. "Find what you needed?" she asked.

Paul nodded. "More or less. Thanks for the help."

He left the evidence archives, pulled out his phone and called Bax. They agreed to meet for lunch at a small Chinese restaurant right near Denver police headquarters. It had been a frustrating morning.

Chapter Forty-Three

Buck finally vacated the corner booth in the restaurant and drove back to his hotel. He was hoping he could get a couple of hours' sleep in. His brain was fried. He grabbed a quick shower and was finishing the last of the warm bottle of Coke on the nightstand when his phone rang. He looked at the unknown number that flashed on his screen, and he almost let it go to voice mail. Almost, but not quite.

"Taylor."

"Good afternoon, Agent Taylor. My name is Morris Keller. I'm a professor of psychology at the University of Colorado in Boulder. I have some information that you might find helpful about the bombings that took place on Christmas Day."

Professor Morris Keller had a soft voice, and his manner of speaking was exact. Buck could sense that this man was highly intelligent.

"What can I do for you, Professor Keller?"

"I had spoken about this to a man at the Federal Bureau of Investigation office in Denver earlier today. I must say that the agent I spoke with was terribly rude and surly. I gave him a detailed explanation of my information, and he told me that though my information was appreciated, they had all the Unabomber sightings they needed. I find it troubling that he just dismissed me like I was some crazy person, and worse than that, he didn't take my information seriously. I do not believe the gentleman listened to what I was saying."

Buck was having trouble focusing. "What information did you attempt to give him, Professor?"

"I believe I know or at least have my suspicions about who wrote that dreadful manifesto that was posted all over the internet."

Buck was now wide awake. "Go ahead, Professor. I'm listening." He opened his laptop, connected it to his phone and opened the recording app.

"Thank you, Agent Taylor. It is rewarding to know that people can still be pleasant in this world. As I said, I am a psychology professor at CU Boulder. I am not some crazy person like the FBI would have you believe. I am also a practicing psychologist, most of my clients being students at the university. I tell you this so you will know that I am a serious person, and I debated long and hard before making the call to the FBI. But you don't need to know all that, do you? Anyway, out of sheer curiosity, I decided to read that god-awful manifesto. I thought there might be some good lecture material in it.

"Anyway, as I read it, I noticed wording and phrases that I had read or heard before. Things I was familiar with. I mentioned my discovery to a friend, who read some of what I had found, and he agreed with my assessment. He suggested I contact the FBI, which I did this morning.

"Since the response I received from the FBI was less than adequate, I spoke with the campus chief of police to see if he could give me any advice, and he gave me your name. So here we are."

"That's great, Professor; Chief Dan Winchell and I go way back. So why don't you tell me what you found."

"As I said, after reading the manifesto in its entirety, I am more convinced than ever that the person who wrote the manifesto is a former colleague of mine. I believe Professor Eldridge Parker is the author of that dreadful piece of dribble."

"This Professor Parker, does he still work at the university?" asked Buck.

"Eldridge was fired, must be going on ten or twelve years ago. He was a brilliant man. Had two PhDs before most of us had our master's degrees.

He was a brilliant theoretical physicist, and he also taught advanced chemistry."

"So, you two didn't work together during his tenure?"

"Oh, no. Different departments, but besides working at the university, we were also neighbors, along with several of our other coworkers. Eldridge was always a little odd, you know, smarter than everyone else, but we all got along. We used to do all the normal neighborhood things, like have neighborhood gatherings, barbecues, things like that. Our kids grew up together. For a time, it was all rather Mayberryish. At some point, Eldridge started to lose touch with reality. Eventually, it affected his marriage, friendships, job and, might I dare say, his mind. Over time, his rantings worsened until he was finally released from his contract at the university. That was the end of a long slide into oblivion."

"Professor, what about the manifesto reminded you of Eldridge Parker?"

"The theme of it, for one. I had, over the years, listened to many of those same rants coming from his backyard as he argued with no one. Yelling about the government taking over, immigrants and illegals taking our jobs. Those same themes are spread throughout the manifesto, which I would assume was written over a long time. But it was also the words and phrases.

"One phrase in particular stood out, and it was repeated over and over again. Functional governmental dysfunction syndrome. Eldridge used that phrase all the time as his mind started to shift. It's something he made up in his head about the way our government works. There were many other such examples."

"Professor, do you know what became of Eldridge Parker?"

"I am afraid I can't help you there, Agent Taylor. After his wife left him and took his children with her, he lost his job at the university, and then he lost his house. I'm afraid he was losing his mind the entire time. The first couple of years, I would see him sleeping in this old pickup truck on campus or showering in the gym. I reached out numerous times to see if I could do anything for him, but he always scurried off like a scared animal. After a time, he was just no longer there. I can't say for certain what happened to him. Never heard another word."

"Does his wife still live in the state? Or does he have any family around?"

"I believe he has a son who teaches at the university in Laramie, Wyoming. His wife passed away a few years back. The rest of the family, I have no idea. I hope this has been helpful, Agent Taylor, and if not, I appreciate the fact that you took the time to listen. In a way, I hope it isn't Eldridge behind these bombings, but I fear it might well be."

Buck wrote down the professor's contact information and thanked him for the call. He promised to keep in touch as the investigation proceeded. Buck hung up and let out a soft whistle. He played the recording of the conversation back a second time and was convinced that the professor might be onto something. Could Eldridge Parker be the Avon mosque bomber? He knew he wasn't going to get any sleep now.

Chapter Forty-Four

Buck got dressed, opened his laptop to the investigation file, attached his phone to the laptop and downloaded the conversation to the file. He picked up his phone and speed-dialed a number.

Max Clinton answered the phone the way she always did when Buck called. "Buck Taylor. How's my favorite cop?"

Dr. Maxine Clinton, Max to her friends, was the director of the State Crime Lab in Pueblo. She was a matronly woman in her late sixties, about five foot five with short gray hair. She probably thought she carried around an extra fifteen pounds she didn't need, but she was still a handsome woman.

Married for over forty years, Max had four children, eleven grandchildren and six great-grandchildren. She lived in a 150-year-old farmhouse in Pueblo, where she liked to tend her garden and sit on her porch and drink iced tea. She was also a bourbon girl and could easily drink most people under the table. She was loud and outspoken, but she knew her job.

Max had received her PhD in biology from the

University of Colorado and worked as a biology professor for twenty years before joining CBI and accepting the challenge of running the lab. Under her leadership, it had become one of the top crime labs in the country. She was a hard taskmaster, but she had a belief system that didn't allow for defeat. Her goal was to give the crime investigator, no matter which department or municipality they worked for, all the information they would need to solve any crime. She held that as a sacred obligation to the victims. She was incredibly dedicated, and her team at the lab practically worshipped her.

Buck would be included in that group. Many times, during a complicated investigation, it had been Max and her team that lit the spark that led to a breakthrough. Max was one of Buck's favorite people, and she felt the same way about him.

Max was Buck's first stop whenever he needed an expert opinion on some odd thing that might come up during an investigation. During one of his odder cases, Buck had been looking for information on sonic weapons—more to the point, infrasound weapons. Within a couple of hours of discussing this with Max, he'd found himself on the phone with a former government scientist that Max had gone to school with, who was able to give him the information he needed.

He always knew he could count on Max when

he was stuck. She was his sounding board, and he knew if he discussed anything about a case with her, it would stay right there.

"Hey, Max. I need some advice."

"That's why we're here. What can I help you with today?"

Buck told her about the call from Professor Morris Keller and his thoughts about the manifesto and its relationship to Professor Eldridge Parker.

"I don't remember Eldridge Parker from when I taught at CU," said Max, "but he sounds like someone with some serious problems. How can we help?"

"Is it possible to find other examples of Parker's writings? He must have written a lot of things while he was a professor. If we can, is there a way to compare those writings to the manifesto and document the findings?"

"Sure, Buck. That's easy. I will have one of the linguistics guys search the internet for his writings, and then we can run them through an editing program. We'll adjust the program to look for similar words and phrases and other commonalities. Depending on how much material is out there, it could take a couple of hours."

"A couple of hours is good, Max. I can work with that."

"Buck. The FBI is going to jump all over this once we post the findings. So you won't have a lot of time to work with it."

"That's all right, Max. Remember, we're on the same team." They both laughed.

"That's not what I heard. Anything else I can do for you?" asked Max.

"There is one other thing I'm curious about. Have you finished running the bomb residue from the mosque and the bomb materials from the unexploded bomb?"

"The FBI lab ran the unexploded material, but we compared the results to the material you sent over from the mosque. I can give you a lot of chemical information, but the bottom line is they are not the same material. The unexploded bomb was straight C-4. The material from the mosque was something we've never seen before. A very exotic mix of chemicals. Definitely something custom-made."

Max stopped for a minute. "Didn't you say that this Parker fella taught physics and chemistry?"

"Yeah, that's what Professor Keller told me. Do you think he mixed up his own bomb materials?"

"My guys have never seen the combination we got from the mosque residue, so yeah, it's a good possibility. Also, this combination is about ten times more powerful than C-4."

"Max, do you have any material that was attributed to the Mountain Bomber in the lab?"

"You think there's a connection?"

"I don't know, Max, but those cases over the last decade are still unsolved, and according to Professor Keller, it's been about a decade since Parker was terminated. Maybe he took up a new hobby after he left CU."

"Okay, Buck. I'll get the team on that right now. It would be interesting if there were similarities. He's been quiet for a couple of years. I wonder why now?"

"No idea, but I think we need to find out. Would you let me know when the FBI has a comparison to the materials they confiscated from Sandoval Earthworks, and let me know if that matches the other bombings and the unexploded material?"

"Will do, Buck. Call if you need anything."

She ended the call the way she always did. "You're a good man, Buck Taylor. God will watch over you. Stay safe."

Buck hadn't been to church since he'd received his confirmation, but he always appreciated Max's little blessing. It wasn't that he didn't believe in God. On the contrary, he wasn't sure what he really believed in. He didn't like organized religion, but he never held that against anyone.

A lot of people had prayed for his wife during the five years she fought metastatic breast cancer, but in the end, Lucy still died. Although he had been mad at first, he soon realized that to be angry at God, he first had to believe in God, and he could never get there.

He always felt there were forces in the world that he couldn't explain, and he always thanked the river spirits whenever he had a chance to do some fly-fishing. He didn't have a place for one God in his life, but he never held Max's beliefs against her. He always figured that it couldn't hurt if she believed he was worthy.

Chapter Forty-Five

Bax and Paul grabbed seats by the front window of the Golden Pagoda Chinese Restaurant, across the street from Denver police headquarters. They figured it must be good since there was a line of cops out the door waiting for takeout orders. So they ordered the lunch special and sipped the green tea that was placed on the table when they sat down.

Paul pulled out his laptop and opened the investigation file. "I don't get it, Bax. There is nothing in the evidence that should have convicted this guy. There is pretty much nothing in the evidence at all. What did the detective have to say?"

Bax took a sip of tea. "I got the impression he was as surprised as anyone that O'Connor was convicted. He and his partner didn't have O'Connor on their radar until the anonymous call came in. He mentioned that O'Connor and Jacky Logan Jr. were close friends, having grown up together. We knew Carly Ryan was O'Connor's girlfriend, but what surprised me was that she married Logan not long after the trial."

"Do you think Logan or one of his guys was the source of the anonymous phone call?" asked Paul.

The waitress came by with their lunch, and they stopped talking for a few minutes and dug into their food.

"I wondered the same thing," said Bax. "It's awfully convenient that the cops got the tip the night of the bombing. I wondered if someone, maybe Logan himself, was trying to distance himself from the crime. It wouldn't surprise me at all if Logan set the entire crime up, and when it went bad, he decided to get out from under it."

"But how do you turn a guy's girlfriend against him? That's a pretty ballsy move."

"Money, power, status. She ended up in a much better place than she would have with O'Connor. Then, of course, there's always the fourth motivator, threats."

"Well, whatever the motivator," said Paul. "It worked. She destroyed his entire defense." Paul pulled up the pictures from the journal found in O'Connor's room at the time of the arrest.

"Look at the handwriting and tell me if you think a man wrote that."

Bax leaned into the screen. "There's not much to go on, but the writing looks more feminine to me. What did you think when you first saw it?"

"I thought the same thing," said Paul. "I think

his girlfriend wrote it. If what we are saying is true, they had this guy buttoned up big-time." He showed Bax the pictures of the wire and the pipe.

"That stuff could have come from anywhere. I don't recall seeing anything about the police pulling prints off the material."

"That's because none of this stuff went to the lab," said Paul. "The seals were signed on the morning of the arrest, and no one ever opened the evidence again."

Bax was quiet for a minute. "I think O'Connor screwed up when he killed the wife and daughter instead of the reporter. This was a huge story at the time, and I think Logan set him up to take the fall, to keep the cops from looking too closely."

"And everyone went along because it was easier than doing it right," said Paul. "Do you think people got paid off?"

"Back in those days, that would not have been uncommon," said Bax. "That was the culture back then, and the Logans were a powerful family. Unfortunately, that doesn't help us locate O'Connor now."

"Yeah. He could be anywhere. I think it's time we put his face on the air. We don't have to be specific to the bombings, just a person of interest in a criminal investigation."

Bax pulled out her phone and sent a text to the director asking if he could get the information officer to send a current picture of O'Connor to all the media and social media outlets. She asked if they could say that he was a person of interest in an investigation. She put her phone away.

"So, what's the connection with this Michael Perez?" asked Paul. "You sure caught Marshall off guard. Bet he hates getting embarrassed in front of his people."

Bax laughed. "I didn't even mean to do that. It just came out. I'm probably on his shit list now too. I'm not sure there is a connection. It sounds like the guy was known to sell explosives to the Seventh Brigade, but I have no idea if it connects to O'Connor. It looks like it might reinforce the FBI theory that the militias are to blame."

"Shit, that's the last thing we need. Confirming a theory for the FBI. Hopefully, it will lead to something solid instead of just speculation. What doesn't make sense is how he ended up dead in Denver."

"Another sacrificial lamb," said Bax.

Paul nodded. "We better head towards Avon. We can hook up with Buck for dinner and see what he's been working on."

They each paid their bill and left a nice tip to

compensate for the fact that they spent so long sitting at the table. They headed for their Jeeps.

Chapter Forty-Six

Buck spent the afternoon going through everything Paul and Bax had uploaded into the investigation file. He was surprised, after reading the trial transcript for O'Connor and then looking at the evidence Paul uploaded, that O'Connor was ever convicted.

Bax's report from her conversation with Detective Ramos was even less enlightening, except for the part about Carly Ryan being O'Connor's girlfriend and later marrying Logan Jr. Buck hadn't expected that piece of information.

He sat back in the chair in his hotel room and thought for a minute: "None of this helps us find O'Connor, but it is a sure bet that Jacky Logan III lied to Bax, since the woman in question was his mother. It only makes sense that he would know she was once O'Connor's girlfriend, although secrets tend to run deep in those kinds of families."

Buck had just leaned back into his laptop when his phone rang. He checked the number and answered.

"Hi, George. What's going on?"

"Got some information for you. That list of names from Paul made a big difference. We have confirmed that eight of the families killed in the Christmas Day bombings either were or had family that had been on the O'Connor jury. So it looks like that theory may be more than a theory.

"Three of the victims of the bombings had been members of the jury. We were able to confirm that information. The other five required some digging. In those cases, the original jurors were all deceased, so we had to go through family. Not an easy task, since several of them were daughters who changed their names after they married. So when we include Jackson Logan Jr., that gives us nine of the thirteen as having some connection to the O'Connor trial."

"Great work, George. Are you still digging into the remaining four?"

"Yeah," said George. "Mel's still working on those. Now, the second reason for the call. Sandoval Earthworks. We dug about as far as we could, and we hit something unexpected. Sandoval is a front. We had to dig through five holding companies and partnerships before we found the actual owner.

"Sandoval Earthworks, Inc., is incorporated in Delaware. It is owned by Enrico Sandoval, et al. Sandoval Earthworks is a partnership with Sandoval Construction, a nationally registered woman-owned general contractor, owned by Pamela Sandoval, Enrico's wife.

"Sandoval Construction is a partnership between Pamela Sandoval, under the name PS Construction Limited, and American Resources, Inc., a company owned by Timothy Shaver. Shaver is the husband of Elena Sandoval, Pamela and Enrico's youngest daughter. American Resources, Inc., is in partnership with Consolidated Constructors. Consolidated Constructors holds the majority interest in all those companies. Here's where it gets interesting. Consolidated Constructors is solely owned by Denise Sandoval."

"So, what do we know about Denise Sandoval?" asked Buck.

"Besides being Enrico and Pamela's oldest daughter, Denise Sandoval's married name is Logan, as in, married to Jackson Logan III."

"Shit," said Buck. "That adds a new wrinkle. So now Michael Perez is not only linked to the militia, but he's also linked to the Logans."

"Yeah," said George. "But how does that fit into the theory that the bomber was after the Logans?"

Buck was silent. "That's the million-dollar question. Let's start digging into the Logans a little more. Maybe they are not only victims."

"You thinking they're involved somehow?" asked George.

"That's what we need to find out. Pull their financials, see what Jacky Jr. was worth, and where that all goes, and see if there's any insurance."

"Oldest reason for murder there ever was. Money," said George.

"Exactly. Maybe we're looking at this all wrong. Keep working it. Thanks, George."

Buck hung up, and his phone rang. He looked at the number. "Damn, Chase. I don't talk to you for years and then twice in one day. What's up?"

"Wasn't sure if you knew, but the FBI is here in force, rounding up all the members of the Seventh Brigade," said Montrose County Sheriff Chase Goodley.

"I had no idea," said Buck. "How many we talkin' about?"

"My guys are reporting that they have nine in custody and are still looking for six more."

"You guys involved?" asked Buck.

"Nope. Not a whisper they were here until they started kicking in doors."

"Okay, Chase. Let me know what happens. Thanks for the call."

Buck disconnected the call and sat back. He took a long sip of Coke from the warm bottle on the desk and closed his eyes. He hadn't slept in over twenty-four hours, and it was starting to get to him. He closed his eyes for just a minute and woke up two hours later, still in the same position in the chair.

He grabbed a quick shower and headed back to the restaurant. Bax and Paul should be there any minute, and they had a lot to discuss, considering the new information George and Melanie had dug up. The little bug in his brain was starting to move around. Not fast, but noticeable. Things were starting to move, but he wasn't sure where they were moving to.

Chapter Forty-Seven

Jacky III was sitting at the dinner table when the evening news came on. As it had been for the past three days, the lead story was the Christmas Day bombings. According to the news anchor, the FBI was in the process of rounding up several members of a militia group out of far western Colorado, called the Seventh Brigade.

The TV station's western slope reporter said that so far, eleven members of the militia were in custody, and they were closing in on several more. Jacky III smiled.

He got up to turn off the TV when a face came on the screen. The news anchor said, "The Colorado Bureau of Investigation is seeking the public's help in trying to locate this man, Connor O'Connor. Mr. O'Connor is a material witness in an ongoing investigation, and they would desperately like to talk with him. Mr. O'Connor was recently released from the state prison in Florence, where he had served over forty years of several life sentences, without parole, for a car bombing. The crime took the lives of the wife and daughter of a *Rocky Mountain News* investigative reporter. According to sources at the prison, he was granted a compassionate release. It is believed that Mr. O'Connor was suffering from stage four pancreatic cancer and only had a few weeks to live. If you have any information on the whereabouts of this man, please call the CBI hotline at 303-744-1177 or your local police department."

Jacky III stood there and stared at the picture on the screen. He thought back to the conversation he had had with the female CBI agent. She had asked him if he knew O'Connor, and he had told her he didn't. Now, he wondered if she didn't believe him.

Dee stepped up next to him. "That's not good," she said. Jacky III looked at her. She could see the concern in his eyes.

"What are we going to do?" she asked.

"I don't know. If they find him before we do, he could tell them a lot. I am going to have to deal with this personally."

"Oh, Jacky. I'm sorry it has come to this. What can I do to help?" she asked.

"Nothing. Let's just go about our business like nothing has happened, and I'll make the drive tomorrow and take care of this."

"Is there anyone who can help? I hate you making that drive all by yourself," she said.

Jacky III thought for a minute. "There is no one I can trust until it's over. No. This I need to do myself. It's better that way anyway. I'll leave first thing in the morning, and I'll be back before anyone knows I'm gone. Anyone asks you, tell them I needed some time off to grieve."

"Okay," she said. "Just be careful; there's a storm coming. Get home before the weather gets bad."

They walked back to the table and joined the kids for dinner. Jacky III had to fake his way through dinner because he had lost his appetite. He had hoped it wouldn't come to this, but now, he had no choice.

Jacky III had a restless night, and sleep didn't come until too late. He looked at the bedside clock, rolled over and kissed Dee on the cheek. He slid out of bed, took a quick shower and put on jeans and a flannel shirt. He made himself a thermos of coffee for the road and slid into his car.

The street was dark, and he looked both ways as he pulled out of the driveway and headed north towards I-70. He never spotted the older blue sedan that was parked on the shoulder a few houses away. The sedan waited until Jacky III passed and then pulled out and followed behind. The driver didn't need to get too close because the tracker was working perfectly, just like he'd expected. Jacky III had no idea he was being followed.

Chapter Forty-Eight

Bax and Paul found Buck seated in the back corner booth in the restaurant. He had his laptop open and was reviewing some notes when they slid into the booth.

"Hey, guys. Busy couple of days, huh?" asked Buck.

"Yeah," said Paul. "Things are starting to get interesting, and it looks more and more like the militia theory is going by the wayside."

The waitress came over and took their order and left to get their drinks. "Before we get started," said Bax. "I spoke with the two Avon officers and Sergeant McKenzie about the arrest you guys made in the bar. They found several bottles of Rohypnol in his car and hotel. They also found some souvenirs that have been identified by a couple of the victims. Max called me on the drive over, and his DNA is a match for the other samples we have. Looks like we can cross the I-70 rapist off our list of priorities. Nice catch, Buck."

"All in a day's work," said Buck with a big smile.

"Any blowback from your argument with Marshall?" asked Paul.

"No. I guess the governor unloaded on the attorney general and the director of the FBI. Of course, they, in turn, unloaded on Hank Clancy. That whole shit rolls downhill thing. Hank has taken an oversight position. Marshall now reports to him."

The waitress dropped off their drinks, and Buck took a big sip of his glass of Coke. Bax and Paul both had coffee.

"So, I read your reports," said Buck. "This guy O'Connor was convicted with nothing in the way of evidence. The more of the transcript I read, the more I think the fix was in. He was probably guilty anyway, but Jacky Logan Jr. and Carly Ryan cemented his conviction. Imagine thinking about that for over forty years."

"Yeah," said Bax, "but that still doesn't explain how he was able to put all this together from prison. I think he had help on the outside. My first thought was Jacky Logan III, but why kill his own family? Doesn't make sense."

"Then we're missing something," said Buck. "We need to go back over everything we know and try to find the hole."

The waitress set their plates on the table, and

everyone took a couple of minutes to dig into their meals. The conversation turned to lighter subjects like the storm predicted to hit the mountains the following day. It wasn't supposed to be a big storm—only a couple of inches of snow were predicted—but it could still slow things down in the investigation.

Paul set his fork on his empty plate. "If O'Connor is the bomber, then this sounds like revenge, but according to everything we've learned, he has no living family, so who would stand to gain?"

"Let's assume for a minute," said Buck, "that this is about revenge. Suppose Jacky Jr. and Carly were the real targets because they turned on him. What was his goal, and why kill all the jurors or their families too? All they did was listen to the testimony and convict him."

"Here's a crazy thought to consider," said Bax. "Carly Ryan was his girlfriend, and they were most likely planning a life together. Suppose he went after the jurors or their families because they took that away from him. With Carly's help."

Paul looked at her. "Makes as much sense as anything we've thought of so far, but where's the proof?"

"Until we find O'Connor, if he's still alive, all we can do is speculate," said Buck.

Bax's phone rang. She pulled it out and checked the number. "Hey, Marcie. What's up?"

"You still in town?" asked Marcie Blackburn.

"No, we're back in the mountains; why? What's going on?"

"Thought you might like to come to another crime scene. Someone did a broad daylight hit at a social club on South Broadway. District three homicide gave us a call."

"Why call me? Something interesting about this scene?" asked Bax.

"Yeah, you could say that," said Marcie. "The social club belongs to Tony Ryan. Ryan was a small-time rival of Jacky Logan Jr."

"Shit," said Bax. "Let me put you on speaker. Paul and Buck are with me."

Bax put the phone on speaker and turned down the volume so they wouldn't disturb the other diners.

"Marcie, this is Buck. Give us a rundown."

"Hey, Buck. Sure thing. Daylight hit. Happened

a few hours ago. Probably used a silencer since none of the neighboring shops heard anything. Five dead, three wounded. Two of those are critical—all double taps to the chest and then a head shot. There was no brass at the scene, so either revolver or pros. No witnesses, so far."

"Marcie, tell us about the connection to Logan," said Bax.

"Tony Ryan had a small operation, covering south Denver and a little bit in the suburbs. Mostly drugs and prostitution. There were rumors several years ago that he was trying to move into Jacky Logan Jr.'s protection racket. A couple of guys ended up getting beat up, but nothing like this. This was ballsy."

"Marcie," said Buck. "Can you ask the district three lead detective to send us the file once he gets it put together? We're not looking to steal his case, just curious."

"Will do, Buck. You guys have a good evening."

Bax disconnected the call. "That's interesting, an Irish mob hit. When was the last time you heard about something like that?"

Buck sat back in the seat. The frown said it all. They were missing something, but he felt like they were close. He pulled out his phone, looked through his contact list and dialed a number. Bax and Paul could hear the phone on the other end ringing, and then Buck hung up. They looked at him with questions in their eyes.

"I'll be right back," he said. He picked up his phone and headed for the door, just as his phone rang. He saw the words "Unknown Number" on the screen, stepped through the door and answered. He would have recognized Frank DiNardo's gruff voice anywhere.

Chapter Forty-Nine

Frank DiNardo was the "godfather" of the west. He had his fingers in everything—drugs, prostitution, gambling, and protection—that went on in Colorado and a good chunk of Utah and Wyoming. He was a cousin of Vincent Scapelli, the mafia boss who controlled everything from Kansas City to Salt Lake City, a guy who ruled his kingdom with an iron fist.

When Buck had first joined the CBI, he was assigned to a task force investigating the Scapelli crime family. It was a region-wide federal and local task force whose sole purpose was to break up the family. They never succeeded. Buck never got all the details, but one day they were running an investigation; the next, they were told to clear their desks and leave all the evidence and documents with the FBI. He wasn't sure what changed, but he never heard another word about the investigation. As far as he knew, no one associated with the Scapelli family ever went to jail due to that investigation.

Over the years, he encountered Frank DiNardo during several investigations, but there was never enough evidence to make a case stick. Which, frustrating as it was, actually helped Buck. Frank DiNardo could be as charming as he was ruthless, but for some reason Buck never understood, Frank had taken a liking to him. He was never a confidential informant, but over the years, Frank had reached out to Buck with information about potential crimes that were occurring around Colorado. Buck had also reached out to Frank when he needed a piece of information he couldn't get from another source. They were never friends, more like adversaries with a vested interest. Frank DiNardo knew enough about Buck that he understood that if Buck ever found enough evidence, he would arrest him in an instant. Still, Frank also knew that it was good business to pass along information to Buck that might get one of his rivals arrested.

Buck would have liked nothing better than to put Frank DiNardo in jail and throw away the key, and he always vowed he would. As far as Buck was concerned, this guy was as dirty and ruthless as they come, but he was also careful.

Frank DiNardo was also helpful since Buck had saved his son from getting killed during a previous investigation into a corrupt mountain town. Frank DiNardo owed him, and he always paid his debts.

"What do you need?" said the voice on the other end of the call.

"A thing went down at an Irish social club this afternoon. Is there more to come?"

"Looks like a little housecleaning to me. There's a new boss in town. People are a little on edge, but I think most of the scores have been settled."

"This new boss staking his claim?" asked Buck.

"I hear it might have been a revenge thing. It might have had something to do with one of the bombings the other day. Terrible thing, those bombings."

Buck could picture Frank DiNardo making the sign of the cross.

"Could the bombings be connected to this thing today?"

"Could be," said Frank DiNardo. "Maybe the kid wanted to move faster than the father allowed. Might have ruffled his feathers. Could be why the kid wasn't there when the bomb went off. The king is dead, long live the king kind of crap. Just speculation, you understand."

"Could there have been enough ruffled feathers that the kid set this whole thing in motion? Make it look like a revenge thing? It takes a special kind of person to do that to your own father," said Buck.

"I think it was business and a revenge thing—a

lot of rumors coming out of that side of the neighborhood. Like maybe people ain't who they think they are. You keep looking that way, and you're gonna find something."

"You want to elaborate?" asked Buck.

"Hey, I can't do all your work for you."

"Did this thing today go through your house?" asked Buck.

There was a moment of silence on the line. "It was nice talking to you. Have a good evening."

The line went dead, and Buck clipped his phone to his belt. Interesting conversation. Even though the conversation was cryptic, Buck had a sense of what was going on. The more he thought about it, the more he was convinced that everything that happened since the bombings was centered around Jacky Logan III. He just didn't understand why.

Buck walked back into the restaurant and slid into his seat. Paul and Bax looked at him suspiciously. "Was that your Italian friend?" asked Bax.

They all knew about Buck's relationship with Frank DiNardo, but no one ever talked about it.

Buck nodded. "There might have been something going on between Jacky III and Logan

Jr. Just not sure about the motivation, but it must have been strong if all that's true."

"Was your friend involved in today's situation?" asked Paul.

Buck looked at him and then at Bax. "No way of knowing. Anyway, we need to look closer at Jacky Logan III."

"Do you really believe he would kill his family and a bunch of other people because he was pissed at his father?" asked Bax.

"I think it's something we can't overlook. There has to be a reason. We just have to find it."

Buck's phone rang. He checked the number and clicked the green button. "Hey, Max."

"Buck Taylor. How's my favorite cop?" asked Max Clinton.

"Good, Max. What's up?"

"First, good call on checking Eldridge Parker's papers against the manifesto. My guys tell me there's a ninety-two percent chance that Parker wrote the manifesto. There are a lot of commonalities, but the thing that moved the needle was misspelled words. All the documents turned up similar misspellings."

"Then why not a higher percentage?" asked Buck.

"That's easy. It's not an exact science. The problem is how we change over the years. Most people stay pretty even throughout their lives. Similar views, pet peeves, etcetera. This guy, over the last decade or so, has lost touch with reality. His radicalization skews the results."

"Well, that's great, Max. That gives us the direction we didn't have. Now, we need to find this guy. How are you going to handle this information with the FBI?"

"How much time do you need?" she asked.

"That's hard to say. He's been eluding every agency in the country for the past decade. We need to get a solid lead, or our chances of finding him are slim to none," said Buck.

"I can give you twenty-four hours before I need to send the information to the FBI. We still have a few details we need to confirm to make sure we are accurate. Use that time wisely, Buck."

Buck thanked her, and she told him God would watch out for him. He put his phone on the table. "So, our bombings are not related?" asked Bax.

"Looks that way. Max said ninety-two percent certainty, but she can only give us twenty-four hours before letting the FBI know. Since there's not much we can do tonight, that doesn't give us a lot of time. So, how do we find someone we've been looking for, for a decade, in the next twenty-four hours?"

"Any luck with leads from the news story on Connor O'Connor?" asked Paul.

Bax pulled out her phone and dialed the CBI office in Denver. She spent a few minutes talking to one of the agents who was working the tip line. She disconnected the call.

"Some information coming into the tip line," she said, "but nothing so far that has panned out. They're following up on a couple of tips, so we may have something tomorrow."

"Okay," said Buck. "Let's put out an all-points bulletin to law enforcement in Colorado, Utah and Wyoming. See if you can find a picture of Parker and include his CV and add what little bit of a description we have of his truck. Let's also get his picture out to the media, same story, material witness in an investigation."

"I wish we had some idea if the guy even lives in the state," said Paul. "He could live anywhere. Your contact from CU said he thought Parker's son was a teacher in Laramie. I'm gonna go back to the hotel and spend some time trying to track him down."

"Good," said Buck. "Let's get some sleep and see if we get any good news on either guy in the morning."

They grabbed their backpacks, they each left a twenty on the table and they headed for their Jeeps. The clock was ticking, and they needed a break.

Chapter Fifty

Jacky III pulled into Montrose just a little before noon. He stopped for a quick bite to eat at a fast-food restaurant and then sat in his car and thought about how to handle what he knew he had to do. The picture of O'Connor on the news the night before gave him pause. He hoped that O'Connor would be dead by the time the cops fingered him for the bombings, but they'd moved faster than expected.

He wondered why the news didn't call him a suspect in the bombings, just a material witness in a CBI investigation. Odd that there was no mention of the FBI in the story either. He started to worry that something he might have said when he talked with that CBI agent might have tipped her off.

He finished his burger and fries and sat back for a minute. He yawned and realized how tired he was. That five-hour drive had taken a lot out of him, but he knew it needed to be done.

He headed for Main Street and found a parking space a block from his destination. He looked out the window at all the Christmas decorations lining the street. With the snowflakes coming down, it made for a pretty picture. "Maybe when I retire, I'll move to a little town like this," he said out loud. Retire, what a laugh. Right now, he just hoped to survive the next couple of weeks.

He reached under the seat and pulled out the twenty-two-caliber pistol. He reached into his backpack and pulled out the silencer. He dropped the silencer into his jacket pocket and put the pistol in the holster clipped to his belt. He slid out of the car, looked up and down the street and started walking back towards his destination.

The snow was coming down a little heavier, and he hoped it wouldn't get too bad. He hated driving in the mountains in the snow. He approached the door to the apartments above the storefronts, looked up and down the block, stepped into the small foyer and headed up the stairs.

Down the street, his shadow stood in the doorway of a small gift shop and watched his prey walk up the block to the small door between the real estate office and the bookstore. He watched him look both ways, and then he watched Jacky III enter the building.

He waited a few minutes, pulled up his collar against the ever-increasing snow and headed for the same door. He looked through the window in the door and stepped inside. He heard footsteps, and then a door closed just above his head. He headed up the stairs, his hand on his pistol.

He stopped in the hallway at the top of the stairs and listened. Hearing nothing, he moved to the apartment at the end of the hall, facing the street. He placed his ear against the door and listened. He could hear Jacky III talking to someone. He tried the doorknob, and it turned in his hand. He slowly opened the door and slid into the apartment.

Jacky III was kneeling next to a frail-looking older man lying crumpled on the floor. "Connor, can you hear me? It's Jacky. I'm gonna pick you up and put you on the bed."

He gently lifted the man and carried him to the bed. He covered him with a blanket, found a small hand towel on the nightstand and wiped the blood from O'Connor's lips.

"Water," said O'Connor, his voice so soft Jacky III had to get close to his lips to hear.

Jacky III picked up the glass from the nightstand and placed it against O'Connor's lips. He sipped a small amount, and some of it dribbled down to his neck. Jacky III used the rag to catch the dribble.

O'Connor opened his eyes and looked up. His face lit up in a strained smile. "Jacky. I prayed I would see you before the end."

"Can I get you something for the pain?" asked Jacky III.

"No," said O'Connor. "The oxy doesn't help anymore. It's getting close to the end." O'Connor's voice showed the strain, and tears formed in his eyes. "I don't want to die like this."

Jacky III wiped the tears from his face and struggled to find the words. "I wish we had had more time. I feel cheated that you didn't come into my life until just a short time ago."

O'Connor reached up and touched his cheek, his hand shaking. "It's okay, son. The visits at the prison and the realization that you were my son made the last few years tolerable. I wish I could have gotten to know my grandchildren."

Jacky III placed his head on O'Connor's shoulders, and the tears flowed like water. He stayed there for a while and then raised his head. He looked at O'Connor.

"The cops know about you. I tried to protect you, but they put your picture and name on the news."

O'Connor got a serious look on his face. He rested his hand on Jacky III's shoulder. "Then it's time for me to go. They can't know of your involvement."

"Are you sure?" said Jacky III. "I could stay a day or two until the end. Take care of you."

"No. You've done enough. You helped me get some of my dignity back, even if we're the only ones who know. I asked God for forgiveness last night for all the people I hurt. His forgiveness won't matter where I'm going, but I won't be alone. Your mom and Jacky will be there. That's some consolation."

He looked up at Jacky III. "I'm at peace with my life, Jacky. It's time to rest. You know what you have to do."

Jacky's hands shook as he pulled the silencer out of his pocket and screwed it on the pistol in his hand. He placed it on the pillow next to O'Connor. He looked the old man in the eyes.

"I'm so sorry, Dad. For all they put you through. I'll never forget you." He wiped the tears from O'Connor's eyes, picked up the pistol and held it next to his head. He kissed him on the cheek and tried to steady his hand, which wouldn't stop shaking.

He laid the pistol on the nightstand, picked up the second pillow from the bed and covered O'Connor's face. He pushed down, O'Connor struggled and within minutes it was over. He pushed the pillow away and looked at O'Connor. He looked at peace. Jacky wiped his tears, leaned down and placed his lips on O'Connor's head.

"I'm sorry, Dad." He kissed him on the forehead and then picked up the pistol.

"He's your fucking father!" yelled the voice from behind him.

Jacky III spun around and, without thinking, fired two rounds into the person standing in the entryway. Jimmy Sullivan stared in disbelief at the two holes in his shirt and slumped to the floor, blood turning his dark blue polo shirt darker as it seeped from the holes. He looked up at Jacky III.

Jacky III walked over and knelt next to Jimmy Sullivan. "Why?" said Jimmy.

Jacky III smiled. "You knew, you bastard, and you never said a word. You knew all along that Connor O'Connor was my father. Well, I found out a couple of years ago, and we've been plotting this revenge ever since."

"I could have helped you," said Jimmy, blood dripping from the corner of his mouth, pain in his eyes.

"Help me. That's a laugh. And then what? Be my right-hand man like you were for Jacky Jr. You were never gonna let me be the boss. It was only a matter of time before you turned on me: you and your buddies. Well, guess what, Jimmy. I win."

Jimmy Sullivan coughed, and blood spattered

the carpet next to him. Jacky III stood up, aimed the pistol and fired one shot into Jimmy's brain. The body twitched, and then his breathing stopped.

Jacky III hadn't expected anyone to follow him to Montrose, but this was okay. Saved him from having to kill Jimmy closer to home. He removed the silencer from the pistol and dropped it in his coat pocket and placed the pistol back in his holster. He looked one more time at Connor, made the sign of the cross and stepped into the hallway, pulling the door closed. He wiped the last of the tears from his eyes, and he headed back to his car for the long drive back to Denver.

Chapter Fifty-One

The ringing phone woke Buck from a much needed and sound sleep. He checked his watch. He always hated when calls came in this early. It was never good. He turned on the light on the nightstand and looked at the number on the phone. He clicked the green button.

"Glad I didn't wake you," said Hank Clancy.

"Nope. I was just lying here waiting for your call. What's got you up so early?"

"You were supposed to keep me posted on any leads."

Buck cut him off. "I will once we have anything actionable."

"Then what's this picture of this guy Connor O'Connor that's on every cable and internet news program?"

"That's just a person of interest in a case we're working on. We still have other crimes we're investigating, not just the bombings."

"Cut the shit, Buck. You're holding out on me. That was not part of the deal."

"First of all, I don't remember any kind of deal. I told you we would share what we have, when we have something, and not before. Second," said Buck. "Oh, fuck second. It's too god-damn early."

"Damn straight, it's too early. I've had people up all night chasing down information on this O'Connor guy. He's a fucking bomber, Buck, and you're gonna try to tell me that he's not related to our case. I have half a mind to send Marshall out to talk to you. See how you like that."

"All right, Hank. I give up. What do you want to know?"

"How did you guys stumble onto this guy?"

"If I tell you it was incredible investigative skills, would you let me go back to sleep?" said Buck.

"Cut the crap, Buck. Tell me how?"

Buck took a sip from the warm bottle of Coke on the nightstand and gathered his thoughts. "It was all luck. Paul interviewed the family that was supposed to die in the blast in Salida. They had no idea why they would have been targeted. It was pure luck that Paul noticed a picture on the fireplace mantel.

"It was from back in the seventies, and it showed a man holding a picture of the *Rocky Mountain News* with the heading, "Guilty." He asked the family about it, and it turned out that the woman's father was a naturalized citizen, and he was so proud of serving on a jury that he took the picture and had it framed. That jury was for the O'Connor bombing case."

"So, you guys just on a whim decided to pursue it?"

"That's what comes from having incredible investigative skills," said Buck. He laughed, and so did Hank.

"Okay, but for real. How?"

"Up to that point, we had nothing. It was a thread, and we started pulling. The more we looked into it, the more that thread led to O'Connor as the possible bomber, but we still aren't one hundred percent sure. That's why we're trying to find him. It's like he's fallen off the face of the earth."

"Okay, now what are you not telling me?"

"So far, we've been able to tie nine families to the trial. Eight jurors and Jacky Logan Jr."

"The Irish mobster?" said Hank.

"That's the one. It was his testimony that

convicted O'Connor because the evidence was nonexistent. Here's the kicker. O'Connor's girlfriend at the time also testified against him. She married Jacky Jr."

"Shit," said Hank, and then there was silence. Buck took another sip of Coke and waited.

"That's a strong motive for murder, but why kill the jurors?"

"That," said Buck, "is one of the many things we do not know."

"Our research says he was released because of pancreatic cancer. You think he's dead somewhere?"

"I wish I knew," said Buck. "The other thing I wish I knew is who on the outside helped him. No way he put this together, by himself, in prison."

"What about the mosque bombing, Buck. He do that one too?"

"We don't think so, and it wasn't the militia like Marshall thinks. We are looking at a potential person of interest, but we don't know enough about him."

"Who is he, Buck?"

Buck was hesitant. "The mosque bombing may

be connected to some other bombings. We're waiting on lab results to see if there's a connection."

Hank was quiet for a minute. "You're not talking about the Mountain Bomber?"

"We think there might be a connection. It's another thread we're pulling on."

"Fuck, Buck. How far ahead of us are you on this thread?"

"Like I said, Hank. Waiting on some lab work, then we'll have a better idea."

"I want to know the minute you have something, and don't hold out on me. I'm gonna have our people start to look at those old bombings as well. Go back to sleep."

Hank hung up, and Buck sat there and looked at the blank wall. The cat, as they say, was now out of the bag. Buck chuckled to himself, slid back under the covers and turned out the lights. He wasn't gonna get a lot more sleep.

Chapter Fifty-Two

The sun was just peeking through the crack between the drape panels when Buck's phone rang. He felt like he had just gotten back to sleep after talking with Hank. He turned on the light and answered his phone.

"Hi, Buck. Hope I didn't wake you," said Montrose Chief of Police Paul Sawyer.

"No, Paul. How ya been? It's been a while."

"I'm good, Buck. Never a dull moment. Listen, we may have a person of interest you're looking for."

"Go ahead, Paul, I'm listening."

"We saw on the news that you were looking for a guy named Connor O'Connor. We have a guy matches his description, but his name is Sean O'Leary. We ran his prints, and they come back to Connor O'Connor. Could be your guy."

"Where is this guy now, Paul?"

"An apartment building on Main Street. He's dead."

Buck was wide awake now. "Natural causes?"

"Won't know for sure until they get him on the table, but I'm doubtful."

"What's causing the doubt, Paul?"

"The guy who was lying on the floor across from your guy with the two bullet holes in his chest and the bullet hole in his forehead. It's possible we've got a double murder or a murder-suicide."

"Has anyone touched the scene?" asked Buck.

"We just got the call about forty minutes ago. Neighbor was supposed to drop off some groceries for O'Leary, and she found the bodies. I remembered the picture from the news last night and called you right away."

"Thanks. Do me a favor and lock up the scene. I'll get the forensic team from Grand Junction headed your way, and I'll get there as fast as I can."

Buck disconnected the call and speed-dialed Franklin Williams, the lead forensic tech. He gave Franklin the info and told him to coordinate with the chief of police and to call the forensic pathologist and the coroner.

Buck grabbed a quick shower, dressed and grabbed his backpack and his go bag. He dialed Bax and told her to meet him in the parking lot in ten minutes. He clipped on his badge and gun and headed out the door.

He ran into Paul in the lobby, and he filled him in. Paul was on his way up to the University of Wyoming in Laramie. He told Buck he had tracked down Eldridge Parker's son, and he was going to try to catch him before classes started. Buck told him to be careful, and Paul headed for his Jeep.

Bax was already in the parking lot when Buck got to his Jeep. He told her about the call from Hank and the call from Chief Sawyer.

"Why would someone want to kill O'Connor? He must have been on his last legs as it was," said Bax.

"Good question. Let's stop at the restaurant and grab a breakfast to go and hit the road."

They each slid into their Jeeps and headed out of the parking lot. The drive from Avon to Montrose was a shade over three hours. The snow got heavier as they approached Montrose, and by the time they arrived, there were five inches on the ground.

They turned off US Highway 50 onto Main Street. It was easy to find the address because the police department had the street in front of the building blocked off. Buck pulled to the curb, and Bax pulled in behind him. They grabbed their backpacks, and they walked to the crime scene tape.

They presented their IDs to the officer manning the tape and signed the form on the clipboard.

The staircase was tight as they made their way to the second floor and walked past several apartments before they arrived at the end unit. Chief Sawyer was standing just inside the door. He was dressed in a Tyvek suit and booties.

He stepped into the hall when he spotted Buck and Bax. They shook hands all around.

"Paul, good to see you."

"You too, guys. Franklin and his team are inside along with Dr. Kalishe."

Dr. Sima Kalishe was a forensic pathologist. She worked under contract to the Mesa County coroner, based in Grand Junction, Colorado, and several of the other counties in the area, including Montrose County.

Colorado was one of about a dozen states that still used the coroner system instead of the medical examiner system. The coroner for each jurisdiction was an elected official, and that person did not have to have any experience or even be a medical professional. Anyone could run for coroner.

The system was gradually evolving so that the coroner was required to complete a formal training program in death investigations, but it was a slow legislative process. Unlike in the medical examiner system, and since the coroner did not have to be a doctor, coroners would contract with a licensed forensic pathologist to handle any investigations that required an autopsy.

These forensic pathologists were highly trained doctors who split their time among several jurisdictions to keep costs down. Many forensic pathologists were current or former medical examiners, and several were retired, working part time to keep their hands in the game. Sima Kalishe, in Buck's opinion, was one of the best.

An officer standing nearby handed Buck and Bax a Tyvek suit and a pair of booties, and they put them on, leaving their backpacks and coats on the floor in the hall. They stepped into the small apartment.

The first thing they saw was the victim lying against the wall in the short hallway, covered with a sheet. Buck knelt and lowered the sheet. Bax stared for a few seconds.

"I've seen this guy before. He was leaving Jacky Logan III's house just as I was pulling up. Who is he?"

Sheriff Sawyer picked up a bag from the counter. The bag contained the victim's personal effects and what appeared to be a 9mm Glock 17. Visible, through the plastic, was his Colorado driver's license. She read the name. "James Sullivan, age seventy-one. Has an address in Lakewood, Colorado."

"He's a long way from home. I wonder what his role here was?" said Buck.

Buck covered the body and walked over to the foot of the bed. "Doc, how ya doing?"

Dr. Sima Kalishe handed a swab that she had just pressed against the victim's forehead to her assistant and stood up. Dr. Kalishe stood about five foot two. She had medium-dark skin and jet-black hair tied up in a bun, but her most striking feature was her blue eyes. Combined with her skin color, it made an interesting and possibly off-putting look. She turned towards Buck.

"Hi, Buck, Bax," she said. "Our victim was most likely smothered by this pillow." She pointed towards the pillow lying next to the body. "I'll know more once I get him on the table."

Bax walked up next to her and got close to the body. She was looking at the forehead. "Is that tears on his head?"

"Probably; I swabbed the entire forehead. It looks to me like someone leaned over and kissed the guy on the forehead. I've called for a special courier to get the sample to the crime lab today. I hope the weather doesn't delay them."

Bax looked at Buck and Sheriff Sawyer. "So, someone takes the time to murder a dying man and then leans over the body, dripping tears, and kisses his forehead. What the hell? And what's the deal with the guy on the floor?" She pointed to Connor O'Connor. "This guy didn't kill him," she said, pointing at James Sullivan, "and then smother himself."

Buck moved next to the bed, on the opposite side from Bax. He kept staring at the two bodies and thinking. Franklin walked over and stood at the foot of the bed.

"If I read this right," said Buck, "someone smothered this guy to keep him from talking. The picture we posted on the news spurred someone to action who couldn't wait for this guy to die from the cancer. The question is, who did our killer not want him talking to, us or that guy?" He pointed to James Sullivan.

"I think Mr. Sullivan here either came into the room unexpectedly or was already here, saw or heard something he shouldn't have and our killer shot him twice in the chest. Small-caliber wounds. Then walked over and put another one in his head. Gun was probably silenced."

He looked at Franklin. "Any of that line up with what you've seen so far?"

"I'd say that's a good guess. Now we just need to figure out who benefits from these two crimes?"

Bax looked up. "The common denominator is Jacky Logan III. We know he either knew or knew of O'Connor, and I'll bet this guy on the floor worked for him. I think we need to have another talk with Jacky Logan III."

Buck held up his hand. "Let's hold off on that until we get the DNA results back. Sima, can you make a note on the lab request to compare the DNA from the swab to the DNA of Jackson Logan Jr. and his wife? The lab should have those from the bombing. Bax, call the office and see if George or Melanie can run background on our friend on the floor."

"I've got a better idea," said Bax. She pulled out her phone and stepped into the hall.

Buck looked at Chief Sawyer. "Can you get a couple of your people to canvass the shops on this and the next block east and see if we spot anyone or anything suspicious? See if they can find any video?"

Chief Sawyer nodded and pulled his radio off his belt and followed Bax into the hall.

"Franklin," said Buck. "Anything initially that might help us here?"

"We already matched the prints on the doorknob to the guy on the floor. Also ran the serial number on the gun, and it's registered to him. Bought it several years ago. You were right about the head wound. There's some stippling around the wound—close shot. Since no one reported hearing a shot, I would bet he used a silencer. We're dusting the entire place for prints, but so far, most of the prints belong to the guy on the bed."

He held up two plastic evidence bags, one containing a bottle and about a dozen pills, the other a cell phone. "We'll get these tested, but I'm guessing it's street oxy. Unregulated and questionable quality, but if this guy was hurting, it might have been all he could get."

He walked towards the small kitchen and opened the trash can lid. "Lots of bloody towels, same thing in the bathroom. This guy was bleeding out. You think this guy pulled off the Christmas Day bombings?"

Buck smiled. "We think he was involved in the individual bombings, but not the mosque." He stepped away from Franklin and walked towards the door.

He stopped before he stepped into the hall. "Doc, any thoughts on the time of death?"

Dr. Kalishe was slipping out of her Tyvek jumpsuit. "They've been dead ten or twelve hours. I can give you a more exact time once we get them back to the morgue."

"Franklin, did Sullivan have a phone on him?"

"Yeah."

"Send both phones to George and Melanie, and let's see what they can find."

Franklin nodded, and Buck stepped into the hall.

Chapter Fifty-Three

Buck pulled out his phone and called Max Clinton. He gave her the rundown and asked her to do a quick DNA test and then compare that to Jacky Jr. and Carly Logan. He also asked her to see if they had Jacky Logan III's DNA on file and to compare that as well. She told him she would get back to him as fast as she got the samples.

He disconnected the call and walked over to Chief Sawyer. "Paul, who found the bodies?"

"Mrs. Endicott. She lives just down the hall."

He headed towards the woman's apartment with Bax and Buck following behind him. The door to the apartment was open, and a female police officer was sitting at the kitchen table whispering to Mrs. Endicott, a small woman with pink hair who wore jeans and an old, tattered sweater. She had a black-and-white cat sitting in her lap.

The officer stood up and told Mrs. Endicott that she'd be right outside if she needed her. Mrs. Endicott looked at Buck and Bax through tear-filled eyes. They sat down, and Chief Sawyer picked up an empty glass from the table, took it into the kitchen and filled it with water. He set it down in front of her and introduced Bax and Buck.

"Terrible thing," she said. "Reminded me of finding my late husband when he died eleven years ago. He died in bed, as well." She used the napkin in her hand to wipe away the tears.

"Mrs. Endicott," said Buck. "How long did Mr. O'Connor live here?"

She looked up. "Who? You mean Mr. O'Leary?"

Buck smiled. "Yes, ma'am."

"He moved in a couple of weeks ago, just before Thanksgiving. He was dying, you know. I didn't tell anyone. Not my business, but I couldn't help but notice. I picked up some groceries for him whenever I went out."

"How did you know he was dying?" asked Bax.

"Fifty-three years as a nurse. He never said anything, but I could tell. Saw enough death in my lifetime." She dabbed her eyes.

"Ma'am," said Buck. "Did you ever spend time getting to know him? Maybe sit down with him and talk?"

"No. I tried to get him to talk, but he was very private."

"Why did you go to his apartment this morning?" asked Buck.

"I was going to run to the store before the storm took hold. I walked down to see if he needed anything, and I knocked, but he didn't answer. I got a bit worried, so I tried the knob, and the door was unlocked, which was unusual. I walked in, and that's when I saw the man lying on the floor. There was nothing I could do for him, so I moved to the bed, but Sean was already gone. I went back to my apartment and dialed nine-one-one."

"Did Mr. O'Leary have any visitors besides you?"

"I don't think so." She stopped for a second, and Buck could see her mind working. "There was this one young fella. Good-looking lad. It was right after Sean moved in. It was odd. I passed him on the stairs when I was going down to check the mail, and he had a heavy backpack on. I heard him leave and looked out my door, and he didn't have the backpack on."

Buck pulled out his phone and stepped away from the table. Franklin answered.

"Did you guys find a backpack in the apartment?" asked Buck.

"Not yet, but we're not done. Why?"

Buck told him what Mrs. Endicott just said about the man with the backpack, and Franklin said they would look closer. He walked back into the apartment.

They spoke for a few more minutes, then Bax thanked Mrs. Endicott for her help, and they left the apartment. They were heading towards O'Connor's apartment when Franklin stepped out the door, followed by his team, Dr. Kalishe and her assistant.

"We need to clear the building and the stores below," said Franklin. "Found the backpack in a vent in the bedroom. There's two blocks of C-4 in the bag and a wire sticking out of the back. I just called Grand Junction to send the bomb squad."

Chief Sawyer pulled his radio off his belt and started barking orders as he headed down the stairs. Buck and the rest of the folks in the hall started knocking on doors and urging people to evacuate the building. He hated to do it with the snow flying, but they were better safe than sorry. C-4 was stable, but they didn't want to take any chances, in case the backpack was booby-trapped. They were already dealing with enough dead bodies.

Bax stopped Mrs. Endicott and held up her phone. "Is this the man you saw?" she asked.

Mrs. Endicott looked at the picture on the phone.

"Why, yes, dear. That's him." She headed down the stairs, and Bax turned and saw Buck looking at her.

She walked over to where Buck was helping an elderly man put his coat on. She held up her phone, so he could see the picture. "Michael Perez, the torture victim in Denver."

Buck looked at the picture. "And the explosives expert in Nucla. Shit."

Bax's phone rang, and she walked away from Buck. "Hey, Marcie. Whatcha got?"

Bax listened for a few minutes, then followed Buck down the stairs. By the time they got outside, Chief Sawyer had a school bus parked in front of the building, and they were loading the residents of the apartments into the bus to take them someplace warm. Several Montrose police officers were leading people out of the stores below the apartments, and the fire department was standing by at the end of the block. A crowd had gathered on the other side of the street to watch what was going on.

Bax caught up with Buck. "That was Marcie Blackburn. I called her and asked her to talk to someone in the Denver Police Department's organized crime unit. James Sullivan was Jacky Logan Jr.'s right-hand man. They'd been together as long as anyone could remember. Sullivan ran everything that happened on the street. That kept Logan's hands clean. He's got a lengthy record from his early years. Nothing recent, and he was a suspect in the 1998 murders at the Pony Lounge in Lakewood."

"I remember that case," said Buck. "The Pony was a Russian hangout. Seven or eight Russians were gunned down in broad daylight. The cops at the time thought it was a gang thing. During the late nineties, the Russian mob started trying to move into Denver. It didn't go over well."

"Sound familiar?" asked Bax. "The social club on South Broadway Marcie told me about."

"A lot of circumstantial evidence lining up against Jacky Logan III."

They stopped and watched as the Grand Junction Police Department bomb squad van pulled up in front of the apartments, and the team started off-loading gear and putting on bomb suits.

"We need a subpoena for Jacky Logan III's phone," said Buck. He pulled out his phone and speed-dialed a number. Bax nodded in agreement.

Chapter Fifty-Four

Paul pulled into the parking lot for the administrative building on the University of Wyoming campus and parked his Jeep. He grabbed his backpack and slid out of the Jeep. A young campus police officer was standing in front of the entrance. He spotted Paul and waved.

"Agent Webber, Officer Granite. Welcome to the University of Wyoming."

"Thanks, but call me Paul."

"Yes, sir, Paul. I'm Jerry. I have the information you need." He pulled a sheet of paper out of his shirt pocket and handed it to Paul. "Professor Parker has his first class at eleven today. We should find him in his office. I called and told him we would be stopping by. Shall we?"

Officer Granite headed out across a large field towards a building with a red tile roof. On the way, Paul gave the officer a quick debrief on what he was hoping to accomplish. Paul looked at the darkening clouds as they approached the building. The snow that was falling on most of the drive hadn't gotten to Laramie yet, but the wind was icy cold.

They walked up the steps and entered through the double doors. Officer Granite led him up the central flight of stairs and turned left down a long corridor. Halfway down the corridor, he stopped in front of a wooden door and knocked.

"Come in," came the voice from behind the door.

Officer Granite opened the door, and they walked into a small office, made even smaller by the piles of books that covered every flat surface. Paul looked at the bespectacled man behind the desk.

Professor William Parker was thin and frail-looking, sitting behind the oversized desk. He wore a heavy wool sweater, and his hair was pulled back in a ponytail that fell to the middle of his back.

The professor looked up. "Good morning, gentlemen. Pardon the mess. My students are working on a research project, and these books are part of their research. I asked them to go get coffee so we could talk. We have about half an hour. How can I help you?"

Paul introduced himself and sat in the only chair that wasn't covered with books. Officer Granite stood behind him. "Thank you for seeing me on such short notice, Professor. I know your time is short, so I'll get right to the point. We are trying to locate your father and were hoping you might be able to help."

The professor took off his glasses and rubbed the bridge of his nose. "This is going to be a short conversation, Agent Webber. I haven't seen nor spoken to my father in over twelve years. What has the crazy old fool done to draw the attention of the Colorado Bureau of Investigation?"

"He is wanted as a material witness for a crime that I wish I could get into but can't. The last time you saw him was when you and your mother and siblings left the family home?"

"Yes," said the professor. "I was sixteen."

"Can you tell me a little bit about him?" asked Paul.

The professor sat quietly for a minute. "We always knew he was brilliant, that was never the issue, but he started to lose his way about four years before we left. My mother tried to stick it out, but his ranting became intolerable, and she was afraid he might get violent. Anything would set him off, no matter the cause.

"The University of Colorado finally couldn't deal with it any longer, and they fired him. That situation only made matters worse until we packed up and left. After that, we never saw or heard from him again."

"Did he ever get violent with you or your mom?" asked Paul.

"Never physically, but verbally and emotionally. In some respects, I think that was harder on my mother than if he had beaten her. The scars from the abuse she suffered were never visible."

"Your father had doctorates in physics and chemistry. Do you know what his master's was in?"

"He had a master's in chemistry and in structural engineering. We always assumed he would become an engineer, but I don't think engineering kept his mind active. He needed bigger challenges, like the entire universe."

"Do you know where your father went after you guys moved out?"

"I heard," said the professor, "that he was living in his truck. He had an old Ford pickup truck that he just adored. Had it the last time I saw him."

"You wouldn't happen to remember the license plate number, would you?" asked Paul.

"Sorry, Agent Webber. I never paid that much attention."

"This may be an odd question, but do you ever remember your father tinkering with chemicals at home?"

Professor Parker looked at Paul. "My father blew out the back wall of our garage one Sunday morning. We lived in Boulder at the time, and he was doing something in the garage. Not sure what he mixed up, but the reaction almost killed him."

Professor Parker stopped talking and grinned. "Do you think my father was involved in the Christmas Day bombings?"

Paul thought about how to answer. "Your father is a person of interest because of his background and political opinions. Do you think he could have been a part of something like that?"

Professor Parker didn't hesitate. "Without a doubt. I don't know if he would have hurt all those families, but blowing up a mosque? That's easy. He hated religious people of any stripe, but Muslims were at the top of his list."

"He hated them that much?"

"Agent Webber, my father was the world's biggest bigot. He never once thought about how his words, or actions, could hurt people. In the end, he would do and say things that were flat-out embarrassing. Yes, I could see him blowing up a mosque."

Paul saw the professor look at his watch. "One last question, Professor. Did your dad own land anywhere, or a second home, fishing shack? Anything like that?"

"My dad would never be caught dead in the great outdoors. He hated all things related to the woods. Now, my uncle Mil—sorry, Milford Parker. He was my dad's older brother. Now, him, you couldn't keep out of the woods. Stayed that way right up until the day he died."

Professor Parker stopped talking and appeared deep in thought. "I do remember going camping once with Uncle Mil. He took us to a piece of land he owned. It had an old cabin on it. Dad hated every minute of the time we were there, but we had a lot of fun. Now, where was that?"

He thought for a few minutes, and Paul didn't interrupt. Professor Parker's eyes lit up. "I believe it was somewhere near Grand Lake. I'm not a hundred percent certain, but I remember we took a day trip into Rocky Mountain National Park. It's been a long time—Uncle Mil died about fifteen years ago, and to tell you the truth, neither one of us ever went to check on the property. As far as I know, it might have been sold for back taxes, because we never got a tax bill." He looked at his watch.

"Any chance your uncle's family might know the location?" asked Paul.

"Sorry. Uncle Mil was a bachelor. My sister and I were his only living relatives, and my sister was seven at the time of the camping trip." He checked his watch again.

"I hope I have been able to help. If I think of anything else, I will be certain to call."

Paul pulled a business card out of his pocket and set it on the corner of the desk. He thanked the professor, and he and Officer Granite headed back across campus. Snow flurries were just beginning to fall.

Paul thanked Officer Granite and slid into his Jeep. He started the engine to warm the inside and pulled out his phone and speed-dialed George at the office. He gave George the information about Uncle Milford's cabin and asked him to check property records in Grand County and the surrounding counties. Then he headed back to Avon.

On the way, he dialed Buck and filled him in on the conversation.

"Any chance Professor Parker could narrow the location down? Lot of land in Grand County, and not all of it is easy to get to."

"I was glad he could remember Grand County. That narrows our search a little. I've got George combing through property records. With any luck, Uncle Mil still owns the property."

"Good job, Paul. Be careful driving, and I'll fill you in on our adventure in the morning. Get some sleep."

Paul hung up and flipped on his wipers. The snow was wet, and he was hopeful he would get back to Avon before the roads iced over.

Chapter Fifty-Five

Jacky III made it home in time to grab a quick shower, throw his clothes in the washer and head for the funeral home for the viewing. By the time he and Dee arrived, the place was already packed to the doors. There was hardly room for the people with all the flowers that surrounded the eight caskets.

Because of the damage from the explosion, he'd had the funeral home cremate the remains, but he still liked the optics of a big show, so instead of placing the ashes in a couple of urns, he had the urns placed inside the caskets. The image was stirring, with the four small white children's caskets on the end. Eight caskets made quite the show.

Also, to keep up his image, he questioned all of his people concerning the whereabouts of Jimmy Sullivan.

"Tommy, where the fuck is Jimmy? People are starting to notice. This is a huge sign of disrespect, and I won't tolerate that from anyone. Let alone my top people. Find him."

Tommy O'Hara held up his hands. "We've been trying to find him all day, boss. His wife is frantic.

He left early this morning, and she hasn't heard from him either. It's like he fell off the face of the earth."

"You think the FBI nabbed him? They might be working a deal with him right now. Call around and see if anyone has him."

"You got it, boss. But you know Jimmy would never sell you out. He's not like that."

"We'll see," said Jacky III.

He walked away and joined his wife at the front of the room. He knelt in front of the caskets and said a silent prayer.

The viewing was only for the family and their closest friends, and even with that, the place was standing room only. Jacky was pleased, and he and Dee shook hands with everyone who had shown up, and by midnight, all the mourners were gone.

The next morning dawned cold and gloomy, with snow showers predicted. Dee made a final check of the kids to make sure everyone looked their best, and then they headed out the door and slid into the limousine for the short drive to St Agnes's Roman Catholic Church.

They entered the church, and Dee was surprised to see how many people were already in place. Jacky III stood on the side of the altar and watched as his friends and enemies entered the building. The church could hold five hundred people, and it was already standing room only.

Jacky III watched his enemies closely. They were all represented. The Italians, the Russians, the Mexicans, and the blacks. The word had gone out that, for today, the church and the cemetery were neutral territory. No weapons were allowed, anyone causing trouble would be dealt with swiftly and they should all smile for the FBI, who were outside the church taking pictures of everyone who arrived and logging license plate numbers. So far, those assembled were living up to the rules. They even intermingled with each other. This could be the start of a good thing, Jacky III thought to himself.

He was surprised when Frank DiNardo walked into the church, surrounded by four hard-looking men, and slid into a pew in the middle of the church. Jacky III had been hoping Frank would show. He wanted to have a conversation with him after the mass and the burial service.

Tommy O'Hara stepped up next to him. "Did you ever think you'd see all these guys in the same room and acting civil?"

Jacky shook his head.

Tommy said, "We checked with everyone we

could think of. No one has seen Jimmy. I don't know where else to look."

Jacky III was about to say something when the priest stepped up to the altar, and the funeral mass began. All the flowers from the funeral home had been delivered to the church, and it looked like the number of flowers had doubled. The altar almost disappeared under all the flowers, and Jacky III couldn't have been prouder.

Jacky Logan Jr. had been extremely popular and had been a big promoter of the city and its various causes. His generosity was what brought out the mayor of Denver, several city councilpersons, entertainers, sports figures, politicians and businessmen and women from all over the state. It was an amazing turnout, and because of all the celebrities and because Jacky III had been targeted, security was tight. Numerous Denver police officers were securing the outside of the church and moving about inside.

The ceremony lasted about an hour, and Jacky III's eulogy brought everyone to tears. When he finished, he looked around the church, and even the hardest men in the building had tears in their eyes.

The procession from the church to the Fairmount Cemetery was just as impressive as the mass at the church. A contingent of Denver squad cars, lights flashing, led the eight hearses, six pickup trucks with their beds full of flowers and over five hundred cars through the streets of Denver.

The service at the cemetery was quicker than Jacky III would have liked, but the temperature had dropped, and snow was falling in earnest. Immediately following the graveside service, the crowd broke up, and everyone headed for their cars.

Jacky stood under the tent at the gravesite by himself and appeared to say a prayer. It was touching for anyone who happened to see it. One of the media photographers took a picture that would appear all over social media. If they knew what Jacky III was saying, they would have been appalled.

Jacky III noticed a presence walk up, and he turned and looked into the face of Frank DiNardo. Frank smiled. "Good move, kid. I'm not sure I could have planned it better myself. Of course, I wouldn't have been this clever to put together a plan like this. Once things calm down, I'll have someone reach out. We can talk." Frank turned and walked away.

Jacky III was stunned. It sounded like Frank DiNardo knew what he had done, but that wasn't possible. Only he and Dee knew the plan. He wanted to run after him and make him explain how he knew, but he knew he would never be able to get close. He shook off the surprised feeling, turned and headed towards his limo. It had been a good day.

Chapter Fifty-Six

Buck and Bax spent the rest of the afternoon watching the autopsies of Connor O'Connor and Jimmy Sullivan. The autopsy confirmed that O'Connor would have probably died within the next twenty-four hours at most. His body was riddled with cancer, and he was bleeding internally.

Jimmy Sullivan was healthy for his age and, except for an enlarged prostate, would have lived to a ripe old age. Bax had the three slugs they removed from Jimmy Sullivan sent to the State Crime Lab by secure courier, and then they headed for a small motel and grabbed a couple of hours' sleep.

Buck's phone rang, and he checked the number and answered. "Hey, Mel. What'd ya got?"

"Hey, Buck. Paul asked us to check property records for anything owned by Milford Parker. We found one property, thirty-five acres off County Road 4, in his name. The property taxes are current, so someone has been paying them. There is no record of a title transfer."

"That's great news, Mel," said Buck. "I know where County Road 4 meets up with Highway 34. Thanks."

Buck was about to disconnect when Mel stopped him. "We found something odd," she said. "On a whim, we took a look at some of the properties surrounding this one. One property that borders this parcel, to the west, caught our attention."

"How so?" asked Buck.

"The property is one hundred thirty-five acres with a small cabin. Like the Parker parcel, the property taxes have been paid religiously."

"Okay, so what's so odd about that?"

"The owner's been missing for almost ten years."

"What do you mean, missing?"

"Ten years ago, a kayak that belonged to the owner, Frederick Jensen, was found in one of the inlets on Shadow Mountain Reservoir. A massive land and water search were undertaken, but his body was never found. Grand County closed the case a few years back. Death by misadventure was the coroner's ruling."

"Lots of boats on those lakes. How certain were they it was his?"

"He was part of a kayak racing club. The other members positively identified the kayak as his. Fingerprints later confirmed it. Everyone was stunned, because he was an adventure kayaker, and according to the coroner's inquest, he was one of the best kayakers around. Always followed the rules."

"Why do you think that fits with our guy?"

"Frederick Jensen was a bachelor, no known family. He was also a professor of literature at CU Boulder, and it looks like he was there at the same time as Eldridge Parker."

Buck was silent, and he checked his watch. "Mel, let me make a call, and I'll call you right back."

Buck opened his recent call list, found the number and dialed. A hesitant voice said, "Hello."

"Professor Keller, Buck Taylor, CBI. I hope it's not too early?"

"Not at all, Agent Taylor. Have you learned anything new?"

"Still working, but I have a question for you. Did you know a Professor Frederick Jensen?"

There was silence on the other end, and Buck thought he had lost the call. Finally, Professor Keller said, "My god, there's a blast from the past. Freddy was a close friend. He disappeared, must be ten years or so now. Why do you ask?"

"Professor, would he have also known Eldridge Parker?"

"Yes. We all lived on the same block in Boulder. Freddy was a bachelor, and he lived the kind of life we all only dreamed about. He was always flitting off on some new adventure to someplace exotic or mysterious. He was the athlete and outdoorsman in our group. What I guess you would call a man's man. He disappeared in a boating accident up around Grand Lake. We all volunteered to be on the search parties, but his body was never recovered. What's this all about, Agent Taylor?"

Buck explained about the search for Parker's brother's land parcel and how they'd stumbled onto the parcel of land that was owned by Jensen.

"To your knowledge, Professor, is there anyone you could think of that would pay the taxes on Jensen's piece of ground? Friends, family, anyone?"

"I can't think of anyone. He had no family, at least as far as we knew. He had many friends, both from the school and from his adventures, but I can't think of anyone who would do something like that. Freddy loved that piece of land. He called it his retirement plan. Is it possible he put it in some kind of trust, or something, to take care of it?"

"We'll look into that, Professor. I appreciate you

taking the time this morning, and again, I apologize for the early call."

Buck hung up and called Mel. He filled her in on the conversation and asked her to look for any kind of trust Jensen might have set up. He got out of bed, grabbed a shower and his cleanest clothes and pulled out his laptop. He opened the mosque investigation file and entered as much of the conversation with Professor Keller as he could recollect.

Finished, he pulled out his phone and speed-dialed a number. Director Jackson answered immediately.

"Buck, what's going on?"

Buck filled him in on the deaths of O'Connor and Sullivan and about the conversation he'd had concerning Frederick Jensen and the piece of property. The director listened without interrupting.

Once Buck stopped to catch his breath, the director asked, "What do you think about all this?"

"I think someone killed O'Connor to keep him quiet since we exposed him in the media. Probably couldn't take the chance he would live long enough to talk to us. I think Sullivan was collateral damage. Anyway, everything leads back to Jacky Logan III. If we get confirmation that the DNA Dr. Kalishe lifted is a match, I think we have the mastermind behind the thirteen bombings.”

“Incredible, but we still don’t know why and how Logan and O’Connor are connected,” said the director.

Buck agreed, and then they got to the mosque bombing. “It’s too coincidental that this guy Jensen disappeared at the same time that Eldridge Parker was coming unglued, that the properties are back-to-back in the middle of nowhere and the property taxes get paid every year. I’m wondering if Parker wasn’t behind the disappearance of Jensen to get his property. I’m gonna call the sheriff in Grand County and see what he recalls.”

“How much of this have you shared with the FBI?”

“Once we are certain of our facts, we will share it with them. But, until we get DNA, we’re still at the conjecture stage. We need corroboration if we’re going to take on Jacky Logan III.”

The director agreed with that plan and Buck’s assessment and told him to be safe. Buck disconnected the call and called Bax, who was already awake, and told her to meet him out front in a half hour.

The little bug in Buck’s brain was dancing a jig.

He felt a shift in the momentum of the case. Things were about to break open.

Chapter Fifty-Seven

Eldridge Parker woke with a start from a sound sleep and remained motionless in his bed. He wasn't sure what he'd heard, if anything, but something had entered his consciousness and woken him up. He reached for the nightstand and picked up his pistol.

He slid out of bed, making as little noise as possible, slid back the worn and tattered material from the front window and, staying close to the floor, looked out.

The almost full moon shining through the trees made the new snow that had fallen during the night glisten. For a moment, he was mesmerized. Then, his mind started to clear, and he scanned the front of the house for intruders. Seeing none, he repeated the process on the other three sides of the cabin.

Confident that no one was sneaking up on his house, he stood up, walked over to the wood-burning stove and prodded the embers, causing sparks to fly inside the stove. He added two pieces of wood and stood, watching the embers turn into a blaze as the logs caught. The additional warmth in the cabin was immediate.

He placed the pistol back on his nightstand and placed a bowl of water on top of the woodstove. Next to the bowl, he placed his old tin coffee percolator, lifted the lid and spooned a couple of heaping tablespoons of coffee into the water.

While his coffee boiled on the stove, he put on a pair of ratty old jeans over his ratty old union suit and slid a wool sweater over his head. The single bulb hanging by a wire over his makeshift kitchen table was dim, and he made a mental note to check the batteries for the solar panels. The snow over the past couple of days might have accumulated on the panels, and if so, he would need to run the generator to recharge the batteries.

He didn't like to run the generator because the government could track the vibration from the engine through the seismic sensor network and pinpoint his location. It was simple sound triangulation. People believed that seismographs were in place around the country to alert officials to earthquakes, but he knew better. The government was sneaky like that and had been fooling the people for years.

Eldridge Parker poured himself a cup of coffee from the pot on the woodstove. It was dark black, strong, and the grounds didn't seem to bother him. He sat down at the table, started his laptop and carved a big chunk of his homemade herb bread.

He still had the carving knife in his hand when his laptop screen opened to his favorite internet news site. He stared at the picture that was on the screen. He knew that face, but from where? The news anchor was talking about the Colorado Bureau of Investigation and their interest in finding this man. The man's name, which he hadn't initially noticed, was the same as his name. How could that be?

He looked closer at the picture, and then something in his mind clicked. He recognized the picture. It was a picture of him. Not a current picture, but a picture from a different time in his life, a happier time.

His anger started to grow, and his face turned a bright shade of red. They were onto him, but how was that possible? The government was going to be coming for him. He knew what would happen. The government would make sure there was never a trial, so he couldn't expose all their dirty secrets. The ones he knew but had kept out of his manifesto. They would make sure he died before the trial if he even lasted through the arrest.

His hands shook, and he threw the carving knife at the cabin wall. It hit hard and buried itself three inches into the log, then wobbled back and forth.

In his angry rage, he swept everything off the table onto the floor. Then he started to pace back and forth, his entire body shaking. It wasn't possible. He had been careful. He was always careful. How could they have possibly figured it out? He was smarter than them. Hell, he was smarter than everyone. He looked at the mess on the floor, picked up his laptop, put it back on the table, walked over and pulled his coat off the peg by the door. He needed to prepare.

He trudged through the foot-deep snow and headed for the workshop. Slamming open the door, he went straight to the storage shelf in the corner. The box he needed was the only box on the top shelf, and he reached up and pulled it down.

He opened the top and looked inside. The box contained four one-gallon plastic milk jugs full of a clear yellow liquid. This was the last of his special explosive mixture. He would need to be careful with it.

He figured he could get another twenty explosive devices out of the explosive mixture he had left. That would just have to be enough. He checked the shelf to make sure he had all the other components he needed, sat down at the workbench and started to build his improvised explosive devices. He'd show those bastards from the government that he was better than them.

When the time came, he'd make them suffer. He'd show them he was not a man to be fooled with. A sick smile crossed his face, and he worked like a man possessed. He'd show them.

Chapter Fifty-Eight

Buck was standing next to his car talking on his phone when Bax walked up. The morning sky was bluebird blue with no sign of snow, but the temperature was hovering around zero. She snugged up her coat and let Buck finish his call. He pointed towards the restaurant across the street from the hotel, and Bax headed in that direction.

Bax was on her second cup of coffee when Buck walked in ten minutes later. He slid his backpack onto the bench seat, took off his Carhartt jacket and sat down. The waitress handed him a menu, but he never looked at it and ordered the bacon and egg platter with a large Coke. Bax ordered the same thing without the Coke.

Once the waitress left, Bax asked, "Who was that on the phone?"

"That was Sheriff Eric Storm of Grand County. I called him this morning to get some more information on a case he worked about ten years back."

"I'll bet this has something to do with our case, doesn't it?" asked Bax.

"Strong possibility, in my mind."

Buck filled her in on the call from Mel he had gotten late the night before and the possible connection to Eldridge Parker. He explained about the missing kayaker and the property taxes being paid on both properties. Bax listened without interrupting.

Buck stopped talking as the waitress set down the two heaping platters of eggs, bacon and hash browns. They each dug in.

Bax looked up from her plate. "So, you called Sheriff Storm to see what he remembered about the missing kayaker?"

"Correct," said Buck. "He gave me essentially the same story I got from Professor Keller last night. He was also able to fill in the missing details. One being that they searched his property to make sure he wasn't hiding, and the place was empty."

"Was it?" she asked.

"Yes, but they encountered a guy, as he describes him, with long hair and crazy eyes. He identified himself as Eldridge Parker and said that he was taking care of his brother's property. The deputy who interviewed him checked the property records and found out the property was owned by Milford Parker and didn't pursue it any further. He didn't want to get too close to the man because he noted in the report that he was filthy and looked and smelled like some kind of mountain man."

Bax was quiet for a minute while she ate some more of her breakfast and washed it down with her third cup of coffee. She put her fork down and looked at Buck.

"You think Eldridge Parker was involved in his neighbor's disappearance?" she said, more as a statement than a question.

Buck nodded. "I think he needed a bigger refuge, and he made Jensen disappear. Everything we know about Jensen says he was a world-class kayaker, and he didn't make mistakes, so how does he die on a flat lake in perfect weather? I think there's more to the story than anyone is aware of."

Bax laughed. "We don't have enough to deal with, with Irish mobsters, bombings, murders, etcetera. Now we're going to take on a closed case from ten years ago."

"Yeah, crazy, huh?" Buck laughed and finished his egg platter.

"We need to track down Eldridge Parker," he said. "My concern is, if he is the crazy mountain man, he may have the entire property wired with explosives. He's had ten years to prepare for us."

"We're gonna need some help," said Bax.

"Yeah. I'm working on that."

Buck's phone rang as he finished the last of his Coke. "Hey, Max." He put the phone on speaker and turned down the volume.

Max started the conversation the way she always did. "Buck Taylor, how's my favorite cop?"

"I'm good, Max. What's up?"

"I've got some news I think is going to make your day. The swab you guys took from the Montrose victim's forehead. The DNA is a fifty percent familial match to Carly Logan."

She paused for effect, and Buck looked at Bax. "The sample matches Carly Logan, but not Jackson Logan Jr.?" asked Buck.

"I thought you'd find that interesting," said Max, "so we ran the sample against Connor O'Connor, and there was a fifty percent familial match to the sample."

"Holy shit," said Bax. "O'Connor was Jacky Logan III's father. That's the link we've been looking for."

"Fortunately," said Max, "we were able to find a DNA profile for Jackson Logan III on a commercial site. It seems he ran a paternity test. The comparison sample is a match for Connor

O'Connor. So, unless Carly and O'Connor had another child, I'd say the odds are huge for Jackson Logan III."

"Great news, Max. We'll get working on a warrant," said Buck.

Bax pulled out her phone and dialed the office, spoke for a minute then hung up.

"Good," said Max. "Now, for the bullets from the Montrose crime scene. Only one of the bullets from the scene is usable. The other two were too damaged to get any kind of comparison. We ran that one bullet against the database and got two hits. One from a recent Denver police case and one from a case from six years ago."

"Which Denver case, Max?" asked Bax.

"The victim was a Michael Perez. He was from . . ."

"Max, I know the case. I was at the crime scene," said Bax. "What's the second case?"

"The second case was a double murder, also in Denver." They heard keys clicking. "Case was from five years ago. Two victims, both black men in their thirties. Looks like they were noted as suspected drug dealers. They were each shot three times. The DPD lab had two usable bullets. No other forensics and no witnesses. I'm uploading the file to the investigation file."

"Thanks, Max," said Buck. "Now, we have to get to work."

"You're a good man, Buck Taylor. God will watch over you," said Max.

Buck disconnected the call.

"A second set of murders. I'll call Marcie and have her pull the file. You think Jacky III has a past?" asked Bax.

"I was wondering the same thing," said Buck. "Maybe a rite of passage. Take out a couple of rival drug dealers."

Buck placed a twenty under his plate and slid his laptop back into his backpack.

"We've got a lot of work to do. Call Chief Sawyer and see if he can spare a couple of officers for a canvass. We need to show that Jacky Logan III was in Montrose at the time of the murder. See if you can find a recent picture of him, check motor vehicle records and get sample pictures of his cars. Then we need to go back and look at all the videos we can find from that day. Have the officers check every store and gas station on Main Street. Go a mile out of town in every direction."

"What are you gonna be doing?"

"I'm running up to Grand County to meet the sheriff. I want to put eyes on this property that Parker might be on. Call Paul and have him work on the internet stuff for you. I'll call you later and let you know where I'm at."

Buck and Bax slid out of their seats, grabbed their coats and headed for their Jeeps.

Chapter Fifty-Nine

Buck's phone rang just as he was passing through Vail. He hit the button on the steering wheel. "Hey, George. What's up?"

"Where are you?"

"Heading to Grand County, I'm just passing through Vail."

"Okay. Couple of things. We checked DMV records, and the last time Eldridge Parker registered a vehicle was seven years ago. It was a 1995 light gray Ford F-150. He registered it to his old address in Boulder.

"Second. Mel said to tell you that there was no trust established by Jensen to pay the property taxes on his parcel. The property taxes on both parcels were paid in cash. Both properties are agricultural, so the taxes weren't that high—seventeen hundred dollars for both.

"Third. The C-4 they found in O'Connor's apartment matches the C-4 from the individual family bombings. Max tried to call you, but you must have been in the canyon. By the way, you guys are lucky. The bag had a trip wire. If anyone had pulled that bag out of the vent, it would have taken out the entire block."

"There was a forty-five-caliber pistol in the bag along with the explosives. So far, it's a ballistic match to four unsolved Denver metro area homicides from the early seventies. I sent the information to Bax's friend Marcie Blackburn."

Buck slowed as he approached the Silverthorne exit and headed north on Highway 9.

"George, any luck with O'Connor's phone?"

"We checked the history, and there were several calls to the same number, a burner phone. It was bought in Littleton, Colorado. Same place his phone was bought. No ID on the buyer."

"Were you able to get a subpoena for Jacky Logan III's phone?" asked Buck.

"Still waiting on the phone company. You know how they are with responding. Might be sometime this afternoon or sometime next week."

"Thanks, George. One more thing. Max said that the mosque explosion was a unique blend of chemicals. Give her a call and see if she thinks any of those chemicals can be traced, and if they can be, check stores in Grand County and the counties around it. We might get lucky and get a picture of Parker buying them."

Buck disconnected the call and turned onto Highway 40 and headed towards the Grand County sheriff's office in Hot Sulphur Springs. He pulled into the lot and parked in one of three visitor's parking spaces. He grabbed his backpack and headed inside.

Grand County Sheriff Eric Storm was sitting at his desk in the small office behind the front counter. He saw Buck and waved him in. Buck walked around the counter and into the office. He shook Sheriff Storm's hand, and Storm introduced him to Deputy Silvia Vasquez, who was seated in the other chair.

"Stormy, good to see you. It's been a couple of years."

Sheriff Storm and Officer Vasquez were both dressed in dark brown uniform pants and shirts. Eric Storm had been Grand County sheriff for over fifteen years and had gray hair and a belly that hung over his belt. Vasquez looked to be in her early twenties with dark brown hair pulled up in a bun. She looked fit, but it was hard to tell with the ballistic vest she wore under her uniform shirt.

"So, Buck. We pulled the Jensen file out of storage. There's little forensic information. Without a body, we got nothing of any real value. Fingerprints on the kayak and the paddles belong to Jensen. The kayak was identified as his, and there was no blood or anything else on or in it. It was written up as a drowning.

"Odd thing is, Shadow Mountain is only sixty feet deep at its deepest. So, the body should have eventually come to the surface. Now, if he was in Grand Lake, as some people speculated, instead of Shadow Mountain, then that could explain it. Grand Lake is the deepest natural lake in Colorado and is around four hundred feet deep. At that depth, the water near the bottom is close to freezing, and the body could stay down there forever."

"No sign of foul play when you checked his property?" asked Buck.

Sheriff Storm opened a manila folder and lifted out a piece of paper. "Like I told you on the phone. According to the report, the deputy found no one home at the cabin, and nothing looked out of place. The deputy noted his encounter with the long-haired man we identified as Eldridge Parker, and that was that. Nothing more to report."

Sheriff Storm looked up from the paper and handed it to Buck. Buck reached into his pocket, pulled out his reading glasses and slipped them on. He took a minute to read the report for himself.

"Buck, what's going on?" asked Sheriff Storm.

Buck removed his reading glasses. "We believe that Eldridge Parker is living on his brother's property here in Grand County. We have reason to believe that he is responsible for the mosque bombing in Avon. I am also beginning to believe that he might be responsible for the death of the kayaker, Jensen."

Buck filled him in on what they had learned so far from talking with Parker's son about his relationship to the internet manifesto and his connection to Jensen.

Sheriff Storm sat forward in his chair. "Shit, Buck. Do you think he was responsible for the other Christmas morning bombings?"

"We don't think so. Bax is in Montrose right now, working on that case, and we think we may be close to solving it. I'd like to see where this property is that we're talking about?"

"That's why Deputy Vasquez is here," said Sheriff Storm. "I went up to the property this morning after we spoke, and there is no way to get onto the property off County 4. The gate's padlocked, and the lock looks like it hasn't been removed or opened in a long time. Lots of no trespassing, shoot on sight signs on the trees."

Vasquez took over. "The sheriff called me in because he thinks there might be a back way onto the property off Highway 125. That's my patrol area, and I think I know what you're looking for. If you're ready to go, we can leave now."

Deputy Vasquez stood, stepped around Buck and grabbed her jacket off the peg in the corner. Buck thanked Sheriff Storm and followed her out the door. Vasquez slid into her GCSO SUV, Buck slid into his Jeep and they pulled onto US Highway 40 and headed east.

Vasquez signaled for a left turn, and they turned onto Highway 125. They drove north for about twenty minutes before Vasquez slowed and pulled over onto the shoulder. Buck followed, and she continued down the shoulder.

She found what she was looking for, pulled completely off the highway and stopped. Buck wondered why until he slid out of the Jeep and walked to the fence line where Vasquez was standing. It was hard to see with the new snow on the road, but she pointed towards a loop in the barbed wire fence.

"If there weren't all this snow, you would be able to see two very faint tracks heading back into the woods," she said. She lifted the loop. "This fence looks continuous until you notice that the loop opens up a path wide enough to pass a truck through. I think this is how he gets out without going out the side road off County Road 4. The cabin is about a mile and a half down this track."

Buck looked at the makeshift gate. "Nice work, Deputy. Care to take a little walk?"

She nodded, walked back to her SUV and pulled a pair of high fur-lined snow boots out of the back hatch. Buck did the same, and they stood next to the loop in the fence.

"We don't have a warrant. So, what's our play?" she asked.

"Welfare check," said Buck. "With all this snow, we're checking on all the residents in the area. Making sure they're okay."

Vasquez smiled and pulled the wire loop off the fence post. They headed up the track. Buck cautioned Vasquez. "We think this guy is a bomber. I'm guessing he has protection in place around the property. Stay on the track and watch for anything out of the ordinary."

They walked for about fifteen minutes before they heard something in the distance. Pulling their weapons, they walked up the track until they could see the roof of the cabin over a slight rise, smoke rising from the chimney. They crouched low and moved over the rise, the soft snow silencing their steps.

Buck pulled a small pair of binoculars out of his backpack and focused on the man they saw next to the cabin. He was old with long stringy gray hair and a full beard.

While Buck watched, the man dug a hole a few feet from the cabin and then placed a short metal-looking tube in the ground. He unraveled a string or wire, hooked it to the tube and ran it in a small trench he had made in the snow. He hooked it to the side of the cabin and then covered everything up with snow. To Buck, it looked like he was talking the entire time, but there was no one else around. The man looked at his handiwork, moved ten feet away and started digging another hole.

Buck handed Vasquez the binoculars, and she watched for a minute. Buck then tapped her on the shoulder and nodded his head back the way they came. They backtracked in the snow until they were well clear of the cabin site.

"Looks like you have your answer, Agent Taylor. He's preparing for war."

"Yeah. If the FBI shows up in force, there's gonna be a lot of dead bodies. We're gonna need stealth."

They reached their vehicles, and Buck told Vasquez to meet him back at the sheriff's office. He slid into his car, pulled out his phone and found a number he had never dialed before. He dialed.

"Good morning, Deputy Taylor. How can I help you today?"

Harriet's voice on the other end of the phone sounded mature, with just a hint of a Southern twang. Buck hadn't used his U.S. Marshals contacts since the Marshals Service had presented him with his federal credentials, but he knew this action was going to require a special kind of help.

"I need a couple of door kickers. We're going after a bombing suspect. They need to be comfortable in the woods, and they need to understand stealth. And I need them as soon as possible. Can you help me?"

"Absolutely. I know just the team. Do you need a federal warrant?"

"Can you do that?" asked Buck.

"Text me your case file, and I will get you what you need. Where would you like the team to meet you?"

Buck gave her the address for the Grand County Sheriff's Office. He could hear computer keys clicking in the background as he opened his investigation file and texted it to the same number.

"I have your text, Deputy. I will get right on it. The team has acknowledged the request, and they expect to be at your location in roughly two hours. I will call you with the warrant information."

Buck thanked her and hung up. He was listening to a message from Bax when his phone rang again. He looked at the number.

Chapter Sixty

While the arrest warrant was being prepared for Jacky III, Bax continued the canvass in Montrose. She was close to calling it quits when she got a call from a Montrose police officer who was canvassing Highway 50 between Montrose and Delta. He thought he might have something at a gas station/convenience store just south of Delta. Bax ran to her Jeep and headed north.

She pulled into the gas station parking lot and parked next to the Montrose patrol car. The officer—Wendover was the name on the tag over his uniform pocket, stepped through the door. A look of excitement filled his face.

"I think we might have something," said Officer Wendover.

She followed him into the store, and he headed back towards the manager's office. The manager was sitting in front of a computer monitor, and Bax took the chair next to her. Without being asked, the manager began playing a section of the video that was already keyed up. Bax watched carefully.

"There," said Officer Wendover.

The manager slowed the feed, and Bax slid in closer to the monitor. She watched as a black Land Rover pulled up to the pump. Bax asked her to stop the feed.

"Can you zoom in on the license plate?"

The manager clicked a couple of keys, and the camera moved in closer to the license plate. It wasn't the clearest picture, but Bax could make out the letters and numbers. She wrote them down and asked the manager to continue slowly. The Land Rover door opened, and a man in a tan jacket stepped out of the SUV, put his credit card into the gas pump, locked the handle and looked around. Right into the lens of the camera.

"Son of a bitch," said Bax. Jackson Logan III was staring back at her on the monitor.

She asked the manager to stop the video. "I need you to email a copy of the video to me." She took a business card out of her pocket and placed it on the desk. The manager pulled up an email account, looked at Bax's card and keyed the address into the open email. She then inserted the video.

Bax told her to wait before she hit send. She pulled out her phone, called Chief Sawyer and asked him to prepare a warrant request for the video and for any receipts and have someone run it by the convenience store. They sat back and waited.

A half hour later a second Montrose police SUV pulled into the lot, and Officer Wendover walked outside, accepted the warrant from the other officer and brought it into the office. He handed it to the manager.

During the wait, Bax had asked the manager to pull up the receipt for that pump. The manager checked the time stamp on the video, opened another screen on the monitor and searched for the receipt. It was a matter of seconds until she pulled up the receipt and attached it to the same email.

Bax asked the manager to go ahead and send the email, and within seconds her phone chimed, indicating receipt of the email. She thanked the manager, and she and Officer Wendover stepped outside. She pulled out her phone and dialed Montrose Chief of Police Paul Sawyer.

"Hey, Bax," said Police Chief Sawyer. "Your office has been trying to reach you. They were able to triangulate that cell phone number you gave them. The phone was here in Montrose at the time of the murders."

"Great news, Chief. I need you to do me a favor. I'm going to call my director and have him work on getting an arrest warrant for Jackson Logan III. I would like you to do the same thing. We need a local warrant for two counts of murder."

"No problem, Bax. I'll call the judge who issued the warrant for the video. I'll get my admin on it right away. I'll call you when it's ready."

Bax hung up, thanked Officer Wendover and headed for her Jeep. She called Buck but got his voice mail and left a message. Then she dialed Director Jackson, explained what they'd found and the evidence she now had against Jackson Logan III for murder and asked him to have someone at the office prepare a warrant request and get it in front of a state judge.

"We're on it, Bax," said Director Jackson. "Smart move getting Montrose to pull a warrant as well. Do you want us to wait for you to make the arrest?"

"No, sir. I don't want the son of a bitch to get away."

"No worries, Bax. I'll pull together an arrest team and get a forensic team ready to roll behind them. Good job, Bax. Anything else?"

"One thing, sir. We're looking for a twenty-two-caliber pistol. It was used in one of the murders here and may be related to several other murders in Denver. We've already given Denver homicide a heads-up, and they're pulling the case files for their unsolveds. If we get the gun, please get in touch with Detective Marcie Blackburn and let her know."

"Will do, Bax. Where are you heading?"

"I'm heading to Grand County to catch up to Buck. He's looking at our mosque bombing suspect, and he can probably use all the help he can get."

Bax disconnected the call and slid into her Jeep. She pulled onto Highway 50 and headed towards I-70. She flipped on her red, white and blue flashers and hit the gas.

Chapter Sixty-One

Buck answered his phone. "Yes, sir."

Director Jackson filled Buck in on what Bax and the locals had discovered in Montrose. He told him that the warrant request was sitting in front of a judge at this very moment, and he had a team ready to make the arrest.

"Is Bax on her way to Denver to assist with the arrest?"

"No," said Director Jackson. "She's heading to you, should be there any minute. She didn't want to lose him, so she asked me to put together a team."

"How about Paul, he's in Avon?"

"Not anymore. I called Paul a little bit ago, and he's heading to you as well. You're not going up against a mad bomber without help."

Buck filled him in on his call to the special number the Marshals Service had given him and that a team was enroute to help. He told him he wanted to keep the arrest low-key, hopefully, to prevent a firefight.

"Good call, Buck. I knew that badge would come in handy. Be safe, and if you need additional help, just yell. We'll be there."

"One more thing, sir. Would you call the governor and have him put a National Guard bomb disposal team on alert? They can stage at the Grand County sheriff's office."

"You got it, Buck."

Buck hung up, and his phone rang again. He looked at the number and frowned. He'd known this call would come eventually.

"Hey, Hank. What's up?"

Hank Clancy was not his usual cheerful self. Not that he ever was, but this time his voice had an undertone that Buck couldn't read.

"That tip from Bax on the deceased Michael Perez paid off. Marshall's team did a number on the poor guy's wife, and once the threats of removing her children sunk in all the way, she caved. Perez received twenty-five thousand to secure the explosives and deliver them to Connor O'Connor.

"Mrs. Perez broke down and showed Marshall's guys where the money was. The backpack was hidden in a space behind a false wall in her husband's workshop. They found the twenty-five large along with another forty K, which Mrs. Perez said came from numerous militia groups."

Hank paused for effect, but Buck stayed quiet.

"Marshall wants to charge Mrs. Perez as an accessory to the bombings. Now, here's the good news. Our lab folks fumed the backpack and came up with a couple of partial prints. All belonging to Mrs. Denise Logan, Jacky III's wife. Mrs. Perez positively identified Mrs. Logan in a photo array. Mrs. Logan does not have a record, but she was fingerprinted when her name was added to the bar's liquor license.

"Marshall has just dispatched a team from the office in Grand Junction to arrest Mrs. Perez. He is also preparing charging documents for Denise Logan. He'll have an arrest warrant in a couple of hours. He is back screaming about militias, and now people are listening. What he doesn't know is what you know. He believes that O'Connor was working with the militias, and he is going to use Mrs. Perez to prove us all wrong, but you and I both know that he will not be able to prove anything without finding O'Connor. Where is he, Buck?"

Buck was silent for a minute. He had never, in all the time they'd known each other, lied to Hank. He decided now was not the time to start, and Hank did not sound like he was in the mood to dance around the truth.

"O'Connor's dead. He died last night in an apartment in Montrose."

"Natural causes?" asked Hank.

"No. He was murdered. He was part of a double homicide."

"Who was the other victim?" Hank sounded exasperated.

"James Sullivan, aka Jimmy Sullivan, the second-in-command of the Irish mob, under Logan Jr."

"What the fuck is going on, Buck?"

"Connor O'Connor is Jacky Logan III's biological father. Jacky III arranged the whole get-out-of-jail thing and then used O'Connor to kill the people that betrayed him and the people that convicted him."

"Why?" said Hank. "You're telling me he killed his entire family out of revenge."

"Partly. It was revenge for his father. The rest was about power. Jacky III saw an opportunity to run the whole show, but from what we heard, he couldn't get out from under the old man. Even though he was retired, he still controlled everything."

"So besides killing his adopted father, his mother and his sister and her family, he also killed his biological father?" asked Hank.

"He couldn't take the chance that someone might recognize O'Connor. Our posting his picture with the news media changed the direction of what was going on. Jacky III had to act so we wouldn't get to him before he died of natural causes, which was probably only hours away anyway. We're not sure why Sullivan was there, but I'm guessing Jacky III wasn't pleased with his presence."

"So how does the militia fit into this, with this guy Perez?"

"It doesn't. The militia had nothing to do with the bombings. Marshall is still barking up the wrong tree."

"Okay, say you're right. What's your next move?"

"Director Jackson is in the process of securing a warrant to arrest Jacky Logan III. He has a team standing by."

"Where are you?" asked Hank.

"We're about to make a move on a guy we believe is the Mountain Bomber and is responsible for the mosque bombing."

"You can't be serious," said Hank. "We've all been looking for the Mountain Bomber for a decade and you think you've found him. That would be great if he's your man. You're certain Jacky III and O'Connor didn't blow up the mosque for sport?"

Buck laughed. "I need to run, Hank. Pull up our investigation file. Marshall had access to it. Read the report. It will tell you everything you need to know."

Buck disconnected the call, started his Jeep, made a U-turn and headed back to Hot Sulphur Springs. He knew this was all coming to a close. He just wasn't sure how it was all going to turn out.

Chapter Sixty-Two

Bax and Paul were waiting at the Grand County Sheriff's Office when Buck pulled into the parking lot. He walked in, put his backpack on the floor next to an empty desk and grabbed a can of Coke out of the small refrigerator in the corner.

Sitting with Bax and Paul were Sheriff Storm and Deputy Vasquez. Vasquez was filling them in on what she and Buck had observed. The sheriff looked at Buck as he sat down at the desk.

"Thought maybe you changed your mind and decided to head home," he said with a smile on his face.

Buck filled them in on his call with Hank Clancy and then told them about the help he had recruited from the Marshals Service. They had at least another hour to kill before the marshals team arrived, so Buck asked Vasquez to run and pick up a couple of pizzas.

They were just cleaning up the desks when Buck's phone rang with the number for Harriet from the U.S. Marshals Service. "Buck Taylor."

"Deputy Taylor, I am emailing you the federal

arrest and search warrants. Please look them over and let me know if there is anything else I can do for you. One other thing, Deputy. Once these warrants hit the system, the FBI was made aware of their existence. You will not have a lot of time. Godspeed, Deputy Taylor."

Buck's phone chimed, and he opened the email from Harriet. He read the warrants and asked the sheriff for the email address for his printer. He forwarded the warrants to the printer, heard the printer in the corner kick on and he walked over and removed the two papers that sat in the bin. He read them and passed them around to the others.

"Must be nice to have federal friends," said Bax. They all laughed, and she was about to say something else when a black Chevy Suburban pulled into the parking lot and parked next to Buck's Jeep.

They spotted two people getting out of the SUV and walking towards the door. Buck stepped over to the counter as the door swung open.

The woman was the first to enter, and she walked up to Buck.

"Buck Taylor?" Buck nodded, and she reached out her hand. "Dorsett," she said. She pointed behind her at the man coming in the door. "That's Schoenberger."

Vicky Dorsett was about five foot seven and had a muscular physique under her coat. She had short black hair and dark eyes.

Ari Schoenberger set down his backpack and took off his jacket. Under his jacket, he wore a black T-shirt. He was bald and stood a shade over Dorsett. His arms were covered in tattoos, and Buck noticed that the tats appeared to be the story of his military career. Buck was impressed.

Dorsett started to say something, but all eyes fell on the third member of the team, who ducked as he walked through the door. The team got the same reaction wherever they went.

"That's Chicago," she said, pointing towards the man who filled the doorway.

"Why Chicago?" asked Paul.

Dorsett smiled, having said the same thing several hundred times. "He was born in Chicago into a Russian family. His family had a tradition, and he was named after his two great-grandfathers, who had unpronounceable names. Couple that with the fact that no human can pronounce his last name. It's just easier to call him Chicago." Chicago laughed as he took off his coat.

Paul was big at six foot four and two hundred and forty pounds, but Chicago made him look tiny in comparison. Chicago was six foot eight or nine and weighed three hundred and fifty pounds. He had shoulder-length dark hair and a scraggly beard, and the muscles under his T-shirt had muscles of their own. He was a mountain of a man.

They all shook hands, and Dorsett pulled a laptop out of her backpack and set it on the table. They all gathered around.

"Buck, if it's okay with you and your team, I'd like to run this operation. We do this kind of thing every day, and we are damn good at what we do." Buck nodded. He had heard about teams like this. These were the people who did the dirty work for the Marshals Service. They were specialists, and Buck had no problem relinquishing control.

She opened the laptop to a satellite view of the cabin and the surrounding property.

"Buck," she said. "Have you guys scoped this place out from the ground yet?"

Buck looked at Deputy Vasquez, who stepped up and gave them a rundown of where the access point was.

Dorsett enlarged the map. "Okay, that's great. Since this guy is a bomber, he probably has other IEDs buried around the property besides what you saw. Gonna be tricky to spot with the snow, so we'll go in the way you guys did. We'll be on ear comms, so keep the talk to a minimum."

She pointed to several locations, and they discussed how to enter the cabin and what the plan was to secure the suspect. They didn't have much time to plan this operation, so they would have to rely on Dorsett's team's experience to get them through it.

"Did the warrant come through?" she asked.

Buck handed her both warrants, which she read and passed on to her team. They discussed the plan for a few more minutes, then Buck stood up.

"I'd like to have Paul find a cover position to shoot from. Paul, grab your long gun and your white camo suit. Bax and I will go with you guys." He looked at Sheriff Storm. "Stormy, I want to keep you guys in reserve. I'd like to have Vasquez and another deputy watch our backs from the road at the fence, and can you position a deputy at the property gate on Road 4 to make sure he doesn't get past us?"

"No problem, Buck." He pulled the mic off his collar and stepped away from the group.

"If there are no other questions, then let's gear up. We're running out of daylight," said Dorsett.

They grabbed their coats and headed for their vehicles. Dorsett stopped them at her Suburban and handed out headsets to everyone. The headsets operated on a secure government frequency so outsiders couldn't hear what was being said. Everyone pulled camo gear out of their vehicles, and within minutes the entire team was outfitted and ready to go. Paul looked like a giant snowman. They pulled out of the parking lot and followed Deputy Vasquez's SUV.

Chapter Sixty-Three

The caravan pulled onto the shoulder around a bend from the makeshift gate. They checked their comms and their weapons and climbed over the barbed wire fence, quickly making their way through the trees to the two tracks Vasquez had shown them on the map. They were about to start up the road when Buck's phone buzzed. He pulled it out.

"What's up, Stormy?"

"Just got a call from the Winter Park police," said Sheriff Storm. "Six black SUVs with lights flashing just blew through Winter Park. I think you've got company coming."

Buck thanked him and put his phone away. "We need to go. Looks like our friends from the FBI are on their way."

Dorsett nodded, and they moved out, single file, following Buck's tracks from earlier. Within minutes they were on the slight rise overlooking the cabin. Buck pointed to a spot higher up a small ridge, and Paul headed off to find a suitable sniper's nest.

Dorsett spotted the shed lean-to and the pickup truck under a dirty canvas cover. "Chicago, disable the pickup," she said through the mic next to her cheek. Chicago nodded and slid off into the woods on the left.

"Paul, are you in position?" she said into the mic.

"I've got a good view of the cabin," said Paul. "No movement."

She looked towards where she knew Paul had headed, but she couldn't see him. For someone his size, he did a great job of blending into the snow.

Just then, her radio chirped. "You're gonna want to see this, skipper," said Chicago. She knew he was over by the shed, so she headed that way.

"Buck, Bax," she said into the mic. "Cover the back of the cabin."

Both Buck and Bax acknowledged and spread out to cover both sides of the cabin. They got low to the ground and waited.

A few minutes later, Dorsett said, "Schoenberger, cover for Buck. Buck, make your way over to the shed."

Schoenberger moved in behind Buck and tapped him on the shoulder. Buck nodded and moved into the woods and headed towards the shed, being extra careful where he placed his feet.

Buck came up behind the shed, out of view of the cabin, and let his AR-15 hang from his harness. He approached Dorsett and Chicago. Dorsett waved him to follow her while Chicago watched the cabin. She walked through the shed and pushed open a door.

Buck stepped past her and was amazed at what he saw. Inside was a full-blown chemistry lab. There were containers of various chemicals neatly organized on the shelves. The inside of the building was rustic but relatively clean.

There was a laptop sitting on a wooden worktable. Buck walked over and clicked a button, and the laptop sprang to life. There was no password required, so he clicked past the sign-in page. The screen was open to the news article about the bombing and a picture of Parker from when he was a professor at CU. Buck looked around.

The lights were burning, which meant he must either be connected to the grid or he had a solar installation someplace on the property. Buck was impressed by the whole setup. For a scraggly old mountain man, he had a lot of modern conveniences.

Dorsett tapped him on the shoulder, and he

turned. She pointed to four plastic milk jugs lying on the floor by the workbench and the array of wires and timers sitting on the bench. Buck looked back at the computer screen.

"He knew we were coming," he said. He looked back at the jigs on the floor. "If those were full of the explosive material he created, there's a lot of bombs out there."

"We need to hit the cabin, now. You stay here and watch the shed," Dorsett said to Buck. She keyed her mic. "Bax, stay where you are. Paul, cover us. We're going in. Chicago, front door. Schoenberger, on me."

She headed out of the shed, and Buck followed, taking up a position behind the covered pickup truck. Dorsett moved to the back door of the cabin. Schoenberger came towards her and then stopped mid-stride. He knelt and brushed the snow away from his foot. He reached down and slowly slid his foot out from under a trip wire, then took a deep breath. He smiled, stepped over the wire and joined Dorsett at the back door.

"Chicago ready," came the voice over the radio.

"Move." Dorsett grabbed the knob, twisted it and pushed the door open. With weapons up, she moved right, and Schoenberger moved left. Buck could hear them moving around in the cabin.

"Clear. Buck, Bax, come forward. Paul, stay and cover," said Dorsett.

Watching their feet, Buck and Bax moved towards the cabin. Inside they found the team looking in and under everything. The one-room cabin was a decent size but with rustic fixtures. There was no bathroom and just a rudimentary kitchen with a wood-burning stove and a water pump over an old metal sink.

Buck touched the woodstove. "Warm, but not hot," he said.

"Okay, any thoughts on where this guy might be?" asked Dorsett.

Buck keyed his mic. "Vasquez, anything moving your way?"

"All clear here, Buck," said Vasquez.

"Buck, this is Stormy. I can't reach the deputy I put on the gate off Road 4. I'm heading over there now, and I've called for backup."

"Roger, Stormy. Be careful. We don't know where Parker is."

Dorsett pulled out her laptop and clicked on the satellite view of the property. She pulled back from the cabin, and they followed a dirt road east onto Parker's original property. She scanned the area.

"There's nothing on this piece but an old rock foundation," she said. "Not a cabin or outbuilding. Just this road leading to this wide spot in the road, about a mile and a half from the east gate. What do you think that is?"

Buck and Bax were looking at the image when his phone buzzed. He pulled it out and looked at the number. "Not a good time, Hank."

"Buck," said Hank Clancy. "I can't reach Marshall or anyone from his team. I think they were heading towards you guys, but he's gone radio silent."

"We got a report about an hour ago of six government SUVs passing through Winter Park, but we haven't seen him," said Buck. "How would he know where we are?"

"I read your investigation file after we talked, and I forwarded it to him. I told him to coordinate with me, and we would work with you and develop a plan for finding Parker. The next thing I hear is that he's left the building along with his team and the SWAT guys."

Buck was about to say something when three explosions echoed through the forest, and semiautomatic weapons fire erupted. Dust floated down from the cabin rafters.

They all ducked. "What the hell was that?" asked Schoenberger.

Buck could hear Hank yelling through his phone.

"Buck, what's happening?"

Buck lifted his phone to his ear. "I think your guys just engaged Parker. We've got to go."

Chapter Sixty-Four

Buck hung up just as Paul stepped through the front door. "I've got tracks off to the southeast." They all flinched as several more explosions rocked the forest, raining down more dust and debris from the rafters.

Paul headed out, following the footprints. Dorsett and her team and Buck and Bax were spread out behind him. The semiautomatic weapons fire was intense, and Buck clicked his mic. "It sounds like a lot more firepower than just Parker. Heads-up, everyone."

The footprints led them through the forest, and when they reached the end of the trail, they were on a ridge overlooking the carnage. They could see several of the government SUVs engulfed in flames and several bodies lying alongside the vehicles.

FBI agents had taken up positions behind the remaining SUVs and were returning fire, only to be pushed into cover by withering fire coming from several directions. Buck watched as several green-clad SWAT agents attempted to outflank whoever they were shooting at, only to have several IEDs go off in their path. Two agents went down and stayed down.

Still hidden in the trees, Dorsett called everyone together. "We need to stay low. Those FBI guys are gonna be shooting at anything that moves. Right now, we have the advantage. If I were a betting person, I'd bet there are no IEDs between us and the cabin. These guys would need an escape route. Let's take advantage of that. Buck, you and Bax take the right flank. Work your way through the trees until you can spot the bad guys. Take them out. You okay with that?"

Buck nodded, and he and Bax headed off through the trees.

"Paul. Head over into those rocks." She pointed to where she wanted him. "Pick your targets carefully and stay down."

She looked at Chicago and Schoenberger. "We need to take out anyone in front of us. Chicago, cover from here. We'll move closer."

With guns in front of them, they crawled forward towards a pile of downed trees. The wildland fire the year before had devastated part of the hill, but it gave them good cover.

Several more explosions went off to the left side of the government SUVs, and Buck spotted two more FBI agents fall back behind their vehicles. One was hit in the shoulder. Buck wasn't sure about the other one.

He worked his way through the snow until he spotted one of the bad guys hiding behind some downed trees. The noise was deafening. Buck crouched behind a tree and lined up his shot. The bad guy stopped to reload as another bomb went off, and Buck took advantage of the situation. He sighted his AR-15 and shot the bad guy in the back of the head. The guy slumped over the log.

Bax was moving off the ridge, on her belly, when she almost fell over the guy hiding in the snow. He was startled to see her and started to roll onto his side to bring his assault rifle around, but Bax never hesitated and put two in his head. She looked over his body and could see another bad guy moving to outflank the FBI. She didn't have a shot and was now taking fire.

Buck spotted the same guy Bax had, trying to outflank the FBI, and he moved sideways down the ridge, trying to make his way through the downed trees, but he couldn't get a clear shot. The bad guy slid into a small ravine that ran towards the south. If he got to the end of the ravine, he would have a clear shot at the remaining FBI agents.

Bax spotted Buck as he moved along the ridgeline, and she could see he was focused on the guy she'd been watching. She was about to move towards him when she heard a bullet from Paul's rifle split the air. The guy's head exploded in a cloud of pink mist, and he slammed hard into the ground.

Paul located several more bad guys and fired twice more. Two more bad guys were dead, but whoever was left now knew they were there, and they opened up on the trees above them. They dove for cover as bullets tore black chips out of the downed trees.

Bax heard Buck engage the shooters, and during a lull in the shooting, she looked over the trees and fired a couple of rounds to where she thought the bad guys might be.

On the other side of her, she heard Dorsett and Schoenberger open fire, and within minutes there was silence. The FBI agents behind the vehicles stopped shooting.

Dorsett took advantage of the momentary silence and yelled at the top of her voice. "US Marshals, holster your weapons."

Buck heard sirens in the distance and keyed his mic. "Stormy, we're gonna need ambulances. A lot of them."

"Roger, Buck. We're coming up Road 4, almost to the gate. Clear to come in?"

"Hold at the gate," said Buck.

A voice came from behind the closest Suburban. "Identify yourselves."

"Deputy U.S. Marshal Victoria Dorsett. There are six of us on the ridge. We're coming down. Put your weapons down."

Dorsett stood up and made herself known to the FBI below. She moved cautiously down the ridge as Bax and Schoenberger moved towards her. Buck stood up and headed towards the ravine. After checking the guy that Paul had dropped, he moved to the end of the ravine and approached the FBI caravan. He holstered his pistol and raised his hands, as had Dorsett and the others.

They arrived at the clearing, and now that the FBI could see the large U.S. Marshals logo emblazoned on their ballistic vests, they moved out from behind the Suburbans.

"Anyone have eyes on Parker?" asked Buck.

Everyone looked around, and then Dorsett said, "Where's Chicago?"

She turned and was about to head back up to the ridge when she saw Chicago step through the trees. He was pushing someone in front of him as he made his way through the downed trees. He stepped into the clearing, blood dripping down his arm.

He pushed his prisoner, who landed face-first on the ground. Eldridge Parker just lay there.

"Silly bastard tried to shoot me," he said with a grin.

Dorsett pointed towards his arm. "Looks like he succeeded."

Chicago looked at the blood dripping on the ground and laughed. "Yeah," he said. "Guess he did."

Buck stepped up and looked at Chicago. "Where'd you find him?"

"I saw movement through the trees and followed him. Caught him trying to start that old truck in the shed. He popped off a round through the side window, so I hit him with the butt of the rifle. Had to wait until he came to before I could bring him down."

Paul came down the ridgeline, looking like a gigantic snowman in his white camo—a deadly white snowman—and joined the group. Bax knelt next to Parker, pulled her handcuffs from her belt and slapped them on his wrists. He lay on the ground and moaned.

Chapter Sixty-Five

Buck called Sheriff Storm as the rest of the group fanned out and started checking on the FBI agents that were on the ground. "Stormy. It's clear to come up."

"Roger," said Stormy.

Buck stepped over to one of the FBI agents. "Where's Marshall?"

The agent pointed towards the first smoldering wreck, and Buck walked towards it. Lying against a downed tree, Deputy Director Marshall was being tended to by one of the SWAT agents. Marshall was in bad shape. The SWAT agent looked at Buck and shook his head. "The first blast hit on his side of the Suburban. His legs and right side took the brunt of it," said the agent.

"Try to keep him stable; we've got ambulances on the way." He stepped away and pulled out his phone. He dialed Director Jackson.

"Sir, we're gonna need air evac for some of the wounded FBI agents, and we'll need the bomb disposal guys ASAP."

"I just spoke to the EOD guys, and they're following one of the Grand County deputies up 125 towards the cabin. Are you guys okay?" asked Director Jackson.

"We're okay, but Marshall is hurt bad. I need to go."

Buck disconnected the call as a helicopter flew overhead and hovered over the trees. It moved off to the north, and Buck saw one of the FBI agents cover his earpiece with his hand. He acknowledged a message and slid into the last Suburban. With several of its windows blown out and full of bullet holes, he turned around and head down the road, stopping to let four GCSO trucks come through, followed by four ambulances. Sheriff Storm slid out of the first SUV and looked around.

He walked up to Buck. "What the fuck happened, Buck? What a mess."

"Before I answer that. Is your deputy okay?"

Sheriff Storm did not look happy. "Fucking FBI handcuffed him to his steering wheel. If I find out who did that, I'm gonna kick his ass."

Sheriff Storm looked at the man lying handcuffed on the ground. "Parker?"

Buck nodded. "Any idea who the rest of these fuckers are?"

Sheriff Storm looked at the closest dead body. He walked back to Buck. "I recognize that one—local kid. Been in trouble before, but not like this. Hangs out with a group of white nationalists. They've got a camp in the next valley. I thought they were just harmless assholes. How the hell did they hook up with Parker?"

Buck was about to answer when the FBI Suburban that had left a few minutes earlier returned. The back door opened, and Hank Clancy stepped out, followed by two stern-looking agents. They looked around in disbelief. Hank spotted Buck and Sheriff Storm and headed their way.

"Where's Marshall?"

One of the ambulances pulled away and headed towards Road 4, siren blaring.

Buck looked at Hank. "I think he's in that ambulance. Not sure he'll survive the trip."

Hank stood, looking at Buck but not saying anything. He turned and looked around. "Looks like they ran into a buzz saw."

"They did exactly what Parker hoped they would do," said Dorsett, as she walked up and introduced herself to Hank. "They came through the gate thinking they had a mile or more before they reached the cabin, drove into this clearing and stepped right into the perfect kill zone, boxed in on three sides. Parker had this all well planned out.

"He just made one miscalculation," she said. "When they hit the clearing, someone must have realized what they were walking into. The blast should have taken out the last Suburban, blocking them in, instead of the middle two, but the first Suburban stopped too soon. These guys are lucky they're not all dead."

Dorsett walked away to see how Chicago was doing. One of Hank's agents walked up. "Sir, I've got a count. Eighteen agents in total. Five are DOA. Eleven are wounded, and five of those are critical and may not make it, including Director Marshall."

Hank walked away; the look on his face said it all. Bax walked up to Buck. "That is not a happy-looking man," she said.

The two agents that had arrived with Hank walked over and picked Parker off the ground. They placed him in the Suburban that had been used to shuttle them from wherever they landed and drove away.

Buck nodded. His comm unit crackled. "Buck, this is Vasquez. The National Guard is here at the cabin. They don't want anyone to come back this way. They've only been looking for ten minutes, and they have already marked six IEDs around the cabin. I can't figure out why you're all still alive. I am heading to your location to pick you all up."

Buck acknowledged the transmission and walked over to Dorsett. She stepped away from Chicago and the paramedics and stopped. She looked at Hank on the phone. "This could be a career killer."

"Yeah. I know. It wasn't his fault, but in the end, this became his op, and knowing Hank, he'll fall on his sword. Marshall jeopardized his entire team because he wanted all the credit for solving this thing. In the end, he got what he wanted. It became about the militia, even though it never was. If he survives, they'll give him a medal, and Hank will get shafted."

His phone buzzed, and he pulled it out and looked at the number. "Yes, sir."

"Buck," said Director Jackson, "tell me what happened. We're getting conflicting reports."

Buck filled him in on what had transpired and about what they'd found in the shed. He told him about the white nationalists and the firefight. As he spoke, he looked around the clearing at the bloodstained snow, the dead bodies and the smoldering vehicles. It was all so senseless.

"So, in the end, Marshall wins," said Director Jackson. "He gets the bomber and the connection to the militias he was looking for, and he has our prisoner."

"That's okay, sir. Let them have him. He'll likely disappear into the system, and no one will ever know where he went or what damage he caused. Maybe the governor can spin it so that the survivors of the mosque bombing and the families of those who died can feel like justice was served."

"Can Hank survive this?"

"I don't know, sir. In the end, it was his team that captured the Mountain Bomber. Maybe that's something. What about the Logans, sir?"

"Dee Logan is in the custody of the FBI. If I had to bet, I think she'll turn on her husband to save her family. Jacky Logan III is in the Denver County Jail. We'll hold him there until his trial. I doubt any judge in his right mind will release him on bail. We arrested him at his office downtown. He was sitting with an architect going over the plans for the new event center he was planning to build to replace the old bar. The FBI found a twenty-two-caliber pistol in his desk drawer at his house and a silencer in his coat pocket."

Bax walked up and listened for a minute. She pulled Buck's hand. "Sir, did you give Marcie Blackburn the information on the unsolved murders?"

"She, and her partner, just left my office. They should have everything they need to solve several old murders and bring closure to the families of the deceased."

There was silence for a few seconds, and then the director spoke. "This has been a hard case on everyone, but you guys did an awesome job. Grab Paul and your marshal friends and have a nice dinner on me. Then take some time off and finish your Christmas with your families. You deserve it."

Hank was still on the phone and looked like he would be for a while. Buck looked up and noticed that the snow had started to fall again. It was almost festive. Buck pulled out his phone, dialed Franklin Williams, gave him directions to the cabin and asked him to bring the entire forensic team. Once the bomb techs finished, it would be a long, tedious process to gather all the evidence they would need.

Deputy Vasquez pulled into the clearing and waved to them. Sheriff Storm walked up and pointed to his SUV, and they split up and each climbed into a vehicle. They rode in silence back to the sheriff's office.

Once at the office, they removed their gear and stowed their weapons. Buck told them about the offer from his boss to take them all to dinner, but no one was in the mood to eat. It had been a long, sad day, and everyone just wanted to head home. Buck realized that he wasn't hungry either.

They shook hands all around, and Buck thanked Dorsett and her team for a job well done. He had no idea where they had come from or where they were going next, but he was grateful they were at his side when the shit hit the fan.

Soon the parking lot was empty, except for Buck and Sheriff Storm. They stood watching the snow come down and looked at the Christmas lights that decorated the town. Buck had almost forgotten it was Christmas. He looked at his watch and realized that Christmas was long gone. It was New Year's Eve, and in a little over four hours, Colorado would welcome in the New Year. He shook the sheriff's hand, thanked him for all his help and slid into his Jeep.

With a bit of luck, and if the snow didn't screw up the roads, he might make it home in time to welcome in the New Year with his family.

Epilogue

Buck made it back to Gunnison in time to celebrate the New Year with his son David and his family. He gave David a quick rundown on what had transpired, and then he settled into the recliner. With a grandchild on each leg, he held them close and toasted to a better year. Tears filled his eyes as they watched the fireworks from downtown Denver, and he thought about starting another year without Lucy.

Jacky Logan III had hired the best lawyers money could buy, but it probably wouldn't make a difference. The government's case was strong, and the evidence was overwhelming. And once he was convicted by the U.S. government, he still had to face the charges of murder and conspiracy in twelve separate jurisdictions in Colorado and two counts of murder in the city of Montrose. Jacky Logan III was in for a lengthy prison sentence.

Just as Buck had figured, Dee Logan, to keep what was left of her family together, took a plea deal in exchange for turning on her husband. Betrayal seemed to run in the family. She would be the government's star witness.

Two months had passed since that day on the

ridge in Grand County. Buck, Paul and Bax spent a lot of that time completing the investigation files on both the O'Connor bombings and the mosque bombing. They gathered boxes full of evidence that they shipped off to the U.S. Attorney's office in Denver. They would be the ones prosecuting Jacky Logan III on the federal charges.

Through a deal with the governor of Colorado, the federal government allowed Colorado to have the first crack at Eldridge Parker. Buck and the team had spent hours in Denver working on the case with the prosecutors from the Colorado Attorney General's office, and they were convinced they had a rock-solid case. Eldridge Parker refused to say anything during the interrogations, leading many who were involved to speculate on whether his mind had finally snapped.

After the National Guard bomb techs declared the area around the cabin safe and all the evidence from the shed had been gathered, George and Melanie had torn apart Eldridge Parker's laptop. They found all the evidence they would need to connect him to the earlier bombings, the manifesto and the mosque bombing. All that evidence pointed to the fact that the bombings were his and his alone. He had no ties to any militia groups, or anyone else, for that matter—just a lonely, crazy old man acting alone.

His only connection to the white nationalists,

who had helped him that day on the ridge, was a call to some like-minded neighbors seeking help from an intrusive government. They had jumped at the chance to help Parker put the FBI in their place. They probably never realized how deadly that encounter would be.

One thing George and Melanie didn't reveal was the exact formula that Eldridge Parker had developed to make his explosives, which they found in his laptop. Even though CBI was being pressured to give that information to the federal government, they refused to turn it over. They made sure the formula never saw the light of day.

The forensics team also discovered a shallow grave near the old rock foundation on Parker's property. The remains had been sent to the State Crime Lab and were being tested to determine if they were the kayaker, Frederick Jensen.

FBI Deputy Director Felix Marshall survived the attack that day. His injuries were devastating. He lost his right leg from just above the knee, and his left leg had been severely damaged in the explosion. The nerve damage in his right arm made the arm useless, and his right eye had been destroyed.

The FBI awarded him their highest honor for bravery and presented him as the man who captured the Mountain Bomber and solved the Christmas

Day bombings. Once out of the spotlight, he was given a tiny office in the basement at the FBI training facility at Quantico, given a fancy new title and put in charge of a task force of one. Periodically the FBI would parade him in front of the news media when they needed a bit of good publicity, but for the most part, he would live out the remainder of his career in obscurity.

Two of the five agents that were in critical condition died of their injuries, bringing the total to seven dead. The other three recovered from their injuries, two choosing to retire with full disability. The last agent, Marshall's assistant, was transferred to a one-person residential FBI office in a small town in Montana, just south of the Canadian border.

Hank Clancy had survived, but he took a beating. Like a good soldier, Hank accepted full responsibility for the entire tragic event. He was demoted too, but he was allowed to remain at the Denver Field Office. His wife had tried to convince him to retire, but Hank wasn't prepared to leave the FBI with a blemish on his otherwise exemplary career.

He would most likely never know that he owed the fact that he wasn't sent to some little backwater office to Buck. Buck had called the governor and asked him to intervene on Hank's behalf, and the governor never walked away from a good fight or a friend in need.

Those few people who sat in the room that day when the governor of Colorado met with the United States Attorney General and the director of the FBI would describe the confrontation as epic. By the time the yelling was over, the governor had walked out of the room with everything he wanted. He would be able to prosecute the Mountain Bomber in Colorado first, and he had a commitment that Hank Clancy would keep his job leading the FBI field office in Denver. It was a good day for the governor.

Jacky Logan III was just as cocky in prison as he had been on the outside. He walked around the cellblock like he owned the place, and it appeared that everyone accepted that and showed him the proper amount of respect. After two months in the joint, Jacky III was king of D block.

The dinner klaxon sounded one Friday night, and Jacky III lined up with his entourage, just like every night. He was in a good mood. He had spent several hours with his team of attorneys, and he was feeling confident he could beat the government's case. He never noticed, while standing in line, waiting to pick up his tray, that his entourage had drifted away from him.

Jacky sensed a presence close in behind him, and he turned to see who was crowding his personal space. An inmate he didn't recognize from the cellblock got right in his face. The other inmates moved in closer and tightened the circle around the two men, hiding them from the view of the guards. Jacky III was about to say something when he noticed a sharp pain in his chest.

The inmate who had crowded him looked in his eyes and smiled. "This is for Jimmy Sullivan," he whispered.

The shiv plunged into his chest several more times in rapid succession, and Jacky III looked down and saw the red stain spreading across the front of his prison-issue shirt. He slumped to the floor, and the crowd separated and moved around him.

It wasn't until the line moved past him that the guards realized something was wrong and sounded the alarm. The mess hall was cleared, and the cellblock was placed in lockdown. All the inmates that had been in the mess hall that evening were questioned, but no one remembered seeing what happened to Jacky III. A thorough search of all the cells in the cell block was conducted, but the shiv was never found.

No one noticed the two guards escorting the unknown inmate back to his own cellblock. Justice had been served, mob-style.

Acknowledgments

A special thank-you to my daughter Christina J. Morgan, my unofficial editor in chief. She devoted a significant amount of time to making sure the book was presented as perfectly as possible.

Thanks to my editor, Laura Dragonette, whose efforts helped turn my manuscript into a polished novel. Her help is greatly appreciated. Any mistakes the reader may find are solely the responsibility of the author.

Also, I would like to thank my family for all of their encouragement. I have been telling them stories since they were little, and I always told them that someone should be writing this stuff down. I decided to write it down myself.

I want to thank my closest friend, Trish Moakler-Herud. She has been encouraging me for years to write my stories down. I hope this will make her proud.

A special thanks to my late wife, Jane. She pushed me for years to become a writer, and my biggest regret is that she didn't live long enough to see it happen. I love her with all my heart and miss her every day. I think she would be pleased.

Finally, thanks to the readers. Without you, none of this would be important.

About the Author

2019 Pacific Book Awards Best Mystery Finalist . . . *Crime Delayed*

2020 Pacific Book Awards Best Mystery Winner . . . *Crime Denied*

2020 Chanticleer International Book Awards: 1st Place Blue Ribbon, CLUE Book Awards for Suspense, Thriller Fiction . . . *Crime Denied*

Chuck Morgan attended Seton Hall University and Regis College and spent thirty-five years as a construction project manager. He is an avid outdoorsman, an Eagle Scout and a licensed private pilot. He enjoys camping, hiking, mountain biking and fly-fishing.

He is the author of the Crime series, featuring Colorado Bureau of Investigation agent Buck Taylor. The series includes *Crime Interrupted, Crime Delayed, Crime Unsolved, Crime Exposed, Crime Denied, Crime Conspiracy* and *Crime Unknown.*

He is also the author of *Her Name Was Jane*, a memoir about his late wife's nine-year battle with breast cancer. He has three children, three grandchildren and a Siberian Husky. He resides in Lone Tree, Colorado.

Other Books by the Author

"Crime Interrupted: A Buck Taylor Novel by Chuck Morgan is a gripping, edge-of-the-seat novel. *Right from page one, the action kicks off and never stops, gaining pace as each chapter passes." Reviewed by Anne-Marie Reynolds for Readers' Favorite.*

Finalist . . . 2019 Pacific Book Awards Best Mystery

*"**This crime novel reads like a great thriller.** The writing is atmospheric, laced with vivid descriptions that capture the setting in great detail while allowing readers to follow the intensity of the action and the emotional and psychological depth of the story." Reviewed by Divine Zape for Readers' Favorite.*

*"**Professionally written in the style of a best-selling crime novelist, such as Tom Clancy, Crime Unsolved: A Buck Taylor Novel by Chuck Morgan is a spellbinding suspense novel with an environmental flair.** Intriguing subplots of fraud, survivalist paranoia, and murder weave their way through the fabric of the plot, creating a dynamic story. This is an action-filled, stimulating tale which contains fascinating details that are relevant in our present climate." Reviewed by Susan Sewell for Readers' Favorite.*

*"**Chuck Morgan has a unique gift for plot, one that makes Crime Exposed: A Buck Taylor Novel a hard-to-put-down book.** From the start, readers know what happens to Barb, but they become curious as they follow the investigation, wondering if the characters will find out what happened to her. The descriptions are filled with clarity, and they offer readers great images. The prose is elegant, and it captures both the emotional and psychological elements of the novel clearly while offering vivid descriptions of scenes and characters. This is a fast-paced thriller with memorable characters and a criminal investigation that is so real readers will believe it could happen."* Reviewed by Romuald Dzemo for Readers' Favorite.

Winner . . . 2020 Pacific Book Awards Best Mystery

2020 Chanticleer International Book Awards: 1st Place Blue Ribbon, CLUE Book Awards for Suspense, Thriller Fiction

"It's really progressive to see a female serial killer portrayed with such intelligent writing and depth of character, and the cat and mouse chase dynamic is thrown off nicely by the switching of genders. What results is a really enjoyable thriller and crime mystery novel, and overall Crime Denied is certain to please fans of both hard-boiled detective tales and action/adventure crime novels."* Reviewed by K.C. Finn for Readers' Favorite.

"This makes for a truly dynamic story where anything is possible, and a hero you can root for even when it looks like all is lost." Reviewed by K.C. Finn for Readers' Favorite.

"This is a book you can't put down, which will entertain you on many levels, and at times make your skin crawl; the kind of book that remains in your thoughts long after you finish reading." Reviewed by Steven Robson for Readers' Favorite.

"I read Crime Unknown in one sitting. The plot is intenseand the main character agent Buck

Taylor is a hero like no other. *This book has everything a thriller needs to be and more. I thought I knew the story at the beginning. Buck will solve a tricky murder case, I thought. But Chuck Morgan adds a twist to this story that expands it and makes it one of the most enjoyable books I've read in this genre. I loved that the lead was such an awesome well-rounded fellow but that he also had a support team who were just as important to the story.*" Reviewed by Maureen Dangarembizi for Readers' Favorite.

"Crime Unknown is a thoroughly enjoyable read and I would not hesitate to recommend this book to fans of the crime genre and those looking for a gateway in." Reviewed by K.C. Finn for Readers' Favorite.

www.ingramcontent.com/pod-product-compliance
Lightning Source LLC
Chambersburg PA
CBHW072038190726
48294CB00005B/1310